Beneath a Dying Sun

This book is dedicated to the memory of my dad who always loved a good Western. I just hope there's one in here.

Beneath a Dying Sun
Western Short Stories

Laughton J. Collins, Jr.

Beneath a Dying Sun: Western Short Stories © 2025 Laughton J. Collins, Jr.

Published by Requiem Press.

https://requiempress.weebly.com/
https://www.laughtoncollinsjr.com

A Requiem Press Book

ISBN: 979-8-9928855-4-5

The Ghost of John Wilkes Booth is a story from an idea I've had rolling around inside my mind for years before I wrote it. Then I started writing it and let it settle awhile before finishing the story. Even then, the story wasn't finished—it wasn't quite what I wanted so I rewrote it. I rewrote it 2 or 3 times before finally getting to the finished version. It is an alternate history story—a 'what if?' story.

There are conspiracy theories that John Wilkes Booth survived and lived for decades after the assassination of Abraham Lincoln under assumed names. This story is based on none of them. The story is fiction but some of the characters in the story are real historical figures that were involved in the historical events. They are fictionalized representations of those people. The historical characters that appear in the story are Abraham Lincoln, Mary Lincoln, John Wilkes Booth, Major Rathbone, Dr. Samuel Mudd, Willie Jett, Ruggles (Mortimer Bainbridge Ruggles), Bainbridge (Absalom Ruggles Bainbridge), David Herold, Richard Garrett, William Garrett, Jack Garrett, Luther Baker, Everton Conger, Boston Corbett, Orwell Swann and Edwin Stanton. James Boyd was the alias Booth used when he was taken to the Garrett farm to hide out. All other characters are completely fictional.

Las Vegas in the story is a town in New Mexico, not the more famous city in Nevada. The Cheyenne Leader newspaper was first published in September 1867, in this story it appears a couple of years earlier.

Table of contents

In the Shadow of Devil's Spine

The sun beat down hard on the cracked earth. Marshal Cole Everett shifted in his saddle, the worn leather creaking. Dust coated his clothes, his face, grit itched in his eyes. Three weeks—three weeks tracking Simon Crowe across half the territory. The name left a bad taste in his mouth—Simon Crowe—accused of putting a bullet in Tom Henderson's chest during a stagecoach holdup outside Red Rock. Tom Henderson was Lily's father.

Cole saw Lily's face whenever he closed his eyes. The shock—the raw grief turning her eyes hollow—the way her hand trembled when she pressed his badge into his palm. "Bring him, Cole. Bring him for Pa." Her voice, usually warm, was now cold as ice. He'd promised—he'd hunt Simon Crowe to the ends of the earth.

He found Crowe's trail leading into the badlands near Devil's Spine—a jagged ridge of rust-colored rock that clawed at the sky. Water was scarce, shade was non-existent. Cole's canteen was light, almost empty—almost dry. His horse, a sturdy buckskin named Buck, plodded with its head low. Cole looked around at the baking landscape. Nothing moved but the shimmer of heat in the distance. Then he saw it—a thin wisp of smoke, barely visible against the pale blue. It was snaking up from a narrow canyon ahead. It was too deliberate for a brush fire.

Cole dismounted a quarter mile out. He ground-tied Buck in a shallow depression, whispering reassurance. He checked his Colt Peacemaker, the metal warm against his palm. He slid the Winchester from its holster. Moving silently, using rocks for cover, he approached the canyon mouth. The smell of woodsmoke grew stronger, it mixed with the scent of cooking meat. His stomach tightened. He edged around a large boulder—his rifle ready.

Simon Crowe sat hunched over a small fire near the canyon wall. He looked older than his wanted poster, lines etched deep around his eyes and mouth. His clothes were ragged and his boots were worn through. A lean-to offered scant shelter. A scrawny jackrabbit roasted on a spit. His rifle lay within arm's reach, but he wasn't holding it. He stared into the flames, shoulders slumped, looking utterly defeated. He looked nothing like the hardened killer Cole expected.

Cole stepped into the open, Winchester leveled. "Simon Crowe. Hands high. Real slow."

Crowe flinched violently, his head snapped up. Fear flashed in his eyes, quickly replaced by a weary resignation. He didn't reach for the rifle. Slowly, he raised his hands. "Marshal," he said, his voice dry. "Figured someone'd come eventually. Didn't reckon it'd be you, Everett."

"You know me?" Cole kept the rifle steady. Ten paces separated them.

"Seen you in Red Rock. With Lily Henderson." Crowe's gaze held Cole's. "I didn't kill her Pa, Marshal."

"Save it for the judge." Cole's voice was flat. "Stagecoach guard saw you clear. Tom Henderson took a bullet meant for the strongbox. Your gang's signature."

"My gang?" Crowe barked a humorless laugh. "What gang? Been ridin' solo near two years. That guard saw wrong. Or he was paid to see wrong." He lowered his hands slightly, gesturing at his meager camp. "Does this look like a successful outlaw's hideout? I been runnin' and hidin', Marshal. Not from the law. From the man who *really* killed Henderson."

Cole's finger tightened on the trigger—lies, desperate lies. "Who? Who'd want Tom Henderson dead? He ran the general store. Lived quiet."

Crowe's eyes burned with sudden intensity. "Ask Lily."

The words hit Cole like a physical blow. "What?"

"Ask her about the money, Marshal. Ask her about the debts. Ask her why her Pa was on that stagecoach in the first place." Crowe leaned forward, his voice dropping low. "He wasn't just deliverin' supplies. He was carryin' near five thousand dollars. Bank notes. Money owed to a man named Jacob Strate. You know that name?"

Cole knew Jacob Strate. He operated out of Silverton—loans, land deals, rumors of coercion. He's a man who collected debts with ruthless efficiency. Cole felt a cold dread start to seep past the anger. "Tom owed Strate money?"

"Not Tom." Crowe spat into the fire. "*Lily.*"

Cole stared with disbelief and a horrible, creeping suspicion. "Lily? Why?"

"Fancy dresses. Trinkets. That big house she wanted her Pa to build." Crowe's voice was thick with contempt. "She ran up debts in Red Rock, then Strate's place in Silverton. Hid it from her Pa. When Strate's collectors came callin', scared her bad. She begged Tom to fix it. He mortgaged the store. Took the money to Strate on that stage. Only Strate didn't want payment. He wanted the store. He wanted Henderson ruined. He hired men to take that money back…and make sure Henderson didn't survive to talk."

Cole's mind raced—Lily's frantic insistence he hunt Crowe. Her strange reluctance to discuss her father's business—her unexplained trips to Silverton. The pieces clicked into a monstrous picture. "You expect me to believe Lily knew her father was walking into an ambush?"

"No," Crowe said quietly. "I don't think she knew Strate would kill him. But she knew Strate wanted that money back. She knew her Pa was carryin' it. She sent him." He looked Cole dead in the eye. "I was there, Marshal. Hidin' in the rocks above the trail. Saw Strate's men – Pike and Dobbs – stop the stage. Saw Henderson try to reason. Saw Pike shoot him down like a dog. I fired, spooked their horses. They grabbed the money bag and ran before they could finish the driver or guard. I went down, checked Henderson. He was gone. The guard was groggy, half-blind from dust. Saw my face as I leaned over Henderson…figured I did it."

Cole felt the ground tilt beneath him. The conviction that had fueled his hunt began to crumble. Crowe's story had the terrible ring of truth. "Why didn't you come forward? Tell the sheriff?"

"With what proof?" Crowe demanded. "My word against Strate's? And Strate's men saw me too. Been tryin' to kill me ever since. Figured if I could get proof…Strate's ledger maybe, showin' Lily's debts…I might clear my name. But they've been houndin' me." He gestured towards the canyon entrance. "They're close. Heard 'em last night. That's why I lit the fire. Figured it might draw you or them. Either way…it ends."

A sharp crack echoed through the canyon—a stone splintered near Cole's head. He dropped instantly, rolling behind the boulder he'd used for cover. Crowe scrambled back, grabbing his rifle, another shot ricocheted off the rocks near the lean-to.

"Crowe! Everett!" A harsh voice yelled from the canyon rim. It was Pike. "Come on out! Strate sends his regards!"

Cole risked a glance. There were two figures positioned on opposite sides of the canyon rim, rifles trained downward. Dobbs had joined Pike—Strate's enforcers, proof that Crowe hadn't lied.

"Looks like you got company, Marshal!" Pike called down, laughter in his voice. "Strate figured you might catch this rat. Saves us the trouble. Hand him over, and maybe you walk away."

Cole pressed against the hot rock. His duty was clear, arrest Crowe but arresting him meant delivering him to Strate's hired killers. And Lily…Lily had lied. She sent her own father to his death. She sent Cole after an innocent man. The betrayal was a knife twisting in his gut. He looked at Crowe, huddled near his pathetic fire, his rifle clutched in his white-knuckled hands. He was not an outlaw, he was a witness. He'd be a dead man walking if Strate got him.

"Everett!" Dobbs shouted. "Last chance! Send Crowe out!"

Crowe met Cole's eyes. There was no pleading, only grim understanding. "Do what you gotta do, Marshal."

Another shot kicked up dust near Cole's boot. They weren't waiting, Cole made his decision. He raised his Winchester, sighted on Dobbs' position, and fired. The shot echoed like thunder. Dobbs jerked back, disappearing from view.

Pike's answering fire was immediate, peppering the rocks around Cole. "Wrong choice, lawman!"

Crowe fired at Pike's position, forcing the gunman to duck. The canyon became a deadly box. Cole and Crowe were pinned down, firing up at the rim. Pike and Dobbs, wounded or not, had the high ground. Bullets whined and sparked off stone. The acrid smell of gunpowder mixed with dust.

Cole ejected a spent shell and slammed a fresh one in its place. He saw movement, Dobbs was crawling, trying to get a better angle. Cole fired, he missed. Dobbs returned fire—a searing pain tore through Cole's left shoulder. He grunted, gritting his teeth, firing back blindly. Crowe fired again at Pike.

Suddenly, Crowe cried out, staggering back. A dark stain bloomed on his thigh. He fell against the canyon wall, sliding down, rifle clattering. Pike had found his mark.

"Crowe's hit!" Pike yelled triumphantly. "Finish them!"

Cole saw Dobbs rise, his rifle aimed directly at the wounded Crowe. Cole fired first—his shot took Dobbs high in the chest. The man crumpled, tumbling partway down the slope before lodging against a rock—motionless.

Pike roared in anger—his fire intensified, focused solely on Cole's position. Bullets chipped away at the boulder around him. Cole pressed flat, pain radiating from his shoulder. He was running low on ammunition. Crowe was down—Pike was enraged and still had the advantage.

A calm came—Pike was reloading. Cole risked a look—Crowe was pale, pressing a hand to his bleeding leg, but he still held his pistol. He nodded towards the lean-to. Cole understood—it offered no real cover, but it was closer to the canyon wall, maybe offering a blind spot.

"Go!" Cole hissed. "I'll cover!"

Crowe hesitated, then started crawling painfully towards the lean-to. Cole rose, firing rapidly up at Pike's last known position, emptying the Winchester. He threw himself down as return fire slammed into the rocks above him. He dropped the rifle and drew his Colt. He saw Crowe almost at the lean-to.

Then Pike stood—he wasn't where Cole expected. He'd moved along the rim, getting a clear line on the crawling Crowe. Pike's rifle came up.

Cole fired his Colt—Pike flinched, his shot going wide, kicking up dust near Crowe. Cole fired again, and again. Pike staggered, clutching his side but didn't go down. He swung his rifle towards Cole.

A single shot rang out. It wasn't from Cole, or Pike.

Pike jerked—a look of profound surprise crossed his face. He dropped his rifle and clutched his throat, then toppled forward. He slid down the steep slope, landing in a heap near the smoldering fire.

Silence descended, sudden and heavy. The dust settled in the smoke filled the air. Cole glanced around the rim, nothing there—it was empty. He looked towards the lean-to. Crowe held his pistol, smoke curling from the barrel—he'd made the shot.

Cole pushed himself up, wincing at the pain in his shoulder. He approached Crowe cautiously, his Colt still drawn but lowered. Crowe leaned against the lean-to's support, breathing hard, his face gray with pain and blood loss.

"You saved my hide, Marshal," Crowe said.

Cole holstered his gun. He knelt, tearing a strip from his shirt to bind Crowe's leg wound. "Proof is dead," he said grimly, nodding towards Pike and Dobbs.

"Strate…" Crowe gasped. "He'll send more. You know it. Lily… she's part of it. Maybe not the killin', but the lies…the debts…"

Cole finished the crude bandage. The weight of everything pressed down—Lily's betrayal, the dead men, the wounded witness, the powerful enemy still out there. His badge felt heavy, tarnished. He'd failed Tom Henderson. He'd failed to see the danger in his own home.

"Can't take you back to Red Rock," Cole said, his voice hollow. "Strate'll have men waiting. Or Lily…" He couldn't finish the thought. "There's a doctor in Mesa Verde. Two days' hard ride. We get you patched up. Then…then we figure out how to get Strate."

Crowe looked at him, a flicker of hope in his exhausted eyes. "You believe me?"

Cole looked at the bodies, at the wounded man before him, at the vast, indifferent badlands. "Yeah," he said heavily. "I believe you."

He helped Crowe to his feet, supporting most of his weight. They hobbled towards the canyon mouth, towards where Buck was ground-tied. Cole whistled and Buck raised his head. They were almost to the horse when Cole heard the distinct *click* of a hammer being cocked behind him.

He froze. Crowe stiffened against him.

"Drop the gunbelt, Marshal. Real slow."

Cole knew that voice—it was Lily. Her voice was cold, hard, nothing like the woman he loved. He turned slowly, keeping his body partly shielding Crowe.

Lily Henderson stood ten paces away, a double-barreled shotgun leveled at his chest. Her face was pale, set in lines of determination he'd never seen. Her eyes shone with a desperate resolve. She must have followed him, tracked him just as he had tracked Crowe.

"Lily…" Cole's voice cracked. "What are you doing?"

"Finishing it," she said, her voice trembling slightly but the shotgun held steady. "You weren't supposed to find him alive, Cole. You were supposed to bring me his body. Proof he paid for Pa." Her gaze flickered to Crowe. "And now you know. You know everything."

The horror Cole felt was absolute. "You sent your own father…?"

"He wouldn't listen!" she cried, the veneer cracking for a second. "I told him Strate would ruin us! He said he'd handle it…handle it by giving Strate everything! I couldn't let him! I couldn't be poor again, Cole! Not after…not after everything!" Tears streamed down her face, but the shotgun didn't waver. "Strate promised…if Pa was gone, the debt died with him. The store was mine. I just had to make sure Crowe took the blame. Strate arranged the…the accident. But you," her voice turned spiteful, "you had to dig. Had to find him. Had to listen to his lies."

"They weren't lies, Lily," Cole said softly, his heart shattering. "Pike and Dobbs are dead back there. Strate's men. Crowe killed Pike. He was telling the truth."

Her eyes widened slightly, a flicker of fear—then they hardened again. "Doesn't matter now. State will know. He'll come for me. Unless…unless the outlaw kills the marshal who hunted him. It's tragic but then I inherit Pa's store…and mourn my brave man." She gestured with the shotgun. "Now drop the gunbelt. Both of you."

Cole moved slowly, his mind racing—he couldn't draw. The shotgun spread would kill them both at this range. He started to lower his hands towards his buckle. Beside him, Crowe swayed, weakened by blood loss and shock. His hand brushed against Cole's holster.

Lily saw the movement. Her finger tightened on the trigger. "Don't!"

It was instinct—years of facing sudden violence. Cole shoved Crowe sideways, away from the line of fire, as he dropped and drew in one fluid motion. The twin barrels of the shotgun roared—a deafening blast in the still air.

Cole felt the impact like a kick from a mule. Hot lead ripped through his side and chest. His own shot, wild and desperate, went high. He crashed onto his back, the world tilting violently. The sky was impossibly blue. He couldn't breathe, agony consumed him.

He heard Crowe cry out, a wordless shout of rage and pain. Then another gunshot—a single, sharp crack. Then silence, broken only by the frantic pounding of his own fading heartbeat and the distant cry of a hawk.

He tried to turn his head. He saw Lily lying a few feet away, her eyes wide and sightless, a dark stain spreading across the front of her dress. Crowe stood over her, Cole's Colt smoking in his hand, his face a mask of anguish and fury. Then Crowe's leg gave way, and he collapsed beside Cole.

Crowe crawled closer, his face contorted with pain. He pressed his hand against the terrible wounds in Cole's chest, trying to stop the flow of blood—it was useless. Cole felt the cold spreading from his core.

"She…she used us both, Marshal," Crowe said, tears mixing with the dust on his face. "I'm sorry. So damn sorry."

Cole tried to speak—he could only manage a wet gasp. He looked past Crowe, past the bodies, towards Buck. The horse stood watching and confused. The sun beat down on the empty land—the hunt was over. Justice was dead, he had brought in no outlaw—he had only found betrayal and death. The blue sky above him began to darken at the edges. The last thing he felt was Crowe's hand on his shoulder, and then nothing. The wind picked up, swirling dust over the three still figures in the shadow of Devil's Spine.

The Hangman's Knot

The rope bit into Ted Finley's neck like fire. It burned deep as he swung from the old oak branch, boots kicking empty air. Below him, the vigilantes watched. Seven men—their faces grim, etched by lantern light. Hatch led them—he spat tobacco juice near Ted's shadow on the ground.

"Rustler. Murderer," Hatch growled. "Judge said guilty. We carry the sentence." He gestured at the others. "Cut him down after he stops. Leave him for the crows. Message needs sending."

Ted choked and clawed at the rough rope. His vision blurred, he saw their hard faces tilt up, watching his death. He saw the stars, cold and distant. He saw the face of the real killer, laughing somewhere safe. Then darkness overtook him—the kicking ceased, his body hung limp.

They cut him down an hour later. His body thudded onto the hard-packed earth. No one checked for breath, no one checked for life. They were confident he was dead, confident the animals would finish him off if not. They rode out, leaving him under the hanging tree.

Dawn painted the sky a pale gray. A sharp pain stabbed at Ted's throat. He gasped, catching too much air in his lungs. The air scraped hard inside his throat. He lived—the rope had stretched just enough. The knot hadn't crushed his windpipe. He rolled onto his side, coughing and vomiting bile. Every movement tore agony through his neck and shoulders. He touched the brutal welt. He remembered the faces—Hatch—the others. Men he knew by sight from the territory. Men who judged him without proof. Men who left him for dead.

Weeks passed in a dusty shack far from the main trail. An old trapper found him, half-dead. The man asked no questions. He brought water, broth, and silence. Ted healed—the physical wounds closed but the rage burned hotter. The injustice festered within. He had been a lawman once, he was good at it. He quit after seeing too much innocent blood spilled, now they spilled his. They called him a rustler, a murderer. They stole his life, left him for dead. Now, he would take theirs. But not like they did, he would take them by the law.

He found his old badge, tarnished, in a trunk. He polished it and pinned it inside his coat, strapped on his worn Colt. He was ready—he rode back into the territory. Not as Ted Finley, rancher, as Marshal Finley. He had warrants now—not for rustling or murder, for attempted murder—for illegal hanging. There were seven names.

The first man was Clem. He ran a way station south of Dry Creek. Ted found him mending harnesses. Clem looked up, his face was drained of color. He dropped the leather he was working on.

"Finley? But…you're…"

"Dead?" Ted's voice was a rasp, scarred by the rope. He showed the badge. "Not quite. You remember the hanging tree, Clem? You held the lantern." Ted pulled the warrant. "You're under arrest. For attempted murder. Illegal execution."

Clem panicked, he grabbed for the rifle leaning against the wall. Ted drew faster, his bullet took Clem in the shoulder. Clem screamed, dropping the rifle. Ted bound his hands and loaded him onto a spare horse. "Trial's in Carson," Ted stated. "You'll face a real judge."

Word spread fast, a ghost marshal hunted the vigilantes. Men whispered in saloons, fear grew. Ted moved methodically, every move carefully calculated. He took the next man, Peters, asleep in his bunkhouse. Peters fought hard, Ted broke his arm subduing him. Peters joined Clem on the trail to Carson jail. Three more followed over the next month. One resisted fiercely, Ted shot him through the leg. The man bled out before reaching a doctor. Justice, some murmured. Ted felt no satisfaction, only grim necessity. Hatch remained free—and the last two.

Hatch hid, he knew the ghost marshal wanted him the most. Ted tracked him to a mining camp high in the Sierra Diablos. Hatch had taken work as a guard—Ted walked into the camp saloon at noon. Men froze— Hatch stood near the bar, his hand hovering near his gun.

"Finley." Hatch's voice held disbelief and hate. "Should've made sure the knot was tighter."

Ted showed his badge. "Marshal Finley. Warrant for your arrest, Hatch. Attempted murder. Illegal execution. Drop the gun belt."

Hatch's eyes darted—he saw no escape. His hand twitched towards his holster. Ted's Colt cleared leather first—the shot echoed. Hatch clutched his thigh, bellowing and crashed to the sawdust covered floor. Ted kicked his gun away and hauled him up. "Carson wants you. Alive. For trial."

The journey back was slow. Hatch cursed him constantly. Ted ignored it the best he could. The scar on his neck throbbed. He thought of the last two names. Two men left, then it would be over.

Three days from Carson, they camped in a box canyon. Ted secured Hatch to a sturdy pine, then built a small fire. Hatch watched him, his eyes burning in the firelight.

"You think this makes you righteous?" Hatch said. "Chasing us down like dogs? We did what needed doing. That rancher, Davis… slaughtered in his bed. His cattle run off. We found your hat near his body. Found tracks leading to your place."

Ted stirred the fire. "My hat was stolen. Weeks before. Tracks were planted. I was thirty miles away, buying stock. Had witnesses." He'd told the vigilantes that night. They hadn't listened.

Hatch sneered. "Easy to say now. We did the territory a service. Davis got justice."

"Davis got murdered," Ted said. "And you murdered justice. You killed an innocent man. You just failed to finish the job." He looked at Hatch. "Who was the seventh man? The one who stayed in the shadows? I saw seven faces."

Hatch looked away. "Doesn't matter now."

"It matters to the warrant." Ted leaned closer. "Who was the seventh man?"

Hatch remained silent—Ted let it go. Tomorrow they'd reach Carson, the jail held the others. The trial would expose it all and he'd have his justice—it would be lawful justice. The thought brought no peace, only exhaustion.

Dawn came and Ted saddled the horses. He untied Hatch's bound hands from the tree, keeping his wrists secured. He helped the wounded man mount. As Ted turned to his own horse, Hatch made his move. He kicked his horse hard, straight at Ted. The animal bolted, knocking Ted sideways. Hatch, hands still bound, yanked the reins with all his strength, veering the horse wildly. It crashed through brush, heading for the canyon mouth.

Ted scrambled up, drawing his gun. He couldn't shoot the horse. He couldn't risk a shot hitting Hatch fatally. The man needed to stand trial. He ran after them. Hatch was disappearing around a bend. Ted reached the canyon mouth and saw Hatch's horse plunging down a steep, shale-covered slope. Hatch, unable to grip properly with bound hands, swayed dangerously.

"Hatch! Pull up!" Ted yelled.

Hatch ignored him and kicked the horse again. The animal stumbled on the loose rock. Its front legs buckled. Hatch flew from the saddle and tumbled down the slope, a rolling mass of limbs. He struck a large boulder at the bottom with a sickening crack, then lay still.

Ted scrambled down the treacherous slope. When he reached Hatch, the man's neck was bent at an impossible angle. Sightless eyes stared at the harsh sky. Ted checked for a pulse—nothing. Hatch was dead.

A hollow feeling opened in Ted's chest. This was not justice—it was a waste. He secured Hatch's body over the saddle of the trembling horse and rode towards Carson. Two days later, he delivered the body to the sheriff. The sheriff looked grim.

"Finley. Got the others locked up. Trial starts next week. Judge is ready." He eyed the body. "Hatch resisted?"

"Tried to run. Horse fell." Ted's voice was flat. "Where's the seventh man? The one who stayed back that night?"

The sheriff frowned. "Seventh? The boys in there…Clem, Peters, the others…they all named six. Them and Hatch. Six men hanged you, they say. Only six warrants."

Ted stared. "I saw seven. Clear as day. Lantern light. Seven faces watching me die."

The sheriff shrugged. "Nerves maybe? Dark night. Or they're lying to protect someone. But they all swear it was six. Even separately."

Doubt, cold and sharp, pricked at Ted. Had he imagined a seventh man? The terror, the choking…could it have played tricks? The men in the cells swore only six rode out. Only six held the rope.

The trial began—Clem, Peters, the three survivors, sat chained in the courtroom—they looked broken. The prosecutor laid out the case. Illegal assembly, attempted murder. The defense claimed righteous citizen action based on evidence. Ted testified—he described the hanging. He named the six men before him and described the seventh shadowy figure. The defense lawyer pounced.

"Seven, Marshal? Yet your own warrants list only six. The accused all state only six participated. Could the trauma of near-death, the darkness…have created a phantom seventh man in your mind?"

Ted looked at the prisoners. Their eyes filled with fear. But there was not a flicker of recognition about a seventh man, only confusion. Had he invented the extra face? Had the rage conjured an extra target? The thought sickened him.

The jury found the men guilty and the judge sentenced them to twenty years hard labor—Justice, the papers called it. Ted felt no victory, only a gnawing void. The phantom seventh man haunted him. Was it a trick of the light? Or had someone truly been there…someone who escaped? Someone the others protected?

He returned to the shack near the hanging tree. He needed solitude—he needed to remember. He walked to the old oak—the rope scar burned. He closed his eyes, forcing himself back to that terrible night. The rough bark against his back, the bite of the rope. The flickering lanterns, the faces…Hatch, Clem, Peters…the three others…and…the seventh man. Standing slightly apart. His hat pulled low, he was watching, not helping. Just… watching.

The memory solidified—it was real, not imagined. There *was* a seventh. The men lied to protect him. Or feared him. But, who was he?

He spent weeks asking discreet questions and following old grudges. Davis, the murdered rancher, had enemies. Ted tracked one name, a man named Ira. He owned the spread bordering Davis's land. They fought over water rights. They had fistfights in town, serious bad blood. Ira vanished right after the hanging.

Ted found Ira's trail—it led south, deep into Mexico—Ted followed. The scar on his neck felt tight. This was the end—the last one—the one who watched—the one who got away.

He tracked Ira to a small cantina in a dusty border town. Ted stepped inside, the air was thick with smoke and tequila. He spotted Ira at a corner table, playing cards. He was older, weathered but the same man. He was the watcher.

Ted walked over. He didn't draw, he just stood at the table. Ira looked up, his eyes widened. The shock of seeing a dead man standing before him spread across his face. Then a slow, grim understanding. He dropped his cards.

"Finley," Ira whispered. "Hell's doorstep."

"You were there," Ted stated. His voice like gravel. "Under the hanging tree. You watched."

Ira nodded slowly, he didn't deny it. He pushed his chair back slightly. "I was. Didn't touch the rope. Didn't say a word for you or against you. Just…watched."

"Why?"

Ira's gaze hardened. "Because Davis was my friend. My only real friend in that godforsaken territory. Someone killed him. Stole his cattle. Hatch and his bunch thought it was you. I…I wanted to see you hang for it." He looked down at his hands. "I hated you. Blamed you for taking water. For the fights. I wanted you dead for killing Davis."

Ted's hand rested near his gun. "I didn't kill Davis."

Ira met his eyes. There was no hatred now, only a deep, exhausted sadness. "I know that now." He paused. The cantina noise faded around them. "After…after they cut you down…after they rode off…I stayed. Watched you lying there. I walked closer. To spit on you. To make sure."

Ira's voice dropped to a whisper. "You weren't breathing. I was sure you were gone. I knelt down. Right beside you. Then…I saw it." He swallowed hard. "Your hand. Clenched tight. Even in death, you held something. I pried your fingers open."

Ted felt the blood drain from his face, a memory surfaced. It was blurry, painful—the fall, the impact—His hand closing over something small and hard in the dirt as darkness took him. He hadn't remembered it, until now.

Ira reached slowly into his vest pocket. He didn't look away from Ted's eyes. He pulled out a small object. He placed it gently on the scarred table between them.

It was a cufflink, silver. It was engraved with a stylized 'I'.

It was Ira's cufflink.

"Found it near Davis's body," Ira said, his voice utterly flat, empty. "Must have torn loose during…during the struggle. When I killed him. Panicked. Rode out. Left it. Then Hatch found your hat…it was easy. Too easy." He looked at the cufflink on the table. "Fell out of my pocket again that night. By the tree. When I knelt beside you. You grabbed it. Held it like proof."

"How could you kill Davis, your friend and not know what you'd done? Ted asked

Ira looked up at Ted, "I was drunk. Blind drunk. Like I was during all of our fistfights in town. Davis was the only friend that stood by me through all of the drinking and fighting."

Ted stared at the silver glint of the cufflink. The truth hit him with the force of a bullet. The phantom seventh man wasn't just a watcher, he was the killer. The man whose crime condemned Ted. The man whose face Ted saw laughing in his mind as the rope choked him and Ted had held the evidence, unknowingly, uselessly.

Ted's hand moved. It was smooth, fast, years of practice. His Colt cleared leather. He leveled it at Ira's chest. The cantina erupted in panic. Chairs scraped the dusty floor. Men shouted, diving for cover.

Ira didn't flinch. He looked past the gun barrel, straight into Ted's eyes. There was no fear, only a terrible resignation. "Do it, Marshal," he said quietly. "Lawman's justice. Like you gave the others. For Davis. For what they did to you. For what I let happen to you"

Ted's finger tightened on the trigger. Justice, for the hanging, for the murder, for the stolen years. The scar burned white-hot on Ted's neck. The faces of the six men he'd hunted flashed in his mind. Clem's terror, Peters' defiance, Hatch's hate-filled eyes as he fell. He saw the courtroom and the hollow victory. He saw Ira kneeling by his body, finding the proof clutched in his dead hand.

He had brought men to justice. He had upheld the law, mostly. He had killed one who resisted. He had hunted a phantom who was real. He had the killer before him. He had confessed and was armed.

Ted Finley pulled the trigger.

The roar filled the cantina. Ira jerked back, a dark stain spreading across his chest. He slumped across the table. The silver cufflink rolled slowly towards the edge, gleaming in the dim light.

Silence crashed down. Men stared, Ted holstered his smoking Colt. He looked at Ira's body, he looked at the cufflink. He had proof but it was useless now.

He turned and walked out of the cantina into the blinding Mexican sun. He was a lawman—he had delivered justice. He had killed the man who murdered his friend and caused his hanging. He had completed his hunt.

Ted Finley mounted his horse and rode north towards the border— towards the hanging tree. The badge felt heavy as a stone against his chest. He had become the thing he hunted—he had hanged himself.

Paid in Blood

The stage rolled in at noon, kicking up dust along the way. One passenger stepped down. He was, tall, lean and wearing a worn duster coat. He wore a single gun belt, the holster tied low. His face held no expression, just a quiet watchfulness that scanned the street. He carried a small canvas bag. He walked directly to the Grand Hotel. The town knew his name, Harlan Stone. They knew his profession and they knew he settled his business with bullets.

The whispers started before he finished signing the register. By supper, fear hung thick in the saloon air. Men drank slower, they talked quieter. Stone sat alone at a corner table, sipping his coffee. He didn't speak, he just watched. He cleaned his pistol methodically at breakfast. He had six bullets laid out, he loaded them back—one-by-one. *Click*. Click. *Click*. Click. *Click*. Click.

"Who's it gonna be?" Ed, the blacksmith, muttered over cards. Sweat beaded on his forehead despite the cool morning. "Carson? He cheated Stone in that land deal last year." Carson, the storekeeper, turned pale and fumbled his cards.

"Could be Miller," the barber offered, sharpening his razor with nervous energy. "Remember that fight over the water rights? Stone near killed him then." Miller, the rancher, stopped mid-stride outside the window and changed direction abruptly.

The sheriff watched Stone from his office. He knew Stone's reputation. He was fast—final. The law wouldn't stop him if he drew first. Stone hadn't broken any ordinance, not yet. The sheriff felt helpless. He couldn't guard every possible target.

Stone moved through the town like a shadow. He bought tobacco and examined a new saddle at the livery. He stood for a long moment outside the bank. Each action fueled the speculation. The bank manager locked his door early. The livery owner hid his best whiskey.

Days passed—the tension stretched thin. Stone ate his meals, he walked the boardwalks. He watched—people avoided his gaze. Mothers kept children inside and men carried rifles openly. Every creak of a sign,

every shout, made heads snap around. Sleep became scarce. Who would he kill? When?

On the fourth morning, Stone walked into the feed store. Sam Carter ran it. He was a quiet man, widowed. He was known for fair prices and helping folks in a bind. He looked up, startled. His hand trembled as he wiped it on his apron.

"Morning, Mister Stone. Need...need some grain?" Sam's voice cracked.

Stone didn't answer immediately, he looked around the store. There were burlap sacks, barrels of nails and the smell of oats and molasses. He walked to the counter, placed a single silver dollar down. "Remember me, Sam?"

Sam frowned, confused. He looked hard at Stone's face. The hard lines, the cold eyes. Then, something shifted. Recognition dawned. Not fear, but surprise. "The boy? At the crossroads? Years back...winter?"

Stone gave a single, slow nod. "Thirteen years. You gave me bread. And a blanket. Told me to head south." His voice was flat. "Only kindness I saw that year."

Sam swallowed—a flicker of hope touched his eyes. "I...I recall. Hard times. You looked starved half to death. Just did what seemed right." He managed a weak smile. "Glad you made it through."

Stone didn't return the smile. His hand rested near his holster. "Made it." He paused. The silence grew heavy. The hope died in Sam's eyes, replaced by dawning horror—he understood.

Stone drew—the movement was a blur. The roar of the gunshot filled the small store, it was deafening. Sam Carter jerked backward. He crashed into sacks of feed. A dark stain spread across the front of his faded blue shirt. He slid down, eyes wide with shock and betrayal, already lifeless.

Stone holstered his gun and picked up the silver dollar he'd placed on the counter. He polished it briefly on his coat sleeve and placed it back down, precisely where it had been—payment in full.

He walked out of the feed store, past the townsfolk frozen in the street by the sound of the shot. He walked straight to the livery, saddled his horse, and rode out—he didn't look back.

The sheriff found Sam Carter dead behind the counter. He found the silver dollar. He heard the confused, terrified whispers of the crowd gathering outside. They had expected a feud, a grudge, a known enemy. They hadn't expected kindness to be the death sentence. The town huddled in the street, staring at the feed store door, the dust settling on the road south, and the terrible, unexpected weight of a debt paid in blood.

The Hole at Red Creek

The sun beat down on the dry earth outside Red Creek. Harlan sat on his stool, rifle across his knees, eyes fixed on the hole. It appeared three days ago, a dark circle just beyond the town's last shack. No one saw it form. It just was. One day it wasn't there but the next day there it was.

He watched it every daylight hour. The townspeople called him crazy at first—then the hole grew. It was wider than a wagon wheel now. Its edge crept closer to the town each day. The dark earth crumbled into its unseen depths.

Harlan ignored the jeers. He ignored the preacher who called it a hell-mouth. He ignored the families packing wagons and leaving. Someone needed to watch the hole, he felt it in his bones. He took shifts with Fred from the saloon, but mostly Harlan sat alone.

The hole swallowed stones whole. It made no sound—its darkness felt heavy, like looking at the bottom of a deep well at midnight. Harlan kept his distance. He prodded the ground near its lip with a long stick. The earth felt loose, ready to give and sometimes it did. Harlan, and Fred would watch the dirt loosen into sand and fall effortlessly into the hole.

By the seventh day, Red Creek was a ghost town. Only Harlan and Fred remained. The hole continued to grow—it now stretched thirty feet across. Its edge was now level with the foundations of the abandoned mercantile. Dust devils swirled above it, then were sucked down into the blackness.

"It's moving faster," Fred muttered, handing Harlan a canteen. His face was gray. "We should go."

Harlan shook his head. He took a sip, eyes never leaving the crumbling rim. "Need to see."

Fred left at dusk but Harlan stayed—he lit a lantern. The hole's edge was only ten feet from the mercantile's sagging porch. The blackness seemed to absorb the lantern light. He heard a low rumble deep underground and the ground beneath his stool vibrated.

He stood up, rifle ready but nothing emerged. The hole just grew. He saw the mercantile's foundation stones crack. A section of wall groaned, tilted, and vanished into the dark without a splash or crash. The hole was eating the town.

Harlan backed up, keeping the lantern raised. He retreated past the empty jail, past the silent saloon. The rumbling grew louder—the hole was getting hungrier—it expanded like ink spreading on wet paper. It consumed the mercantile, then the jail. Dust filled the air—boards snapped and fell silently into the hole.

He reached the edge of town near the livery. The hole was immense now, a widening pit of nothing. It reached the saloon—the building leaned, groaned, and slid silently into the void—the ground shook violently. Harlan stumbled, dropping the lantern. It shattered, plunging him into near-darkness lit only by starlight on the dust cloud.

The rumbling became a roar. The earth heaved as the hole expanded even more. Harlan scrambled backwards on hands and knees. He looked towards the center of town, towards his own small shack near the now-vanished saloon. The hole was everywhere. It stretched from where the mercantile stood to the edge of the livery yard. It was swallowing Red Creek whole.

He got to his feet. He needed to run. He turned towards the open desert, the only direction left—he took one step.

The ground beneath his feet disappeared. He fell into silent, absolute blackness. Above him, the last pieces of Red Creek crumbled and vanished into the void. The desert wind blew dust over a vast, smooth pit where a town and its watcher once stood.

The Last Prayer

Samuel wiped the worn wood of the pulpit, the scent of lemon oil mixing with the faint, comforting smell of old hymnals and dust dancing in the Sunday morning light. Outside, the sounds of Cedar Flats waking up drifted through the open church doors—a wagon creaking, Mrs. Henderson calling her chickens, the distant clang from the blacksmith's shop. It was peaceful, he breathed it in. For twelve years, this had been his world: small, contained, good. He preached kindness, mended fences, sat with the sick, and buried the dead. The town respected him, they trusted him. They knew him only as Preacher Sam, a gentle man who arrived one dusty day seeking a quiet place to serve.

No one in Cedar Flats knew about the man called Silas Quick. Silas Quick, whose name once sent a cold ripple through saloons from El Paso to Cheyenne. Silas Quick, whose gun hand was faster than a rattlesnake strike, who left a trail of graves across the territories. That man died the day Samuel found a Bible in a burned-out homestead, the words inside searing his soul more than any desert sun. He buried his matching Colts deep in his saddlebags, along with the name—he chose peace.

He kept the guns, though. One pair of beautiful, deadly things. He locked them in a heavy oak chest beneath his bed in the small house beside the church. A reminder of the darkness he fled, and a silent vow never to unlock it again. He swore to leave the violence behind, he was now a man of peace.

The trouble rode in on a Tuesday, kicking up a thick curtain of dust that hung brown and choking over Main Street. Three men rode in that day. They moved with a lazy arrogance, their horses lean and hard-eyed like their riders. The leader, a man with a face like scarred leather and eyes the color of dirty ice, was called Boone. His brothers, Wyatt and Zeke, flanked him, they were smaller echoes of his cruelty. They didn't announce themselves. They just *were*, a sudden, ugly presence against the town's quiet rhythm.

It started small—things like knocking over old man Peterson's apple cart with a careless nudge of a horse. Loud, mocking laughter in the saloon that silenced the usual afternoon murmur. A deliberate bump that sent young Tommy Carter sprawling into the dirt, his schoolbooks scattering. The boy scrambled up, eyes wide with fear, but said nothing. Cedar Flats held its breath.

Samuel saw it from the church steps. He felt the familiar cold knot form in his gut, a feeling he hadn't known in years. It wasn't fear for himself, but a dread for the fragile peace of his town. He walked down, his long black coat brushing the dust. He approached Boone, who was leaning against a post outside the saloon, picking his teeth with a splinter of wood.

"Afternoon," Samuel said, his voice calm, steady. "Welcome to Cedar Flats. I'm Preacher Sam. Anything we can help you gentlemen with?"

Boone looked him up and down, a slow, insolent appraisal. He spat near Samuel's boot. "Preacher, huh? We ain't needin' saving. Just passin' through. Lookin' for some entertainment." His gaze drifted to where Sarah Miles was sweeping her porch. She quickly turned and went inside.

"Entertainment's scarce in a quiet town like this," Samuel said evenly. "Best found further down the trail. We value our peace."

Wyatt snickered. "Peace looks awful dull, Preacher." He nudged Zeke. "Don't it?"

Samuel kept his eyes on Boone. "Dull keeps folks safe. Keeps folks alive. I'd suggest you move on. Find livelier pastures."

Boone's smile faltered. "We'll move on when we're ready, Preacher. When we've had our fill." He pushed off the post, his bulk looming over Samuel. "You run your church. We'll run the street. Keep your sermons to Sundays."

The preacher didn't flinch. "This town is my church, Mr. Boone. Every day. And I'll preach peace on any day it's threatened." He held the bigger man's stare, a quiet challenge in his own steady gaze.

For a moment, tension crackled in the air. Boone's hand twitched near the gun on his hip. Then he barked a laugh, harsh and empty. "Holier than thou, ain't ya? Fine. Preach your peace. See how long it lasts." He turned and shoved through the saloon doors, his brothers following. The doors swung shut with a bang that echoed down the suddenly silent street.

Samuel exhaled slowly—the cold knot tightened—he knew that look in Boone's eyes. The look of a man who enjoyed breaking things. He spent the next two days walking a tightrope. He was a constant, calming presence, talking down hotheaded ranchers like Bill Hooper who wanted to

run the troublemakers out with buckshot, soothing frightened shopkeepers, checking on the families who lived closest to the saloon where the Boones had taken up residence. He offered them food, water and a listening ear. He preached patience, reason and non-violence, the words feeling both true and desperately fragile against the ugliness brewing.

He tried again with Boone, approaching him as he watered his horse at the trough. "No need for any unpleasantness," Samuel said, keeping his voice low. "The stage comes through tomorrow. It's heading west. A clean break. Fresh start."

Boone didn't even look at him. He poured water over his horse's neck. "Told you, Preacher. We leave when we're ready." He finally turned, water dripping from his hand. "Maybe we like it here. Maybe we think this town needs…shaking up. Maybe," his voice dropped to a menacing whisper, "we think you need shaking up. Man of peace. Bet you weren't always so soft."

Samuel felt a chill that had nothing to do with the water. "The past is buried, Mr. Boone. Let it lie."

"Some graves ain't deep enough," Boone murmured, his eyes boring into Samuel's with unnerving intensity. Then he grinned, a predator's smile. "Afternoon, Preacher." He led his horse away, leaving Samuel standing by the trough, the cold knot now a block of ice in his chest. Boone knew—or suspected—how? It didn't matter. The knowledge was a weapon.

The shaking up began that evening. It started with Wyatt and Zeke stumbling drunk out of the saloon. They targeted the general store. They smashed the front window with a thrown bottle, the crash shattering the twilight quiet. They kicked over barrels of flour and sugar on the porch, laughing as the white clouds billowed. Old Man Peterson rushed out, yelling. Zeke backhanded him, sending the frail man sprawling into the dirt, blood trickling from his lip.

A crowd gathered, murmuring and angry. Bill Hooper pushed forward, his face dark, his hand on the worn stock of his rifle. "That's enough!" he roared.

Boone appeared in the saloon doorway, leaning against the frame, his own gun loose in its holster. His face was calm and watchful. "Problem, farmer?" he drawled.

"You're the problem!" Bill shouted, raising his rifle slightly. "Get your mangy dogs on their horses and ride! Now!"

Wyatt and Zeke stopped their destruction, turning towards Bill, hands hovering near their own guns. The air crackled—one nervous twitch, one shouted word, and the street would become a killing ground. The townsfolk were frightened and angry, but unarmed except for Bill. They were farmers, shopkeepers, families. They were lambs facing wolves.

Samuel stepped into the widening space between Bill and the Boones. He held up his hands, palms out. "Bill, lower the rifle. Please." His voice cut through the tension, clear and firm. He turned to Boone. "This stops now. You've made your point. Take your brothers and go."

Boone pushed off the doorframe and walked slowly towards Samuel, stopping a few feet away. The street was utterly silent. "Or what, Preacher? What's the holy man gonna do? Pray us away?" He laughed, a short, ugly sound. "We ain't leaving. We like it fine right here. We think we'll stay. Maybe take over." His gaze swept the frightened crowd. "Starting with showing you all who gives the orders now."

He turned his back deliberately on Samuel, addressing the crowd. "This town has a new sheriff. Me. My rules. First rule: no weapons. You," he pointed a thick finger at Bill, "drop that rifle. Now. Or Zeke puts a bullet in that old man's head." Zeke instantly drew his pistol, pressing it against Peterson's temple where he still lay dazed in the dirt. Peterson whimpered.

Bill Hooper's face contorted with rage and helplessness. His knuckles were white on the rifle stock. Samuel saw the calculation in Boone's eyes—he wanted Bill to resist—he wanted the excuse to kill, to break the town's spirit completely. He wanted Samuel to watch.

"Bill," Samuel said, his voice low and urgent. "Do as he says. For Peterson. For everyone."

Bill's shoulders slumped. He slowly bent and laid the rifle on the dusty street. The sound of wood meeting earth was final.

Boone smiled. "Good. Smart farmer." He turned back to Samuel. "See? Peace through strength, Preacher. Your way?" He spat at Samuel's feet. "Weak. Useless." He stepped closer, his voice dropping to a spiteful whisper only Samuel could hear. "I know who you were, Silas Quick. Heard the stories. Fastest gun west of the Pecos. Killed twenty men. More?" He chuckled. "Look at you now. Hidin' behind a cross. Makin' nice." His eyes glittered with malice. "Bet you still got the speed. Bet you got those fancy guns stashed somewhere." He leaned in. "I want to see it. I want to see the devil in the preacher. Draw on me, Silas. Give me an excuse to put you down in front of your precious flock. Or…" He looked meaningfully at Sarah Miles, who stood frozen on her porch, clutching her young daughter. "…maybe I start with them. Slow."

Samuel stared into Boone's eyes. He saw the absolute certainty there. Boone would kill Peterson—he would kill Sarah and her child—he would burn Cedar Flats to the ground for the sheer pleasure of it. He would do it slowly, savoring the terror, unless Samuel stopped him. The words of the Bible, the years of sermons, the hard-won peace—they were sand against the tide of Boone's evil. The vow he made, locked away with those guns, felt like a noose tightening around the town's neck.

The cold knot in his gut dissolved into a terrifying, familiar clarity. The clarity of the gunfighter assessing angles, distance and threat. It flooded back, spontaneously, like a sickness. He saw not Boone, but a target. He saw Wyatt and Zeke, their positions, their readiness. He saw the terrified townsfolk, frozen statues in a picture of impending massacre. There was no reasoning—no prayer would stop this—Boone wanted blood. His, or the town's.

The path Samuel walked for twelve years ended right here, in the dust of Main Street. To save Cedar Flats, he had to become Silas Quick one last time. He had to break his sacred vow. The cost would be his soul, but the town…the town might live.

He met Boone's mocking gaze. His own eyes, usually warm and patient, were flat and empty. The eyes of a man looking at the dead. "Alright, Boone," Samuel said, his voice devoid of emotion, a stranger's voice. "You want the devil?" He took a slow step back. "You'll see him."

Boone's smile widened, triumphant and eager. He expected Samuel to go for a hidden gun—he expected a quick draw—he expected Silas Quick.

Samuel didn't draw. He turned and walked away, not towards the church, but towards the small path leading to his house beside it. His steps were measured and unhurried. The silence was absolute, broken only by the crunch of his boots on the gravel. Every eye followed him—confusion flickered on Boone's face, replaced by irritation. "Where you goin', Preacher? Scared? Run to your prayers?"

Samuel didn't answer. He didn't look back. He walked up the path, opened his front door, and disappeared inside.

Boone spat. "Coward." He turned to the crowd. "See? Your holy man ran. Left you to us." He gestured to Zeke. "Shoot the old man. Show 'em we ain't playin'."

Zeke grinned, tightening his finger on the trigger pressed against Peterson's head. The old man closed his eyes.

The sound of the preacher's front door opening again stopped Zeke cold. Samuel stood framed in the doorway. He wasn't wearing his black coat. He wore a simple, faded work shirt. And in his right hand, held low against his thigh, was a revolver—not just any revolver. It was an old Colt Peacemaker, its ivory grips worn smooth, its blue steel catching the last rays of the setting sun. It looked like an extension of his arm. He held another, identical, in his left hand, dangling loosely.

A gasp rippled through the crowd. Shock registered on every face, even Bill Hooper's. Preacher Sam…with guns?

Boone stared, a slow, predatory grin spreading across his face. He chuckled, then laughed outright. "Well, I'll be damned! Silas Quick lives! Knew it! Knew you was hidin'!" He spread his arms wide. "Welcome back to hell, Silas! Been waitin' a long time to meet the legend!" His hand hovered near his own holstered gun. Wyatt and Zeke shifted, their hands dropping to their pistols, forgetting Peterson. The focus was entirely on the two men now.

Samuel walked slowly down the path towards the street, the guns hanging loosely at his sides. His face was a mask, stripped of the kindness and patience. It was the face of a man who had walked away from death too many times to fear it. He stopped at the edge of the street, maybe twenty paces from Hatch. Wyatt and Zeke were off to Boone's right, ten paces apart.

"This ain't your fight, Silas," Boone taunted, though his eyes were calculating, watching Samuel's hands. "This is between me and this pissant town. You could still ride out. Take your fancy irons and go. Live your little lie somewhere else."

Samuel's voice was low, gravelly, utterly unlike his preaching voice. "This town is my fight, Boone. You made it so. You don't get to break what I built." He raised his head slightly, his gaze locking onto Boone's. "Call your dogs off. Send them away. This is between you and me."

Boone laughed. "Think I'm stupid? Think I'll face Silas Quick alone? Wyatt! Zeke! You see him? That's the real deal! The fastest gun who ever lived! Let's see if he's still got it!" His voice rose to a shout. "Take him!"

The command was the spark. Wyatt and Zeke went for their guns, hands blurring towards leather. They were fast—professionals. But Silas Quick was already moving.

He didn't seem to draw—the guns in his hands simply roared—two shots, impossibly close together, like a single, thunderous crack. Samuel's body was a fluid twist, turning sideways, presenting the narrowest target. Wyatt took the heavy .45 slug high in the chest, the impact slamming him back against the saloon wall before he could clear leather. Zeke, his gun half out of its holster, jerked as Samuel's second shot punched through his throat. He dropped to his knees, gurgling, blood fountaining over his shirt.

The speed was terrifying. Less than a heartbeat and two men down.

Boone had drawn. He wasn't as fast as his brothers, but he was deliberate. He fired as Samuel turned back towards him. The bullet whipped past Samuel's ear, close enough to feel the wind. Samuel fired again, a single shot from his right-hand gun. Boone flinched, but the shot went wide, kicking up dust near his boot. Boone's second shot slammed into Samuel's left shoulder. Samuel staggered, grunting with the impact, the left-hand gun falling from his suddenly numb fingers into the dust. Pain, white-hot and fierce, lanced through him.

Boone grinned, advancing, his gun leveled. "Not so fast now, are ya, old man? Shoulda stayed retired!" He steadied his aim.

Samuel ignored the pain and the blood soaking his shirt. He focused solely on Boone's gun hand, the slight tremor as the man prepared to fire the killing shot. Samuel's own right-hand gun came up, not with the blinding speed of before, but with a terrible, cold certainty. He squeezed the trigger.

Boone's shot roared out almost simultaneously. Samuel felt the hammer blow high on his right side, near the ribs. He stumbled back, gasping. Boone stood frozen for a second, a look of profound surprise on his face. Then a small, dark hole appeared in the center of his forehead. He crumpled forward, dead before he hit the dirt.

Silence—deafening—absolute silence. The acrid smell of gunpowder hung thick in the air, mixing with the coppery tang of blood. Three bodies lay in the dust of Main Street. Samuel stood swaying, clutching his bleeding side with his left hand, the smoking Colt still dangling from his right. Blood soaked his shirt on both sides. The shocked faces of the townsfolk stared at him, not with relief or gratitude. Their faces were filled with horror and fear—they saw the guns—they saw the dead men—they saw Silas Quick.

He looked at them—at Bill Hooper, who wouldn't meet his eyes. He looked at Sarah Miles, clutching her daughter, her face pale with terror—terror of *him*. He looked at old man Peterson, struggling to sit up, staring at Samuel like he was a stranger—a monster.

He saw the peace he had built, shattered like the general store window. He saw the preacher dead in the street, killed by the gunslinger. He saw only revulsion in the eyes of the people he loved, the people he just saved.

The strength left his legs. He sank to his knees in the dust beside Boone's body—the Colt slipped from his fingers. He looked down at his bloodstained hands. The hands that had just killed three men—the hands that had held the Bible, comforted the sick and built fences. The vow was broken—the peace was gone—the darkness he thought he'd escaped had swallowed him whole, right here in the sunlight.

He didn't hear the footsteps approaching. He didn't look up until Bill Hooper stood over him, holding his own recovered rifle. Bill's face was hard, unreadable. Samuel looked into the eyes of the man he'd saved, searching for a flicker of understanding, of the old friendship. He found only cold resolution.

"Sam…" Bill's voice was rough. "Preacher…what did you do?"

Samuel tried to speak, to explain, to apologize. Only a wet, rasping cough came out. Blood bubbled on his lips, the wounds were bad. He knew it. The world started to gray at the edges.

Bill Hooper raised the rifle. Not towards any new threat, towards Samuel. His finger tightened on the trigger. "We don't want your kind of peace," Bill said, his voice thick with grief. "Not after this."

Samuel closed his eyes—he didn't see the rifle muzzle. He saw the sunlight on the pulpit. He heard the distant clang of the blacksmith's hammer. He smelled lemon oil and dust. He was at peace—he let out a breath. The last sound he heard wasn't a gunshot. It was the collective gasp of Cedar Flats as Bill Hooper, the man Samuel saved, pulled the trigger.

The Sheriff's Price

The desert wind carried dust and the sour smell of fear. Sheriff Granger tracked the lone rider across the bone-dry flats, closing the gap near sundown. He found the man huddled by a dying fire, hands raised and eyes wide.

"Easy, Sheriff," the outlaw said. "The money's right here. Take it. Just let me ride." He gestured to a worn saddlebag.

Granger kept his rifle steady. "You killed two men in Cold Creek."

"Self-defense!" The outlaw's voice cracked. "They drew first. Check the bag. It's all there."

Granger lowered the rifle slightly, stepping closer. He reached for the bag's strap. The outlaw watched, his breath shallow. Granger pulled the bag open, peering inside. He saw the bundled cash, then his eyes narrowed.

He raised the rifle again, fast. The shot echoed across the empty land. The outlaw fell back, surprise frozen on his face. Granger spat near the body. "Defense don't matter," he muttered, holstering his weapon. "Dead men don't collect bounties." He dragged the saddlebag free.

The Sun, the Wind
and a Man Named Flynn

The sun burned Flynn's neck. It pressed down, a heavy, white-hot weight on his back. He squinted against the glare bouncing off the endless sand. His horse, a dusty bay, plodded with head low. Water sloshed low in the canteen. Flynn tasted grit—he only wanted silence…silence and distance.

Three towns lay behind him now—places he meant to pass through unseen. Trouble found him anyway. In Dry Creek, two bandits hassled the storekeeper's daughter. Flynn saw the fear in her eyes, the way her knuckles whitened on her apron. He hadn't drawn fast—he was just faster than them. He left before the marshal arrived, the girl's thanks ringing hollow in his ears. Whisper Rock brought a crooked sheriff shaking down miners. Flynn watched a week's wages disappear into the lawman's pocket. He confronted him behind the saloon at dusk. The sheriff drew first—Flynn's bullet found its mark. He rode out under cover of night, the miners were silent witnesses. Then there was Sandy Flats. There, a rancher's cattle were being rustled. The rancher pleaded and offered money but Flynn refused. Then he found the rustlers' camp. There were three men, careless around their fire. He didn't kill them all, one ran. Flynn shot their horses instead, he scattered the stolen herd—he knew the rancher would find them. He collected no reward, never expected to. He tried to stay out of it but something always pulled him in. Now the exhaustion weighed him down. He just wanted rest, just wanted to be left alone.

Now the desert lay before him. It was vast and treacherous, a gamble he might not win. It was a shortcut away from people, away from eyes that might know his face or his reputation. It would take him away from the need to act. The heat warped the horizon—his vision swam. The wind started that morning, it was a dry, rasping breath across the dunes. It kicked up sand and scoured his skin. It stole the sweat before it could cool him. It flung stinging sand into his eyes and his mouth. He pulled his bandana up but it offered little relief. The sun ignored the wind, it was relentless. It baked the air, made it hard to breathe. His canteen emptied faster than he planned. He rationed the last of his water. His tongue felt thick, swollen.

The bay stumbled, Flynn reined in hard. The horse stood trembling, legs splayed, its head hung lower. Flynn dismounted, his own legs were stiff. He patted the horse's neck. "Easy, boy," he said. The words scratched his throat. He uncorked the canteen, poured a trickle into his cupped palm. The bay lapped it up weakly. Flynn took a smaller sip himself. The water was hot—it did nothing. He glanced around at the shimmering wasteland. There was nothing but dunes and the bleached bones of something long dead. The wind howled around them, pushing sand in drifts against his boots. The sun hammered his hat brim. He felt dizzy—he knew the signs, his horse wouldn't last much longer, neither would he.

He walked, leading the stumbling horse—hours blurred, he lost track of time, didn't even know what day it was. The sun reached its peak, a molten rock in a washed-out sky. The wind grew stronger and hotter. The breeze should have been cooling but the desert sun was relentless—it heated the wind—it felt like a furnace blast. Flynn's vision narrowed, he saw dark spots all around. His legs were heavy and tired. The bay stopped—it wouldn't move, Flynn tugged at the reins. The horse sank to its knees with a low groan, then rolled onto its side, ribs heaving. Flynn stood over it, helpless. He pulled his knife—it was quick, merciful. He cut a strip of leather from the saddle, took his canteen and his worn blanket—he left the rest. The wind whipped sand over the bay's still form almost immediately. Flynn turned his back and walked, each step was an effort. The sand dragged at his boots. The sun pressed him down hard—the wind sucked the moisture from his skin. He focused on putting one foot in front of the other, he staggered. He thought of cool streams and deep shade—the images faded, replaced by the glaring white of the sand. He tripped over a rock he didn't see—he fell hard into the sand. He lay there, the sand hot against his cheek. He didn't have the strength to get up. The wind howled and whirled over him. The sun blazed, its relentless heat baking the wind, the sand and the man. This was the end—he closed his eyes.

A shadow fell across his face—Flynn flinched, forcing his eyes open. A figure stood over him, blocking the sun. He was lean, wrapped in faded, sand-colored cloth. His face was shaded by a wide-brimmed hat. Flynn saw dark eyes watching him, a sharp nose. It wasn't a face he knew. A canteen appeared, held out, Flynn's hand trembled as he reached for it. The water was warm, but it was water. He gulped, choked, gulped again. The man took the canteen back. "Slow," a voice said, low and calm, not unkind. The man helped Flynn sit up, then stand. He was surprisingly strong. He draped Flynn's arm over his shoulders, taking most of his weight—Flynn saw no horse. The man pointed—a small rock outcrop broke the monotony of the dunes ahead—it seemed impossibly far. They walked,

Flynn stumbled but the man held him firm. The wind tore at them. The sun continued to beat down—the man never faltered, he never wavered. He moved with a steady stride, ignoring the elements.

They reached the rocks—the shade was a deep, cool shade—it was the kind of shade Flynn needed. He collapsed against the stone. The man knelt, uncorked his canteen again and gave Flynn another drink, then wet a cloth and wiped Flynn's face. He unwrapped a bundle—dried meat and bread. He offered some, Flynn ate mechanically. His strength seeped back slowly and painfully. "Why?" Flynn finally managed, his voice a croak. The man studied him. "Saw your tracks. Saw the horse." He shrugged. "Bad place to die alone." He didn't ask Flynn's name and didn't offer his own. He just sat, chewing his own portion, watching the desert. The wind howled outside their shelter, flinging sand against the rocks. Inside, it was still—it was bearable.

The man shared his water sparingly, his food carefully. He knew the desert. He showed Flynn how to find moisture in certain roots, how to read the wind for shifts. He spoke little. Flynn learned his name was Rafe. He said he was a prospector, looking for a lost claim. Flynn didn't believe him—there was a stillness about Rafe, a watchfulness Flynn recognized— this man knew violence. They rested through the worst of the heat. When the sun dipped lower, painting the dunes in orange and purple, Rafe stood. "Can walk now?" Flynn nodded, though he felt weak. They set out, walking through the cooling dusk. The wind died down, leaving an eerie silence. The stars began to prick holes in the darkening sky. Rafe led with unerring certainty. Flynn followed, grateful but wary.

They walked for hours under the stars. Flynn's strength slowly returned—the vast silence pressed in. He thought about Rafe—why would he help a stranger? Why risk his own water?—strangers can be very dangerous this far out west. Flynn carried death with him, maybe Rafe sensed it, maybe he didn't care. The moon rose, bathing the desert in a cold silver light. Up ahead, Flynn saw a darker smudge appearing on the horizon. It was a town, or what passed for one out here. It was just a cluster of low, dark shapes. Rafe stopped. "Solace," he said. "Got a well. Bad water, but water." He looked at Flynn. "You make it from here." He turned to go, back towards the vast emptiness.

"Wait," Flynn said, the word surprised him. "Obliged. You saved my life." Rafe paused and looked back, his face shadowed by the moon. "Don't make me regret it." Then he was gone, melting into the moonlit dunes as silently as he appeared. Flynn watched him vanish—the unexpected kindness sat heavy in his gut, it was an unfamiliar feeling. He turned towards Solace.

Solace was barely a town. It was three crumbling adobe buildings huddled around a central well. A single light glowed in a window. The place felt deserted, haunted. The wind had picked up again, sighing through gaps in the walls—it felt colder now. Flynn approached the well, the pulley creaked as he lowered the bucket. He hauled it up—the water smelled sour, but he drank deep—he filled his canteen. He needed rest—the building with the light seemed the only option. A faded sign proclaimed it "Solace Saloon". He pushed the door open, it squeaked on rusty hinges.

The air inside was thick with dust and the smell of cheap liquor. A single oil lamp burned on the bar. A man stood behind it, polishing a glass, he looked up, his eyes wary. He was thin and balding. The only other occupant sat slumped at a table in the corner, head buried in his arms, snoring softly. "Whiskey," Flynn said, his voice still rough. He dropped a coin on the bar. The barman poured without a word, slid the glass. Flynn downed it, the burn was a welcomed feeling. He felt Rafe's water and food battling the exhaustion. "Room?"

"Back," the barman gestured with his chin. "Pay first." Flynn paid. The barman handed him a key. "Quiet night," Flynn observed, glancing around the empty room. The barman's eyes flickered to the sleeping man, then back to Flynn. "Usually is." Flynn took the key. The room was small, bare, containing only a narrow cot and a chair. That was probably more than he needed. He dropped his saddlebags, sank onto the cot. He just sat and listened to the night. The wind howled outside—the saloon was silent below. He thought of Rafe, out there in the dark. He thought of the desert sun. He slept.

A shout woke him, a crash. Flynn was on his feet instantly, gun in hand. He pressed himself against the wall beside the door, listening. He heard angry voices below—two, maybe three men—demanding. The barman's voice was scared. "I told you, he ain't here! Left days ago!" There was a thud and a groan, Flynn cursed silently. He didn't need this—he could slip out the back—disappear. Let Solace deal with its own troubles. He moved to the small window and looked out. The desert stretched out forever, silver under the moon. Escape was there, he could feel it. But he saw Rafe's face in his mind. *Don't make me regret it.* The barman cried out again, Flynn sighed. He holstered his gun. He wouldn't draw first but he would draw fast. He opened the door.

He walked down the rickety stairs slowly. Three men stood near the bar. They were rough, trail-dirty. One of them held the barman by his shrt, shaking him—another kicked the sleeping drunk, who groaned and curled up. The third man saw Flynn first. "Well, lookee here. Who's this?" The others turned. The one holding the barman shoved him hard against the bar. "You lied, old man." The barman whimpered. "Didn't know he was here! Swear!"

Their leader, a thick-necked man with a scar across his cheek, stepped towards Flynn. "You know a fella called Rafe? Skinny fella, quiet?" Flynn kept his hands visible, near his sides. "Passed through. Didn't stay." The man's eyes narrowed. "He stole from us. Gold dust. Took it right outta our claim shack while we was sleepin'. We tracked him." He said. "Track ended near here. You know where he went?" Flynn shook his head slowly. "He went back into the desert. Hours ago." He saw the disbelief in their eyes. "He saved my life out there. Gave me water. That's all I know."

The scarred man laughed, a harsh sound. "Saved you? That's rich. Rafe don't save nobody. He kills 'em. Takes their water, their gear. We found bones out there, mister. More than one set near places Rafe frequented." He took another step closer, the other two fanned out. "You're lyin'. Maybe you helped him. Maybe you got the dust." Flynn felt the familiar cold knot settle in his gut. The desert sun, the wind, Rafe's unexpected kindness—it was all a lie? Or was this man lying? It didn't matter—trouble was here. "I don't have your gold," Flynn stated, his voice flat. "Rafe is gone. Leave it."

The scarred man sneered. "Or what? You gonna make us, gunslinger?" He saw Flynn's worn holster, the way he stood. "Yeah, I know the look. Think you're fast?" He dropped his hand towards his gun. Flynn didn't move. "Draw on me," he said, very quietly, "and you die." The threat hung in the air, cold and final. The scarred man hesitated—his hand hovered near his holster. The other two watched, tense. The wind outside rattled the loose shutter. The barman froze with fear and the drunk whimpered. The scarred man's eyes flickered. He saw the emptiness in Flynn's stare, the absolute lack of fear. He saw his own death, he swallowed. His hand moved away from his gun, slowly. "This ain't over," he growled. "We'll find Rafe. And if we see you again..." He didn't finish. He jerked his head. "C'mon." The three men backed towards the door, eyes locked on Flynn, then they slipped out into the night.

Silence descended, it was broken only by the wind and the barman's shaky breathing. Flynn let out a slow breath. He hadn't drawn, no need to. He walked to the bar. "More whiskey." The barman poured with trembling hands. "Thanks, mister. They...they meant trouble." Flynn didn't answer, he just drank. Rafe, a killer? Bones in the desert? The man who shared his water, who bore Flynn's weight for miles under the sun? It didn't fit. Or did it? He thought of the stillness he'd noticed in Rafe, the watchfulness. The desert changed men, it twisted them. Maybe kindness was just another way of survival.

He finished the whiskey. He needed sleep, real sleep. He turned to go back upstairs. The drunk in the corner stirred. He lifted his head, blinking blearily. His eyes focused on Flynn. They weren't the eyes of a drunk. They were sharp, clear and filled with a terrible sadness—it was Rafe. He hadn't left, he'd been right here, listening. He stood slowly, his movements fluid and quiet. He looked at Flynn, then at the door where the men had gone. "You didn't have to do that," Rafe said, his voice low. "I can handle my own trouble."

Flynn stared—the pieces clicked, like a puzzle being solved right before his eyes. Rafe hiding, the barman's fear, the men tracking gold. "Did you steal it?" Flynn asked, his voice tight. Rafe met his gaze. "Does it matter?" He walked towards the bar, poured himself a water. "They work for Eliot Porter. He owns most of the land around here. Found gold on my claim. My legal claim. Sent those coyotes to run me off. Took my papers. Killed my partner." He drank the water. "I took back what dust I could find in their shack. Belonged to me anyway." He looked at Flynn. "They'll be back. More of them. Before dawn. Porter doesn't tolerate thieves, especially ones who steal from him." He said it with bitter irony.

Flynn felt the trap closing—the desert hadn't killed him—this might. "Why stay? Why not run?"

Rafe turned, his eyes were hard. "Run where? Deeper into the sand? They'd hunt me. Porter has reach. This ends here." He looked at the door. "They saw you stand them down. They know you're here. They'll come for both of us now." He picked up a worn rifle leaning against the wall near his table and checked the action. "You should go. Out the back. Now. While you can." He met Flynn's eyes again. "You owe me nothing."

Flynn looked at the door. He heard the wind rising, he could go—he could slip away into the night. He could leave Rafe to his fight. It wasn't his gold, wasn't his claim. Rafe might be a killer, might not be. Either way, it didn't matter. He thought of the crushing heat, his horse dying, the sand filling his mouth. He thought of the shadow blocking the sun, the arm around his shoulders, the shared water. He thought of the barman's terrified face. He thought of the three men backing down. He was tired, tired of walking away. He was tired of the sun and the wind and the ghosts. He walked to the bar, poured himself the last of the whiskey. He drank it down and turned to face the door. "I'll stay," he said.

Rafe looked at him for a long moment. He nodded once. "Barricade the windows." They worked quickly and silently. Flynn tipped the heavy table onto its side and shoved it against the shuttered front window. Rafe did the same with another table for the side window. The barman dragged crates, barrels, whatever he could find. They blocked the back door with a heavy wardrobe dragged from the barman's room. The saloon became a fort, a poor one but a fort nonetheless. They positioned themselves. Flynn near the front, behind the overturned table, his Colt ready. Rafe took the side window, his rifle steady. The barman crouched behind the bar, clutching an old shotgun. The wind howled, a constant presence. They waited.

The first shot shattered the stillness. It blew a hole through the shutter near Rafe, splinters flew. Rafe fired back instantly. There was a cry from outside. Flynn peered through a gap in the barricade. Shapes moved in the moonlight near the well. There was more than three, six, maybe eight. Muzzle flashes lit the night. Bullets thudded into the adobe walls, ripped through the shutters. Flynn fired, he saw a man stagger. Rafe's rifle cracked again. The barman fired the shotgun blindly through a hole in the barricade. The roar was deafening. Flynn reloaded, his fingers steady. The wind carried the smell of gunpowder—men shouted outside. A bottle crashed through the shattered front window, shattering on the floor—kerosene. The smell hit Flynn's nostrils. A second bottle followed, spraying liquid. A match flared in the darkness outside—it arced through the broken window.

Flames erupted with a whoosh, spreading across the spilled kerosene, licking up the dry wood of the barricade. Smoke billowed, thick and choking. Flynn fired at the shapes near the window. Rafe coughed, firing towards the side. "Front's going!" Flynn yelled. The heat from the flames was intense, the barricade burned fiercely. Light filled the room, flickering. Flynn saw the figures moving closer, silhouetted against the fire. He shot one, another took his place. The barman screamed as a bullet caught him in the shoulder. He dropped the shotgun, clutching his arm.

Rafe moved, he grabbed a blanket and threw it onto the flames near the front, stamping it down. It smothered part of the fire, but smoke choked them. Bullets tore through the thinning smoke. Flynn felt a hot sting along his ribs, he ignored it. He fired again, empty click—he reloaded, his movements fast. Rafe was coughing violently now. He fired his rifle, it clicked empty, he reached for his pistol. A figure lunged through the gap near the burning barricade, gun raised. Rafe shot him point-blank. The man fell back, another appeared behind him. Flynn shot that one. The heat was unbearable and the smoke stung their eyes. The wind fanned the flames, driving them deeper into the saloon. The back door shuddered under heavy blows. They were surrounded.

Rafe stumbled towards Flynn, grabbing his arm. "Back room! Window!" He pointed towards the rear. Flynn saw the logic—the fire blocked the front, men were at the side and back. The small window in Flynn's room was the only way. They could try to break out—maybe get one shot. The barman was down, moaning, he couldn't move. Flynn looked at him, then at Rafe. "Go!" Rafe yelled, shoving him towards the stairs. "I'll cover!" Flynn hesitated. Rafe fired his pistol towards the back door, which was splintering. "Go, damn you! You owe me that much!" Flynn turned and ran for the stairs, bullets whined past him. He reached the top, threw open his room door. He ran to the small window, it was barred with old, rusted iron. He grabbed the chair and smashed it against the bars. They held, he hit them again, rust flaked. There were shouts coming from outside, they knew. He heard boots on the stairs.

He turned—rafe stood in the doorway, his back to Flynn, firing down the stairs, he emptied his pistol. There was a cry from below. Rafe slammed the door and he threw the bolt, it was flimsy. He looked at Flynn, at the window. "Bars won't budge," Flynn said, breathing hard. Rafe nodded. He leaned against the door, reloading. The door shuddered under an impact. "They're coming through," Rafe said calmly. He looked at Flynn, there was no fear in his eyes, only resignation and something else. Regret? "Should've let the desert have you," he said, almost a whisper. "Cleaner end."

The door splintered around the lock. A gun barrel appeared through the hole, firing blindly into the room. Plaster exploded from the wall near Flynn's head. Flynn dropped to one knee and fired through the hole. There was a grunt outside. Rafe fired twice more at the door, it burst open. The scarred man filled the doorway, gun blazing. Flynn shot him—the man fell back, another pushed past him. Rafe fired, he missed. The man's bullet caught Rafe high in the chest. He staggered, hit the wall. Flynn shot the attacker in the face. More men crowded the doorway. Flynn fired again—*Click*—empty. He fumbled for his last bullets. He was too slow—a rifle appeared, aimed at him.

A shot rang out—it wasn't from the doorway, it came from behind Flynn. The rifleman dropped, Flynn spun around. Rafe was slumped against the wall, his own pistol smoking in his hand—he'd fired. His eyes were already glazing. He met Flynn's gaze, then his head slumped forward. Flynn jammed bullets into his Colt and fired at the doorway. The men scrambled back, he fired again. There was silence, smoke filled the hallway. The fire roared below, eating its way up the stairs. Heat washed over Flynn—the wind screamed through the broken window, feeding the flames. He looked at Rafe's still form. He looked at the burning doorway. He had no more bullets—he heard shouts outside—they were regrouping. The fire was the only thing holding them back now. It wouldn't hold long. He walked to the window and gripped the rusted bars, he pulled with all his strength— nothing. He pulled again, bracing his foot against the wall—the iron groaned and bent slightly. He pulled again—a bar snapped near the base. Hope surged—he grabbed the next bar. He pulled—it held. He heard boots on the burning stairs. He was out of time.

He turned, the flames flooded through the doorway. A figure appeared, silhouetted against the inferno below. It wasn't one of Porter's men. It was the barman, his face was blackened, his shirt smoldering. He clutched his wounded arm. In his good hand, he held the old shotgun. He looked at Flynn, his eyes wide with terror. He looked at Rafe's body. He raised the shotgun, not towards the door, towards Flynn. "Gold," the barman said. "Rafe hid it. Told me. Before...before he came down. He hid it in your room." His eyes darted around the small space. "Where is it? Give it to me! I can buy my way out!" Flynn stared. The greed, the stupidity, in the face of death. "There is no gold here," Flynn said flatly. "He lied."

The barman's face twisted. "Liar!" He screamed it. He leveled the shotgun. "Give it to me or I blow you to hell!" Behind him, the stairs collapsed in a shower of sparks and burning timber. The fire roared, climbing the walls. The heat was suffocating—the wind howled like a banshee through the broken window. Flynn saw the barman's finger tighten on the trigger. He saw the madness in his eyes. He had no gun, no cover. There was only the burning room, the dead man, the wind, and the greedy fool pointing a shotgun. He braced himself—the barman screamed again, wordless rage. He pulled the trigger. *Click.*

The old shotgun misfired. The barman stared at it, stunned. Flynn moved, he lunged towards the window. He grabbed the broken bar, wrenched it sideways with a final surge of desperate strength. It tore free and he threw it aside. He grabbed the next bar—it bent—he kicked it—it snapped. He had an opening, not much, but enough. He turned back just in time to see the flames engulf the doorway. The barman fumbled with the shotgun, trying to cock it again. He didn't see the burning beam above him groan and crack. Flynn shouted a warning that was lost in the roar of the fire. The beam fell, it struck the barman, crushing him instantly, pinning him to the floor in a shower of sparks. The fire closed over him.

Flynn didn't hesitate, he shoved his saddlebags through the window opening. He squeezed through headfirst, scraping his shoulders on the rough adobe. He dropped the few feet to the ground outside. The night air, thick with smoke, felt almost cool. He grabbed his bags and ran, he ran away from the burning saloon—away from the shouts of Porter's men who were now converging on the front, drawn by the inferno. He ran into the desert, back the way he and Rafe had come. He ran until his lungs burned, until the firelight was a glow on the horizon. He collapsed behind a dune, gasping, coughing smoke. He looked back—Solace was a torch against the black sky. The wind carried the smell of burning wood. The sun would find him soon, rising over the ashes. He was alive, Rafe was dead, the barman was dead. Porter's men would find only bodies and fire. He had escaped again—the wind whipped sand around him. It felt colder now. He pulled his blanket tight, closed his eyes. He saw the shadow blocking the sun. He heard the quiet voice. *Don't make me regret it.* The sun would rise. The wind would blow. He would walk—alone.

The Drifter Behind the Bar

The saloon in Flat Ridge hadn't changed in twenty years. The same warped floorboards. The same cracked mirror behind the bar. The same air heavy with dust and whiskey. It's the kind of place where men didn't ask questions because they didn't want to answer any.

A man walked in near sunset. He was wearing a long coat, worn hat and a clean revolver in his hand. His name was Emmett Rourke. He didn't speak as he crossed the room, he didn't nod, didn't smile. He just stood behind the bar and waited for someone to move.

No one did.

Rourke pulled out the bottle nearest his left hand—whiskey, half full—and poured himself a glass. He drank it in one motion, then poured another. His eyes glanced the faces at the tables. Six men, two women, and one drunk passed out on the floor. No one looked him in the eye.

Someone finally stood.

"Didn't know this place hired new barkeeps," said the man.

"They didn't," Rourke replied.

The man sat back down.

Rourke wasn't there to work. He was there to find a man and the only way to find that man was to wait in the place he was most likely to come back to.

Everyone knew who Rourke was—not from Flat Ridge—not from the county—maybe not even from the territory but there was something about his stillness that made men nervous. He carried his revolver like it belonged drawn. He didn't drink like someone looking to forget, he drank like someone about to act.

By nightfall, no one else came in. The piano player packed up—the women left through the back. The six men trickled out one by one, quiet and slow.

Rourke locked the door.

He spent the night behind the bar, sitting on an overturned crate, watching the door. He didn't sleep, didn't yawn, he just waited.

By the next morning, folks had heard.

They came to see him through the windows—no one came inside. The saloon owner, a man named Tiller, tried once. Rourke turned him around with a glance. Tiller didn't try again.

Rourke was hunting a man named Warren Keach.

Keach had once ridden with the 3rd Kansas Rifles during the war. When the fighting ended, he'd moved west and turned to robbing payroll coaches and burning homesteads. He was smart, mean, and careful…very careful. He vanished for years at a time but every lead ended in Flat Ridge.

Ten years earlier, Keach had been part of a five-man job on a Union Pacific car near Junction Hollow. Three guards were killed, a telegraph boy was shot in the back. The fifth man in that job was Emmett Rourke's younger brother, Miles, he never came back.

They said Keach did the shooting—no one proved it. Then the others disappeared and so did Miles.

Emmett waited six years, quiet. Then he started hunting, state to state, county to county—one name at a time. Two years later, he found one of them in a jail in El Paso—another he dragged out of a brothel in Silver Bluff. Each one gave him something—names, towns, places to check. The trail always pointed back to Flat Ridge.

So he came. He took over the saloon and he waited.

On the third day, a telegram came. Rourke didn't open the door. Tiller slid it under. It was from a sheriff two towns over.

"Keach seen headed west. Might be Flat Ridge. Riding alone."

Rourke folded the note and put it in his coat. He set out a second glass on the bar. He poured it and left it full.

The message was clear.

On the fifth night, Keach walked in.

He didn't rush, he didn't blink. He just crossed the room like he owned it and stopped six feet from the bar.

"I heard someone's been looking for me," he said.

Rourke poured a fresh glass. "I'm not looking anymore."

Keach smiled. "Then I suppose we drink."

They did—one drink, then another. Keach stood the whole time.

"You're Miles' brother," Keach said.

"I am."

"I liked him. He had guts."

"You shot him in the back."

Keach tilted his head. "He made a move. Got scared. Grabbed the money and ran. Couldn't let that slide."

Rourke said nothing. His hand stayed near his gun.

"You came a long way," Keach said.

"I had time."

Keach looked around. "All these people think you're going to shoot me. Right here."

"They're not wrong."

"You know I've killed better men."

"You're not going to kill me."

Keach stepped forward, slow. "I'm faster than you think."

Rourke didn't move.

"Or maybe you want to wait," Keach said. "Maybe you want to drag it out. Do it slow. Like I deserve."

"You do."

Keach reached for his gun.

Rourke drew and fired once. The bullet hit Keach in the throat.

Keach fell forward into the bar. He didn't cry out, didn't make a sound. He just bled, then dropped.

Rourke stood over him, watching.

No one came running.

He left Keach where he fell and walked out the front door into the morning light.

Tiller came in later with a shovel and two men. They dragged the body out back and buried it under the oak.

People asked why Rourke didn't leave.

He didn't say.

Instead, he stayed behind the bar.

Days passed. Then weeks.

He didn't talk much. He just poured drinks, took coins, cleaned up blood when fights broke out.

Some said he stayed because he had nothing else to do. He had nothing left.

Others said he knew something.

A month later, a U.S. Marshal named Deltry came to town. He wore a coat long as Rourke's and carried iron on both hips.

He walked into the saloon and took a seat.

"You Rourke?" he asked.

"I am."

"You killed Warren Keach."

"I did."

"I'm not here for that. He had warrants. You did us a favor."

Rourke nodded.

Deltry took a folded note from his pocket.

"This came out of the Arizona office two days ago. A name showed up. We've been hunting this man for fifteen years."

Rourke poured a drink.

Deltry laid the note on the bar.

Rourke read it. Then he read it again.

The name on the note was Miles Rourke.

Alive.

Wanted for murder. Wanted for train robbery. Alias used: Warren Keach.

Emmett looked up.

"No mistake?"

Deltry shook his head. "Descriptions match. He's been using that name since 1875. Keach was the alias. Miles is the man."

Rourke stared at the bloodstain still dark behind the bar.

"You sure?"

“I am.”

Deltry stood. “You want to come with me? We can clear your name. You helped us.”

Rourke didn’t answer.

Deltry tipped his hat and left.

Rourke stayed behind the bar the rest of the day.

When the saloon closed, he cleaned the glass his brother had used. Polished it slow. Then he pulled out his revolver.

One shot echoed through the street.

By the time Tiller found him, the bar was clean, the bottle was empty, and Emmett Rourke was slumped behind it, gun still in hand.

They buried him beside the man he’d spent ten years hunting.

Flat Ridge didn’t speak of them much after that.

But men passing through still ask who ran the bar back then.

Tiller always says the same thing:

“A man with good aim and bad luck.”

The Dustwater Bones

The sun hammered the earth outside Dustwater. Sheriff Ethan Deeds wiped sweat from his brow, squinting at the dry creek bed. A boy herding goats had found something. Something white poking from the dirt. Ethan knelt, brushing away dust and gravel. It was bone, then another. A chill cut through the heat despite the glare.

The sheriff worked carefully. More bones emerged, tangled in the roots of a mesquite tree. Then, caught on a rib, there appeared a tarnished shape. He pulled it free, it was a tin star. The metal was dented, the pin bent. He knew this badge—every man in town knew it, sheriff Jack Tolliver wore it. He's been missing sixteen months. Some people whispered he cracked under the border chaos and ran. Others muttered even darker things—now they knew.

The undertaker confirmed it later, pointing to a healed break in the left arm bone matching Tolliver's old injury. Personal effects sealed it: a pocket knife with Tolliver's initials, a worn leather wallet, empty.

Ethan walked back to his office. The familiar weight of his own badge felt heavier. Tolliver wasn't weak, he was tough, maybe too tough. Ethan started digging—he pulled old reports Tolliver filed in the months before he vanished. They were mostly routine, drunks, stray cattle, minor thefts but one thread appeared too often. Tolliver noted strange movements near the old Garcia place, a crumbling ranch house five miles out, abandoned since the drought. He suspected smuggling—the reports stopped abruptly.

Ethan rode out at dusk. The Garcia place stood skeletal against the fading light. Inside, dust choked the air, the floorboards creaked and groaned under the weight of his footsteps. He found nothing obvious at first. Then, near the cold fireplace, there was a loose stone—behind it, wrapped in oilcloth, there was a ledger. It wasn't Tolliver's handwriting. There were columns of dates, weights, and cryptic symbols. Payments—maybe—smuggling. Likely guns heading south, silver heading north. Tolliver had found this or gotten close—maybe he was too close.

Back in town, the air thickened, eyes followed Ethan. Conversations died whenever he entered the saloon. He questioned known troublemakers.

They just offered shrugs and sneers. He pressed Maria Ruiz, who ran the boarding house near the creek. She'd seen Tolliver arguing fiercely with someone the night he vanished. It was a man, she thought, tall but the shadows were deep. She couldn't say who it was.

The ledger pointed to local involvement. Big money flowed through those pages, enough to kill for. A lot of people have killed for a lot less. Ethan kept the book hidden in his office safe. He only trusted his deputy, Clay, a steady man who'd served under Tolliver too. Ethan always shared his findings with Clay. Clay listened, face grim. "Jack always pushed too hard," he murmured. "Should've let some things lie.

Days passed, Ethan felt watched. His horse spooked one night, his saddle cinch was mysteriously cut. Then a shot shattered his office window, missing him by inches. He doubled down. He traced a symbol from the ledger—a stylized 'C'—to Clem Darrow, a surly freight operator with known connections south of the border. Ethan brought him in. Darrow sweated but denied everything. He had an alibi for Tolliver's disappearance night—he was playing cards at the saloon, verified by three men. Ethan had to release him. The pressure mounted—the town felt like a coiled spring.

One stifling afternoon, Maria Ruiz sent word—she remembered something else about that night. She'd heard a horse leave the creek area later. Its gait sounded off, like it favored a front leg. Ethan's pulse quickened. Clay's horse had gone lame around that time. Clay said it stepped in a gopher hole. Ethan dismissed it then, now it hooked into his mind, sharp and cold.

He walked back to his office, thoughts churning. Clay was there, cleaning his pistol at Ethan's desk. The safe door stood slightly ajar. Ethan froze. Clay looked up, calm, too calm—he held the smuggler's ledger.

"Looking for this, Ethan?" Clay asked, his voice flat. "Shouldn't leave your safe combination where folks can find it."

Ethan's hand drifted towards his holster. "Clay?"

"Jack found the ledger," Clay said, standing slowly. "He found it because I got sloppy. He came to me. Thought he could trust his own deputy. Wanted to bring me in, give me a chance." Clay's smile was thin, humorless. "He didn't understand the money. The power. This town runs on silver and lead, Ethan, not law. I tried to reason with him. Down by the creek." He tapped the ledger. "He wouldn't listen."

The truth hit Ethan like a physical blow. The trusted deputy—the man who knew every move Ethan made—the man who cut the cinch. The man who fired the shot—the man who listened patiently as Ethan laid out his case. "You killed him," Ethan said. "You buried him."

"Had to," Clay said simply. He lifted the pistol he'd been cleaning. Ethan's own Colt. "Just like I have to do this. You dug too deep, Ethan. Just like Jack." Clay's finger tightened on the trigger. "Should've let some things lie."

Ethan lunged sideways, drawing his own gun. The roar filled the small office. Wood splintered near Ethan's head, he fired back. Clay staggered, clutching his shoulder, but he didn't go down. He fired again, pain exploded in Ethan's chest. He crashed against the wall, sliding down. His gun clattered away, he couldn't breathe.

Clay stood over him, Ethan's smoking pistol steady in his hand. Blood seeped through Clay's shirt, but his aim didn't waver. "Sorry, Ethan," Clay said, no trace of regret. "Needed the job done right. Needed someone folks trusted to take over when Jack vanished. You were perfect." He glanced at the ledger on the desk. "Now it all stays buried. For good."

Ethan gasped, tasting blood. He saw Tolliver's tarnished star on his desk, where he'd left it. Clay followed his gaze and picked up Tolliver's badge, then dropped it onto Ethan's chest. The cold metal pressed against Ethan's shirt.

"Keep it," Clay said. He turned, holstering Ethan's pistol. He picked up the ledger, tucked it inside his jacket and walked out of the office, leaving the door open. Ethan heard his boot heels fade on the boardwalk. The tin star felt heavy as a tombstone on his chest. Outside, the relentless sun beat down on Dustwater. The town's secrets, deeper and darker than the dry creek bed, remained safely buried. Silence filled the office, broken only by Ethan's ragged, failing breaths. Darkness closed in. The last thing he saw was the dented tin star, glinting dully in the dusty light.

Blood and Iron

The South Western Railroad Company had swallowed half the territory in ten years. Its black trains cut through land once ruled by silence and sky. Its agents—men dressed in sharp coats and heavy boots—arrived ahead of the tracks, clearing paths with bribes, contracts, or bullets.

One of them stood in front of the Dry Bluff station, revolver in hand. His name was Harmon Strake. Nobody called him anything else. He didn't speak much, didn't drink much, and didn't blink when things turned ugly. He wore black from head to heel, kept his beard thick, and carried a Colt Dragoon like it was part of his arm.

Most folks assumed he was a hired gun for the company, but they were wrong.

He was the company.

No one signed off on a rail extension without his approval. He answered only to a man back east who stayed behind curtains and sent letters with no return address. Strake showed up, scouted the land, evaluated the risks, and removed obstacles.

Obstacles usually meant people.

Strake arrived in Dry Bluff under a rising sun. The station was new, still smelling of cut lumber. Beyond it lay the town: a mix of weather-beaten storefronts, a half-built church, and two dozen ranchers who didn't want tracks running through their pastureland. The town council had rejected three offers already. The last one came with a veiled threat. The next wouldn't bother with the veil.

Sheriff Tobin met him outside the telegraph office.

"You with the railroad?" he asked.

Strake nodded once.

"We got your papers yesterday," Tobin said. "But I'm telling you plain—this town ain't selling."

"I'm not here to negotiate."

Tobin looked him over. "That so?"

Strake didn't answer. He just walked past him, boots crunching over dry earth, his long coat flapping behind. He made straight for the saloon.

Inside, the place went quiet as he stepped in. He didn't need to say who he was—they knew. He sat at the bar and laid the revolver in front of him. Not as a threat—just truth.

A man slid off his stool and left. Two others followed.

Strake ordered coffee.

By dusk, he'd visited every property marked on the rail map. Fourteen owners—he left notes with each. Only one sentence:

"Survey begins Monday. Prepare."

That night, someone tried to burn the station.

They failed, Strake had posted guards. The fire was put out quick. No one was caught, but he didn't need a name. He just needed a message.

The next morning, a man was found dead in the creek behind the saloon. He was a rancher, shot twice. He owned thirty acres near the proposed cut line and had a history of raising hell.

No one said Strake pulled the trigger but no one doubted it either.

By the week's end, five landowners had accepted compensation. Two others disappeared, the rest stayed put.

Then came Amos Cutter.

Cutter owned the largest parcel in the area—flat land, clear soil, perfect for track-laying. He was old, hard as nails, with one eye and no fear. He lived alone in a stone house and kept three rifles loaded by the door.

Strake rode out to see him.

They met on the porch. Cutter sat in a rocking chair, watching the horizon.

"You're wasting time," he said before Strake could speak. "I don't sell. Not to you. Not to anyone."

"You'll need to move."

"I've been here since before the war. Before your trains. Before your company."

Strake didn't respond. He looked past the house, glanced around the land.

"I buried my wife out there," Cutter said, pointing with his pipe. "Ain't nobody moving me off it."

Strake stared at him a moment. "Survey begins Monday."

"Then you'll need coffins ready."

Strake rode off, he didn't look back.

That night, someone fired two shots through Cutter's window. He returned fire but hit nothing. The town blamed Strake—he said nothing.

Sheriff Tobin came to the saloon.

"You want a war?" he said.

Strake didn't answer. He just drank his coffee.

"You'll get one if you keep this up. These people aren't just landowners—they're neighbors."

"I'm here for the company," Strake said. "Not for neighbors."

"You think they'll let this happen?"

Strake stood. "They won't have a choice."

The sheriff looked him over. "You'll be dead before the rails reach this town."

Strake stared at him. "Maybe. But they'll still reach it."

The sheriff left.

On Monday, the survey began. Three men with flags and tools marked the cut. They had rifles with them.

No one interfered.

By Tuesday, the church was burned to the ground. No one took credit but everyone had an opinion.

By Thursday, Strake returned to Cutter's land.

This time, Cutter waited with a shotgun across his lap.

"Not one inch," he said.

"I'm not here to talk."

Strake raised the revolver.

Cutter fired first, missed by inches. Strake didn't miss.

The old man fell backward into the dust. The shotgun clattered down the steps.

Strake stood over him. Cutter coughed once. He tried to speak.

Strake walked away.

They buried Cutter on the land he wouldn't sell.

By that weekend, the last holdouts signed. The track was cleared.

But the town had changed. People looked at each other like strangers. They didn't gather in the saloon anymore—the sheriff stopped wearing his badge—kids didn't play in the street anymore.

Everyone knew what Dry Bluff had become.

The rail crews arrived three days later.

Strake didn't stay to watch the first spike driven. He never did. His work was done.

He rode east along the rail line, through the dust and heat, toward the next town marked on his map.

He didn't make it five miles.

They found him slumped over his horse near a dry ravine. Shot through the back. It was clean, one shot. There were no witnesses, no trail.

His revolver was gone, so was his coat. Someone took them both.

The company sent word but no one claimed the body. Sheriff Tobin had him buried outside town, no marker.

Weeks passed. The tracks moved on, so did the trains.

Dry Bluff kept its silence.

But every so often, someone would find a fresh bullet lodged in a post or see a shadow watching from the hills. The land remembered. The blood stayed in the dust.

Strake became a name not spoken aloud. Just a story passed between men who knew better than to ask too many questions.

And the railroad kept moving.

The Man Who Rode Alone

The wind dragged dust across the main road of Dry Creek as noon struck. The town sat still under the hard sun. A few shapes moved under wooden awnings, keeping to the shadows. At the far end of the street, a lone man walked with steady steps. He wore a wide-brimmed hat, worn duster, his revolver resting low on his hip. His name was Emett Thorne. No one called him Emett. Most folks just called him Thorne

He had shown up six months earlier. Paid for his room at the saloon with gold. He said little. He worked odd jobs—fixing fences, guarding payroll, tracking rustlers. People called him reliable, though no one called him a friend. He drank alone, he rode alone, and he kept to himself like a man with no future. Or one he didn't want to talk about.

In truth, Emett Thorne didn't exist.

His real name was Matthew Cain. Five years ago, he killed a federal marshal in Dodge City. He shot him in the back behind the Silver Bell saloon. The marshal had recognized him from a botched bank job. Cain had panicked and fired, then he ran. He changed his name, burned his old coat, and vanished. The law never stopped hunting. Cain learned to live like a ghost. But even ghosts leave tracks.

That morning, Emett stopped by the sheriff's office. Sheriff Mallory leaned back in his chair, boots on the desk, his coffee gone cold.

"Stage from Abilene comes through at three," Emett said. "Word is it might be carrying something."

"What kind of something?"

"Payroll. Forty head of cattle sold up north. Buyers wired ahead."

Mallory scratched his jaw. "I'll bring Yates. You ride with us."

Emett hesitated. "You sure you need three?"

Mallory gave him a look. "More eyes, fewer holes."

Emett nodded and stepped outside. The air was dry and hot. He turned toward the saloon and caught sight of a man standing on the hotel balcony. He was young, well-dressed, clean boots, and a narrow face. He was new in town. His name was Russell Finch. He said he was a tax agent doing an audit on the county books. He seemed harmless but Emett had noticed him asking too many questions.

Two nights ago, Finch had cornered the saloon barkeep. He asked where Emett came from. He said he thought he recognized the face—that set off alarms.

Emett had run long enough to know the signs. Finch wasn't just nosy—he had found something. Finch watched Emett from under his hat brim. The way he lingered when Emett passed, he had that look of someone getting too close.

That afternoon, Emett rode out with the sheriff and Deputy Yates. They waited on the ridge above the main road. When the stagecoach came, it was on time and carried two passengers and a single crate of feed. There was no ambush, no sign of trouble.

"False alarm," said Yates.

Mallory sighed. "Or someone changed their mind."

Emett didn't answer. His mind was elsewhere. He kept looking back toward town.

That night, Emett sat in the saloon with a bottle he drank slowly. He was watching the stairs, waiting.

Finch came down after dark. Emett stood and walked over.

"We need to talk," he said.

Finch raised an eyebrow. "About what?"

"Not here."

They stepped out into the alley behind the saloon. The night was quiet, only the sound of piano music from inside and boots on boards overhead.

"You've been watching me," Emett said.

Finch gave a small smile. "Been trying to place your face."

"You figured it out?"

"I think so. Your name's not Emett Thorne."

Emett stayed silent.

"You're Matthew Cain. Shot a U.S. marshal in Dodge City. You've been on the run since '72."

"What do you want?"

Finch didn't hesitate. "Gold."

"How much?"

"You've got more than most. Give me enough to leave, and I won't say a word."

Emett didn't blink. "You ride out tonight?"

Finch nodded. "First light."

Emett's hand moved fast. The gunshot echoed through the alley.

Finch dropped without a sound. Emett looked around. There was no one, just the dust and darkness. He dragged the body behind the stacked crates, covered it with a feed sack. His heart beat steady—there was no panic, just action—he'd done worse.

Upstairs, he packed quick. He took the gold from under the floorboards, he counted it once. It was enough to run, but not far. The pistol he'd used in Dodge was still wrapped in cloth. He touched it, then closed the satchel.

By morning, Finch was gone. Folks said he left early, headed east. The sheriff asked around. Emett helped search the room. He looked concerned, played it calm.

Three days passed.

Then a new rider came into town. He rode in on a gray horse. He had a long coat, square jaw and eyes like cold steel. His name was Alder. He said he was a Pinkerton.

The sheriff let him in—Emett watched from the porch. Alder asked about Finch. He checked the hotel, read the ledger. He found the name, asked who'd seen him last.

That night, Alder knocked on Emett's door.

"You're Emett Thorne?" he asked.

"That's right."

"You talked to Finch before he vanished?"

"We all did."

"I've seen your face before. Dodge City. Matthew Cain."

Emett's hand was on the bedpost.

"I'm not here to argue," Alder said. "But I'm taking you in."

Emett looked him in the eye. "You sure about that?"

"I am."

They both drew. The first shot blew out the lamp—the second hit the wall. Emett rolled low and came up firing. Alder took one in the arm, dropped behind the door. Emett ran—out the back—into the dark.

He rode out that night. He took the trail west into the hills. He slept under brush and drank from streams—he moved fast.

By the end of the week, Emett knew he was being hunted.

He circled back—he needed more ammo and supplies. He rode in under rain and slipped into the stable behind the saloon.

The sheriff was waiting.

"You shouldn't be here," Mallory said.

"I came to settle," Emett answered.

Alder stepped from the shadows. His arm in a sling, gun still on his hip.

"You had your chance," Alder said.

Emett looked around. The street was empty, rain was falling hard. The town had gone quiet again—watching.

Emett stepped forward. "Let's finish it."

They faced off in the open. It was just the two of them. The sheriff didn't interfere, he knew how this had to go.

Alder moved first. His draw was quick—clean.

But Emett was faster.

The first shot hit Alder in the leg, the second grazed his side. He dropped hard, he didn't get back up.

Emett walked forward, gun still raised.

"Do it," Alder spat. "End it."

But Emett didn't. He lowered his gun.

Behind him, the sheriff raised his rifle.

"It's over," he said.

Emett turned slow. He dropped his revolver and put his hands up.

They chained him that night. They locked him in the jail and sent word east.

Three days later, the federal marshal arrived.

Emett didn't speak on the ride to Wichita. He just stared at the dust and sky. There was no trial, no appeal. He'd been running too long. The law wanted it quiet.

He never made it to the gallows.

Two nights before the hanging, a man slipped into the jail. They found Emett's body at dawn, a knife in his ribs. Blood on the stone floor.

The guards said he took his own life.

Others said Alder paid for it.

The truth didn't matter.

His gold was never found. Some said he'd buried it in the hills, others said it never existed. The truth was probably somewhere in the middle.

Back in Dry Creek, no one spoke his name. The hotel burned the ledger—the saloon painted over the bloodstains.

But some nights, when the wind blows just right, old-timers talk.

They say Emett Thorne was a man with a past too heavy to carry.

A man who rode alone.

And couldn't outrun what followed.

The Saint of Mercy Flats

Dust devils spun across Main Street as the rider approached Mercy Flats. He moved slow, his hat pulled low and saddlebags thin. He called himself John Hale. He paid cash for the abandoned livery stable at the edge of town, a place needing more work than it was worth. He spoke little but worked hard. Hammer strikes echoed from the stable at dawn, replacing the sound of gunfire that once followed him.

John Hale was born Thomas Klash. He wore that name like a scar. He'd robbed stages, held up banks, left men bleeding in the dirt for a handful of coins—violence was his trade, indifference his armor. Then he met Anna, a schoolteacher with eyes that saw the ghost of the boy he might have been, not the monster he'd become. She spoke of kindness, of roots, of a life built instead of taken. She died in a fever outbreak two years back, her last words a plea: *"Find peace, Thomas. Be someone else."* Mercy Flats was his attempt.

He kept to himself—he repaired Widow Miller's porch without being asked. He pulled the Cartwright boy from the collapsed well shaft, his hands bleeding on the rope. He fixed harnesses, shoed horses, and never raised his voice. The townsfolk saw a quiet, capable man, a good neighbor. They called him Mister Hale or John—they didn't see the Colt Peacemaker, worn smooth from use, wrapped in oilcloth and buried beneath the stable floor. They didn't see the flinch when a door slammed too loud.

The first lawman came in the dry heat of late summer. Marshal Ellis, his star gleaming and dust coating his boots. He watered his horse at the trough outside the stable. Hale was mending a wagon wheel. Ellis watched him work, his gaze sharp, assessing. Hale felt the weight of that look, familiar as the grip of his hidden gun.

"Passing through?" Hale asked, keeping his voice level, his eyes on the iron rim he was shaping.

"Chasing a shadow," Ellis replied. His voice was neutral. "Heard tell of a man fitting a certain description settling down somewhere quiet. Robbed a bank over in Red Rock few years back. Killed two guards. Nasty piece of work." Ellis paused. "Name of Thomas Klash. Ring any bells?"

Hale hammered the metal. The clang was loud, echoing. "Can't say it does, Marshal. Mercy Flats is mostly farmers and shopkeepers." He straightened, wiping sweat with his forearm. He met Ellis' eyes and held his gaze—it was a gamble. The eyes were the hardest thing to change—Ellis stared back, searching for the cold killer behind the smith's calm demeanor.

"You been here long, Mister Hale?"

"Near on a year now."

"Came from?"

"Back east. Work dried up." A rehearsed lie, smooth as river stone.

Ellis nodded slowly. He looked Hale up and down again—the worn work clothes, the calloused hands and the steady gaze that held no apparent malice, only weariness. The poster in Ellis' saddlebag showed a younger man, harder, with eyes like flint. This man…fit, but didn't fit. He had no proof, just a feeling. Ellis tipped his hat. "Well, if you hear anything about this Klash character…you let the next lawman know. Good day."

Hale watched him ride out, the knot in his stomach tightening only after the dust settled. The past wasn't buried, it was hunting.

A month later, two bounty hunters arrived. They were lean, hungry men with calculating eyes. They drank at the saloon, asking casual questions. They watched Hale as he fixed a broken axle for the general store owner. They followed him back to the stable, he found them poking through his meager belongings inside.

"Looking for something?" Hale asked, blocking the doorway. His hand rested near the heavy wrench on his workbench.

The taller hunter smiled, showing stained teeth. "Just curious, friend. Heard you were new. We're lookin' for a man. Worth a lot of money. Name's Klash. Thomas Klash. Mean son of a gun. Looks…a bit like you."

Hale didn't blink. "Lots of men look like other men. You find what you wanted in my things?"

The shorter hunter spat. "Nothin' but junk. You sure you ain't him? A man changes his name, tries to hide…"

"I'm John Hale. I fix things." He picked up the wrench. "Now, you finished trespassing?"

They saw the shift in him—the stillness that wasn't peace, but control. The way his knuckles whitened on the wrench when his grip tightened. They saw the potential for violence, carefully leashed but undeniably present. It spooked them—proof was needed for a bounty, and tangling with a man who looked ready to fight over nothing wasn't worth the risk, not yet. They backed out, muttering.

The encounters left Hale rattled—he started sleeping less, listening more. Every stranger's glance felt like an accusation. He helped Doc Peterson set a broken leg, his hands steady but his mind racing. He rebuilt the schoolhouse roof after a storm, the townsfolk praising his skill, unaware he was scanning the horizon for riders.

The secret festered—it was Widow Miller who finally spoke the fear aloud, after the bounty hunters left. She'd seen them watching Hale— she'd seen his tension. Gossip, sharp as a knife, did the rest. Whispers became questions—questions became a quiet delegation: the store owner, the schoolmarm, the blacksmith who Hale had helped when his forge chimney collapsed. They found him at the stable, sharpening a drawknife.

"John…" the store owner, Mr. Evans, began, twisting his hat in his hands. "Folks…folks are talkin'. About those men who came lookin'. About…who they were lookin' for."

Hale stopped sharpening. He looked at their faces—concern, fear and uncertainty. He saw the fragile trust he'd built cracking—he set the knife down.

"Thomas Klash," he said. "That's who they were looking for. That's who I was." He didn't embellish, he stated it flatly. He told them about the crimes, the violence, the running. He told them about Anna, about her death—about the promise he'd made. "I came here to be someone else. To leave that man buried." He looked at the dirt floor. "I kept it from you. I understand if you want me gone. I'll saddle up tonight."

He expected anger, fear, demands for him to leave. He braced for it.

Mrs. Holt, the schoolmarm, a woman who'd lost her husband to a mining accident, stepped forward. "Where would you go, John? Back to running? Back to that life?"

Hale shook his head, weary. "No. Somewhere else. Try again. Maybe fail again."

The blacksmith, a burly man named Henderson, spoke next. "You pulled my boy from that well. You fixed Widow Miller's roof before the rains came. You rebuilt the schoolhouse. You sat with old man Peterson when he was dyin', just so he wasn't alone." He looked around at the others. "The man who did those things…that's the man we know. That's the man who lives here."

Mr. Evans nodded. "We know what you were, John. But we see what you *are*. Mercy Flats needs men who fix things. Men who help. We need *you*."

Hale stared at them, with disbelief and a fragile, painful hope. "After what I told you? What I did?"

"You told us," Mrs. Holt said firmly. "You didn't hide it when we asked. That counts. Stay."

He stayed—the weight didn't vanish, but it shifted. He wasn't just Thomas Klash hiding anymore. He was John Hale, trying to be worthy of the name Mercy Flats gave him.

The reckoning came with the first frost—Marshal Royce rode in, a different breed from Ellis. He was younger, harder, with eyes that missed nothing and a reputation for shooting first. He stopped at the saloon and showed the worn poster of Thomas Klash. He'd heard whispers from Ellis, rumors from the bounty hunters. He *knew* Hale was Klash. He just needed to prove it, or provoke him into revealing himself.

Royce confronted Hale outside the stable. Hale was repairing a plow blade.

"Klash," Royce stated, hand resting near his pistol. It wasn't a question, it was an accusation.

Hale straightened slowly. "Name's Hale, Marshal."

"Save it. I know who you are. Ellis had a soft touch. I don't." Royce's gaze swept the stable entrance. "You're coming in. Now. For the Red Rock job. For the men you killed."

Hale kept his hands visible, palms out. "You've got the wrong man, Marshal. I've been here over a year. Ask anyone."

Royce sneered. "Anyone? Like these sheep? You think they'll protect a killer?" He raised his voice, addressing the few townsfolk who had gathered, drawn by the confrontation. "This man is Thomas Kash! Wanted for murder and robbery! Step aside. Law's business."

There was only silence—then Widow Miller stepped off the boardwalk. She stood beside Hale, small and frail but chin held high. "That's John Hale. He fixed my roof."

Doc Peterson stepped forward. "He helped me tend the sick during the fever. Saved young Billy Henderson's leg."

Mr. Evans moved next. "He runs this stable. Honest work. Pays his bills."

One by one, the people of Mercy Flats stepped forward. The blacksmith. The schoolmarm. The farmer whose plow Hale was fixing. They formed a loose line between Hale and the marshal—no weapons drawn, just people.

Royce's hand tightened on his pistol grip. His face flushed with anger and disbelief. "You people are fools! He's playing you! He's a viper!"

"Maybe he was someone else, once," Mrs. Holt said, her voice clear and steady. "But the man we know? He's John Hale. He helps. He builds. He belongs here. You have no proof otherwise."

Royce glanced around at their faces. He saw no fear of Hale, only resolve and defiance—directed at *him*. He saw Hale standing there, hands still open, not reaching for a weapon, his eyes holding a plea not for himself, but for the fragile peace these people offered. The proof Royce craved—a quick draw, a desperate move—wasn't coming. He couldn't shoot them all. He couldn't arrest a man an entire town vouched for, not without evidence.

"This ain't over, Klash," Royce spat, his voice thick with fury. "I'll be watching."

He holstered his pistol with a sharp snap, mounted his horse, and spurred it savagely out of town. The dust he kicked up hung in the cold air.

Hale let out a breath he hadn't realized he was holding. He looked at the faces turned towards him. Widow Miller patted his arm. Henderson clapped him on the shoulder. They didn't crowd him—they just stood with him for a moment longer in the quiet street. Then, one by one, they drifted back to their lives.

Hale turned back to the plow blade. He picked up his hammer. The cold metal felt solid and real. The rhythmic *clang* echoed again in the stable yard. It wasn't the sound of gunfire—it was the sound of a man building something. It was the sound of home. Mercy Flats hadn't just given him shelter; it had given him a shield forged from trust, and a chance to keep his promise. The hammer fell again. John Hale worked.

The Ghost Leader

Dust hung thick over Silver Creek. Jesse Colton leaned against the saloon's hitch rail, squinting against the midday sun. He'd come for supplies and nothing more. He was a drifter, a decent hand with cattle, looking for the next job. Peace was his only currency.

The peace shattered with the clatter of hooves. Six riders stormed into town, kicking up a choking cloud of dry dust. They were men with hard eyes and sweat-stained bandanas pulled low. They didn't stop at the saloon. They headed straight for the bank.

Jesse knew trouble when he saw it. He stepped back into the deeper shadows beside the saloon, hand resting near the worn grip of his Colt. Inside the bank, shouts erupted, followed by two sharp gunshots. The riders burst back out moments later, saddlebags bulging. One man, taller than the rest, wearing a distinctive black duster with a torn right sleeve, paused. His gaze swept the street, lingering for a fraction too long on Jesse's shadowed figure. Then they were gone, thundering back the way they came.

The town marshal, Jed Hawkins, stumbled out of his office too late, rifle in hand. His face was flushed with anger and helplessness. Townsfolk emerged, faces pale. The bank teller, clutching a bleeding arm, pointed a shaky finger not just down the road, but directly at Jesse.

"Him! He was watchin'! Signalin' them! I saw him look right at their leader!"

Jesse stepped forward, hands spread. "Hold on. I just got here. Saw them ride in, same as you."

Hawkins' eyes narrowed. He knew the descriptions—it was the Blackwood Gang. They were ruthless, responsible for the Cedar Flats massacre and a dozen robberies. A thousand dollars dead or alive on their leader, known only as "The Ghost." The teller was adamant.

"You fit the build," Hawkins stated, his voice hard. "Stranger in town right when they hit. Seen conferring with them."

"Conferring? I was fifty yards away in the shade!" Jesse protested, but the seed was planted, suspicion hardened the faces around him. A drifter was easy prey for blame.

Hawkins gestured with his rifle. "You're comin' in, mister. Till we sort this."

Jesse saw the trap closing, innocent men died in cells waiting for sorting. He moved fast, a sharp kick sent Hawkins stumbling back. Jesse vaulted onto his waiting horse and spurred it hard down the alley before the stunned lawman could raise his rifle. Shots cracked, kicking up dust behind him—he was a fugitive.

The wanted posters appeared fast. "Jesse Colton. Wanted for Murder, Robbery. Leader of the Blackwood Gang. $1,000 Reward." The crude sketch barely resembled him, but the name was like poison. He became The Ghost.

He rode hard, avoiding towns, living off the land but the West had eyes—bounty hunters, lean and hungry, picked up his trail. The first two found him at a creek bed. Jesse didn't want bloodshed. He called out, tried to explain. They drew—he drew faster. He buried them under rocks, a sick weight settling in his gut.

Days bled into weeks—exhaustion gnawed at him. He needed supplies. He risked a small trading post at dusk, his hat pulled low. He was trading a silver pocket watch for jerky and shells when the door burst open. Three rough-looking men filled the doorway, guns drawn. Not bounty hunters—they were worse.

"Well, lookee here," sneered a man with a scar across his cheek. "The boss hisself. Collectin' his cut early?"

Jesse froze. The Blackwood Gang. Recognition flickered in their eyes, mixed with confusion and hostility. The man in the black duster with the torn sleeve wasn't among them.

"I'm not your boss," Jesse stated, hand hovering near his Colt. "You boys got the wrong man."

Scarface laughed, a harsh bark. "Wrong man? Poster's got your face, Colton. Or 'Ghost', if ya prefer. Heard you been enjoyin' the fame while we do the work. Time to settle up…or maybe we just collect the bounty ourselves. Easier."

Jesse saw the calculation in their eyes—betrayal was cheaper than sharing. He moved quick, his draw was a blur. His first shot took Scarface high in the shoulder, spinning him. The second man fired wild as Jesse dove behind a barrel of flour—wood splintered near his head. The third man scrambled for cover. Jesse shot him through the leg. The trading post owner cowered behind his counter. In the chaos, Jesse grabbed his meager supplies and bolted for his horse, bullets whining past. The gang wanted him dead as much as the law did—he was both a liability and a prize.

Hunted from both sides, Jesse grew desperate—he needed proof. He remembered the leader's gaze in Silver Creek, the torn sleeve—he needed to find that man. He backtracked towards the gang's known haunts, a ghost hunting a ghost. He found their abandoned camps, the cold ashes of fires and the debris of violent men. He avoided posses, doubled back on bounty hunters, a shadow in the vast emptiness.

Finally, near the badlands, he found a fresh trail—five riders. He followed cautiously, using the rocks for cover. They led him to a box canyon, a dead end perfect for a hidden camp. He crept to the rim, looking down—four men sat around a fire. The fifth, the man in the black duster, stood facing the canyon wall, his back to the camp. The torn sleeve was clearly visible. Jesse's heart hammered—he saw his proof standing before him. He just needed to get the drop on him, force a confession, maybe turn him over to a lawman not blinded by the poster.

He began his careful descent, picking his way silently down the steep slope. He was halfway down when a loose rock clattered—four heads snapped up. The man in the duster turned slowly.

Jesse froze—the face beneath the hat wasn't a stranger's. It was familiar, cruelly so. Hardened by years, scarred by violence, but undeniably...Marshal Jed Hawkins.

Hawkins smiled, a cold, humorless stretch of his lips. He didn't draw—he didn't need to. His men had their rifles trained on Jesse.

"Colton," Hawkins said, his voice echoing slightly in the canyon. "Took you long enough to find your way home. To the *real* gang."

The world tilted, obscured, askewed. The lawman—the one who first pointed the finger. The one who controlled the narrative in Silver Creek.

He *was* The Ghost. Jesse had been the perfect scapegoat—anonymous, present, expendable.

"Why?" Jesse said, his hand itching near his gun, knowing it was suicide.

"Why not?" Hawkins shrugged. "Wearin' a badge opens doors. Closes eyes. Makes folks trust you while you clean out their safes. And when things get hot?" He gestured dismissively at Jesse. "You make sure the heat lands on someone else. Someone like you. Poster did its job. Kept the real hunters lookin' in the wrong direction. Pity you survived this long. Made it messy."

Cole saw the trap he'd ridden straight into. Hawkins needed him silenced, permanently. Proof wouldn't matter down here—there would be no trial, no exoneration—just bodies in a forgotten canyon.

"Finish it," Hawkins ordered his men, turning his back again, dismissing Cole as already dead.

The rifles came up, Jesse drew—he was fast, incredibly fast. His first shot took the nearest gunman in the throat. His second clipped another's arm but there were too many. A bullet slammed into his side, knocking him back. Another tore through his thigh. He fired again, hitting nothing. The world blurred. He saw Hawkins turn with a look of mild annoyance on his face, drawing his own pistol calmly.

Jesse tried to raise his Colt, it felt like lead. Hawkins fired—white-hot pain exploded in Jesse's chest. He fell backwards, the rough stone scraping his back, the vast, indifferent sky spinning above him.

Hawkins walked over, looking down. Cole was choking, tasting blood. "You…won't…" he gasped.

Hawkins knelt, his voice low, for Jesse's ears only. "Course I will. You're Jesse Colton, the Ghost Leader. Killed in a shootout with a brave posse led by Marshal Hawkins after a fierce chase. Tragic end to a violent man." He patted Jesses cheek. "Rest easy, 'Ghost'. Your story's been written."

Hawkins stood, holstering his gun. He nodded to his remaining men. "String him up over there. Make it look right for when the 'posse' finds him.

Then burn the place down." He turned and walked away, adjusting his badge on his chest.

Jesse Colton, innocent cowboy, stared sightlessly at the sky as the Blackwood Gang prepared his final scene. The last sound he heard, fading with the light, was the crackle of the fire starting to consume the evidence, and the distant jingle of a lawman's spurs walking away. Justice wouldn't ride today. The West had claimed another soul, and the real monster wore a star.

Redemption

The desert wind scuffed grit across Redemption Creek's main street, carrying the smell of dust and baked wood. Sheriff Eli Thorne stood on the boardwalk outside his office, a solid figure in a worn duster. He scanned the quiet street. Years of relentless effort had carved this order from chaos. Gone were the open gunfights and the drunken brawls spilling from saloons. Peace wasn't flashy; it was the absence of fear. Eli took a slow breath, the dry air catching in his throat. He saw Mrs. Henderson sweep her porch without glancing over her shoulder. He saw old Tom Fletcher sit outside the mercantile, whittling without his shotgun across his knees. This was his work.

A rider emerged from the shimmering heat haze at the far end of town. Eli's hand drifted towards the worn walnut grip of his Colt. Strangers were rare now, and often trouble. The horse moved slow, its head low. The rider slumped in the saddle, hat pulled down. Eli's eyes narrowed. Something familiar in the set of those shoulders, the careless drape of the man's legs against the horse's flanks. Recognition struck like a physical blow—Cole. Eli hadn't seen Cole Turner in ten years—not since the day Cole rode out chasing dreams of quick money. Now, posters plastered across three territories bore Cole's likeness beneath the stark word: *WANTED. Murder. Stagecoach robbery. A trail of violence.*

Cole reined in before the sheriff's office—he pushed his hat back slowly. Dust caked his face, etching deep lines around eyes that held no warmth, only a weary defiance. He looked older than his years—hardened. "Eli," he rasped. The single word hung heavy.

"Cole." Eli kept his voice flat. His hand stayed near his gun—years of training screamed at him: draw, arrest, uphold the law. But the memory of shared boyhood scrapes, of hunting rabbits in the hills, of Cole pulling him from a flash flood, tangled his thoughts. "You shouldn't be here."

"Needed water. For me and the horse." Cole's gaze swept the quiet street, the clean boardwalks, the absence of armed men lounging. "Heard you cleaned the place up. Looks…different."

"It is different." Eli didn't move. "Law rules here now. My law."

Cole managed a dry, humorless chuckle. "Your law. Fancy that. The kid who couldn't shoot straight, holdin' the reins." He swung down stiffly.

The horse nudged his shoulder. "Just water, Eli. Then I'm gone. You won't see me again."

The lie was obvious—Cole was exhausted. His horse was exhausted—he needed more than water; he needed rest, supplies and a place to hide. Eli weighed the town's fragile peace against the man standing before him. A fugitive—a murderer—his oldest friend. The conflict knotted his stomach. "Water's at the trough," Eli said, nodding down the street. "Use it. Then ride out. Fast. Marshals are lookin' for you."

Cole led his horse towards the public trough. Eyes appeared in windows—faces pressed against saloon glass. The news travelled silent and swift: Cole Turner was in Redemption Creek and the sheriff was talking to him.

Eli watched him drink, the tension coiling tighter with every passing second. He felt the town watching and judging. Years of building trust could unravel in minutes. He couldn't let Cole stay—he couldn't just let him ride away, either. The law demanded action. Loyalty demanded…what? Forgiveness? Complicity? He stepped off the boardwalk and followed Cole to the trough.

"They're sayin' you killed those men on the Carson Stage," Eli said, keeping his voice low.

Cole splashed water on his face, the grime turning to muddy streaks. "They shot first."

"The posters say different. Say you ambushed it. Killed the guard, the driver, a passenger."

Cole turned, water dripping from his chin—his eyes met Eli's. "Things got messy. Wasn't supposed to go that way." There was no remorse, only a cold statement of fact. "Need more than water, Eli. Need supplies. Need to hole up for a day, maybe two. Just till the horse recovers. Then I vanish."

"No." The word felt like stone in Eli's mouth. "You ride out now. This town…I can't let you stay. You bring death with you."

A flicker of anger crossed Cole's face, quickly masked. "After all we been through? You'd turn me away? Turn me *in*?" He leaned closer, his voice dropping to a harsh whisper. "Remember the Sanderson brothers?

Remember who stood beside you when they cornered you in Rattler Canyon? I took a bullet for you, Eli. Or did cleanin' up this town wash that memory clean too?"

Eli remembered. The searing pain in his own leg, the crack of Cole's rifle, the Sanderson brothers falling. Cole dragging him miles to safety. The debt was real—it stood in stark contrast with the badge on his chest and the oath he'd sworn. "That was a lifetime ago, Cole. You're a wanted man. You killed innocent people."

"Innocent?" Cole spat. "That passenger was carryin' a ledger full of names—men set to hang if it got to the marshal. Men who paid good money for that stage *not* to arrive. Guard was in on it. Driver too. They drew down on me. It was them or me." He saw the doubt in Eli's eyes. "Check the passenger's name. Horace Pettigrew. Telegraph the marshal in Carson City. Ask him why Pettigrew was comin' to see him. Then decide if I'm just a murderer."

It was plausible—Pettigrew was known as a fixer for wealthy ranchers. Eli felt the ground shift beneath him. Was Cole a cold-blooded killer, or a man caught in a deadly game, forced to fight? The debt, the possible justification…it gnawed at his resolve. The town's peace felt suddenly fragile, a thin veneer over the old violence Cole represented.

"You can't stay in the open," Eli said finally, the words tasting bitter. "Get your horse. Bring him around back of the jail. Use the lean-to. Out of sight. I'll bring food, water, grain. You get *one* night, Cole. One. And you stay hidden. If I confirm your story…maybe I look the other way when you ride out. But if you're lyin' to me…" He let the threat hang. "One night."

Relief washed over Cole's face, it was quickly replaced by wariness. "Alright, Eli. One night. Appreciate it." He gathered his reins.

Eli walked back to his office, feeling every eye on him. He shut the door, leaning against it. He'd just harbored a fugitive. Betrayed his oath. For what? A debt? A story? He grabbed paper and pencil, composing a telegraph to the Carson City Marshal: *REQUEST INFORMATION HORACE PETTIGREW STOP PURPOSE TRAVEL STOP CONNECTION CARSON STAGE ROBBERY STOP URGENT STOP SHERIFF THORNE REDEMPTION CREEK STOP.*

He handed it to young Danny Miller, his part-time deputy, who'd been sweeping the cells. "Take this to the telegraph office, Danny. Fast as you can. Wait for a reply. Bring it straight back. Tell no one."

Danny's eyes widened at the sheriff's tone. "Yes, sir." He snatched the paper and darted out.

The hours crawled—Eli paced the small office, his gaze constantly drawn to the barred window overlooking the alley where Cole was hidden. He checked his gun, the weight familiar and heavy. Doubt was a serpent coiling in his gut. Had he made a catastrophic mistake? Was Cole playing him? The town felt unnaturally quiet and watchful—he heard whispers and saw curtains twitch.

Dusk painted the sky in bruised colors when Danny burst back in, breathless. He thrust a telegraph flimsy at Eli. Eli scanned the words, his blood turning cold: *PETTIGREW CARRYING EVIDENCE AGAINST CATTLE BARONS STOP INCLUDING COLE TURNER FOR EARLIER RUSTLING STOP TURNER KNOWN ASSOCIATE STOP GUARD AND DRIVER CLEAN RECORDS STOP NO KNOWN CONNECTION TO BARONS STOP CONSIDER TURNER ARMED AND EXTREMLY DANGEROUS STOP MARSHAL ENROUTE STOP HOLD HIM IF POSSIBLE STOP.*

Cole had lied—Pettigrew wasn't the villain; Cole was. The guard and driver were innocent. Cole murdered them to silence Pettigrew and destroy evidence against himself. The debt Eli felt dissolved, it was replaced by a cold, hard fury. He'd been manipulated—used. He had a killer hiding behind his jail.

He grabbed his shotgun, checked the loads. "Danny," he said, his voice tight. "Go home. Lock your door. Don't come out till morning. Tell no one what you saw or heard."

The boy paled but nodded, scrambling out. Eli moved to the back door, his shotgun held low. He eased it open—the lean-to was empty. Cole's horse was gone—panic flared, then died. Cole wouldn't leave without supplies, he was here somewhere. Eli scanned the deepening shadows of the alley. He looked behind building, stacked crates and the narrow gap between the jail and the blacksmith's. He found nothing, only silence.

"Cole!" Eli called, his voice echoing harshly. "I got the wire! I know what you did! Come out! Now!"

A figure detached itself from the deep gloom beside the blacksmith's, stepping into the fading light. Cole held a revolver loosely at his side—his face was unreadable. "Took you long enough to check, Eli." He sounded almost disappointed.

"You lied to me," Eli stated, leveling the shotgun. "Pettigrew was the target. Those men were innocent. You murdered them."

Cole shrugged. "Details. Pettigrew had the proof. Proof that would've seen me hang. Them others…collateral damage. Had to be done." He took a step forward. "You gonna shoot me, Eli? Your old friend? The man who saved your life?"

"You're not that man anymore," Eli said, his finger tightening on the trigger. "That man died the day he ambushed that stage. Drop the gun, Cole. Hands high."

Cole laughed, a short, sharp bark. "Drop it? So you can be the big hero? Hand me over to the marshals? After lettin' me hide back here?" He shook his head. "Nah. See, I didn't just come for supplies, Eli. I came for you."

Eli frowned. "Me?"

"That debt," Cole said, his voice dropping to a venomous whisper. "The one you conveniently remembered when it suited you. The one from Rattler Canyon. You ever wonder *why* the Sandersons cornered you?"

A cold dread seeped into Eli's bones. "They were trouble. We crossed them."

"They were trouble *I* hired," Cole hissed. "Paid 'em good money to scare you off Mary Carter. Remember her? The rancher's daughter you were sweet on? The one *I* wanted. Only you, brave Eli, wouldn't scare easy. They got carried away, cornered you for real. I had to step in, play the hero. Saved your life, yeah. To cover my tracks. To make sure you never suspected it was me who sent them." Cole's smile was a knife slash. "You owe me a debt for cleanin' up my own mess. And you've been livin' off that debt in your head for years. Makin' you soft. Makin' you hesitate."

The revelation hit Eli like a physical blow. The foundation of their friendship, the bedrock of his guilt, was rotten—a lie—a manipulation. Cole had orchestrated the very event that bound Eli to him. The fury crystallized into something cold and lethal. "You're poison, Cole."

"Maybe," Cole agreed, raising his revolver slightly. "But I'm walkin' out of here. You're gonna lower that scattergun, Eli. You're gonna let me walk to my horse. And you're gonna stand there and take whatever happens next. Because if you don't…" He gestured vaguely towards the town with his free hand. "…I've got friends ridin' in. Men who don't care much for sheriffs who've cleaned up their town. They'll burn it down around you. Startin' with that widow Henderson's place. You want that blood on your hands too? After failin' to stop me?"

Eli hesitated—was it another lie? A bluff to make him lower his guard? Or was Cole capable of unleashing that kind of hell? He saw Cole's finger tighten on his own trigger. He saw the flicker of triumph in Cole's eyes. The town's peace, the lives he'd sworn to protect…they hung in the balance. Cole's threat against innocent people was real. The man before him was pure, distilled evil. The debt was meaningless—the friendship was ashes.

Duty—loyalty—both demanded the same thing now.

Eli made his choice—he squeezed the shotgun's trigger. The roar was deafening in the confined alley. Cole jerked violently, a look of profound shock spreading across his face as the heavy buckshot tore into his chest. He stumbled back, his revolver firing a single, wild shot into the dirt before slipping from his grasp. He hit the ground hard, coughing blood onto the dust.

Eli broke open the shotgun, ejecting the smoking shells, reloading with swift, practiced movements. He kept the weapon trained on Cole as he approached. Cole stared up at him, blood bubbling at his lips. "You…shot me…" he gasped, disbelief mingling with the pain.

"For the guard," Eli said, his voice devoid of emotion. "For the driver. For Pettigrew." He racked the shotgun closed. "For Mary Carter." He leveled the barrels at Cole's head. "For Redemption Creek."

Cole's eyes widened with a final flicker of fear. Eli pulled the trigger. The second blast was final—absolute. Cole's body went still.

Silence descended, broken only by the ringing in Eli's ears and the frantic barking of a dog somewhere down the street. He stood over the body of his oldest friend, the man he had just executed. He had upheld the law—he had protected the town. He had settled a decade-old betrayal. He felt nothing—no relief—no sorrow—only a vast, hollow emptiness.

He heard the back door of the jail creak open. Danny stood there, his face white as paper, having disobeyed orders and heard the shots. He stared at the sheriff, then at the ruined body in the alley.

Eli lowered the shotgun. "Fetch Doctor Pryor, Danny," he said, his voice flat and distant. "Tell him…tell him we have a body." He turned away from Cole, from the boy's terrified stare, and looked down the darkening alley towards the street. Lanterns were being lit—doors opened cautiously. Figures gathered at the alley's entrance, drawn by the gunfire. He saw their faces—confused, frightened, then slowly hardening as they saw the sheriff standing over the dead fugitive. They saw the violence, not the reason. They saw the execution, not the threat extinguished.

He had saved them—he had done his duty. But as he met the eyes of his townspeople, their expressions shifting from fear to a dawning, cold judgment, Eli Thorne understood the true cost. He had killed his past, and with it, the trust he'd spent a lifetime building. The peace he'd forged was shattered, not by Cole's violence, but by his own necessary, brutal act. He was the law—he was the killer—he was alone. The hollow silence inside him echoed the silence of the watching town. His redemption was complete, and it was ashes. He walked towards the gathering crowd, the shotgun heavy in his hands, the weight of his choice settling upon him like a tombstone. The street, once a symbol of his victory, now felt like the beginning of a long, desolate road. He had chosen—he had acted—he had lost.

The Desert

The drifter headed west and the cowboy followed. The desert was a deadly place that could kill any man at any time and the cowboy knew that. He didn't know if the drifter knew it but that didn't matter because he did. The drifter seemed strange to the cowboy, almost like a spirit floating across the desert sands.

They had been in the desert, four days now and the cowboy's horse was weary from the heat and his canteen was almost dry. He hadn't eaten anything for two days. The cowboy knew he would lose his horse pretty soon. The desert sun is a murderer that cares for nothing. The drifter on the other hand seemed to be untouched by the desert and its treacherous sun. He had neither horse nor water and he moved across the desert with a graceful ease that to the cowboy seemed a bit unfair.

The sky began to darken. The clouds turned purple as the sun began to set. The drifter disappeared over the horizon as the cowboy followed. The cowboy followed and his horse fell dead to the ground. He knew that if he didn't find something to eat pretty soon, he would be next. He was hungry, his stomach grumbled and ached. He thought about eating his horse, but he just couldn't bring himself to do it. That would be like eating an old friend. His horse had been his constant companion for years. He took off his hat, held it in front of his chest and had a moment of silence for his fallen friend. He had to move on. He had no choice, the drifter was moving farther away every second. He had to continue his journey but he couldn't take his horse with him. So he left it.

The cowboy was tired and wanted to set up camp and sleep through the night, but he couldn't do that. He knew that if he was going to get through the desert alive, he would have to travel through the night. If he had waited until morning, he'd never get out of the desert before the sun reached its full pinnacle in the sky and beat him down with its uncontrollable force.

A rattlesnake slithered its way across the desert. The cowboy drew his pistol and fired one shot. The hot lead from the cowboy's bullet hit the snake in the head. The snakes body wiggled about uncontrollable for a moment. He squeezed off another shot, hitting the snake in the head again, this time separating the head from the body and throwing the snake into the air. The snakes lifeless body fell silently to the desert ground. The cowboy stopped long enough to eat and then he was on his way.

He would not be able to catch the drifter now. All he could do was travel on until the two of them meet again. So the cowboy, with his belly full, headed west in hopes of freeing himself from the monstrous desert that had engulfed him and swallowed him whole. With a small hope that one day he would come face to face with the drifter who had put him in such a deadly situation.

Last Light

Hay prickled Cash's neck, the barn stinking of dung and gunpowder. Outside, Sheriff Vale's voice boomed: "Come out, or we burn it!"

Cash's revolver held one bullet—suicide or surrender? Neither suited a man who'd outrun Apache territory.

He spied the kerosene lanterns.

"Burn it!" Vale yelled.

A match hissed. The flame met fuel. Flames spread out, running towards the barn.

Cash fired into the nearest lantern. The fire roared, swallowing walls. Lawmen scattered as the barn exploded, timbers screaming.

Through the blaze, Cash ran—not toward the hills, but into the inferno's heart, his laugh echoing where the shots couldn't follow.

At dawn, they found only his shadow, scorched into the earth, forever mid-stride.

Sanctus

Bleakwater sprawled beneath a crimson moon, its skeletal buildings swallowed by the silence. Dust devils spiraled through empty streets, carrying the faint cries of those long lost. Jackson Spade's boots crunched over gravel as he walked, his face a map of shadows beneath the brim of his hat. The wind tugged at his coat, it was as threadbare and weathered as the town itself. Ahead, the saloon's sign creaked on rusted chains—*The Scarlet Rose*. Its paint had peeled, but the stench of death lingered. Three nights prior, the barkeep's body had been found shriveled and pale, throat punctured like parchment.

Spade's hand drifted to the revolver at his hip. Sanctus—its ivory handle bore tiny crosses, worn smooth by time. Six notches marked the barrel—one for each encounter with the creature who'd haunted him from Abilene to the Badlands. Laszlo Varga—a specter in a frock coat, a devil who'd slipped through Spade's fingers like smoke. But tonight, beneath the bleeding sky, the hunt would end.

The church bell rang midnight. A breeze swept through the cemetery, reeking of decay and wilted flowers. Varga was perched atop a crumbling crypt, angels with chipped wings weeping at his feet. His coat swallowed the moonlight; his grin was a knife's edge. "Jack," he cooed, voice slick as oil. "Still playing shepherd to the damned?"

"Your last dance," Spade said, thumbing Sanctus' hammer.

Varga's laughter echoed like a shovel on stone. "You swore that in Laredo. And Cheyenne. And—"

The gun roared.

The bullet tore through Varga's forehead. He reeled, then steadied himself, the wound knitting itself shut. "Silver and scripture?" He said with annoyance in his voice, leaping down without a sound. "I've danced with conquerors and kings. You're a gnat with a pistol."

Spade fired again. A hollow click—empty.

Varga's fangs gleamed. He surged forward, but Spade was ready. The hunter dropped, yanking an ashwood stake from his boot. He thrust upward—Varga twisted, the stake grazing his ribs. "Stubborn," the vampire hissed.

They circled, boots scraping stone. Varga's claws raked Spade's arm, drawing blood that pooled black in the moonlight. Spade barely blinked. He'd spilled more than this for Marisol, her body cold in the Texas dirt—for the families butchered in their beds.

"Why her?" Spade snarled, dodging another lunge. "Why Marisol?"

Varga paused, brow furrowed. "You think I mourn the cattle I slaughter?" He struck again, but Spade was quicker. A vial of holy water shattered against the vampire's face.

His flesh hissed and bubbled. Varga shrieked, clawing at his melting cheek. Spade didn't wait. The stake plunged deep, piercing the monster's heart with a wet crack.

Varga stiffened, eyes wide. "Impossible…"

"Not for her," Spade said.

The vampire collapsed, skin flaking to ash. Dawn crept over the desert, painting the sand gold. Spade holstered Sanctus, his breath ragged. But as he turned, a whisper slithered through the graves—a cold, familiar laugh.

On the crypt lay a single rose, petals black as midnight, its stem oozing red.

Spade spat blood into the dust—some curses refused to die.

But neither would he.

He mounted his horse, gaze fixed on the horizon. The sun rose, relentless. Somewhere, a clock ticked. Somewhere, a coffin lid creaked.

Bleakwater faded behind him, but the hunt—the hunt was forever.

The Hollows of Mercy

The canyon walls of Mercy Gorge leaned close, their striated faces scorched amber by a sun that seemed to linger out of spite. The town huddled below had no name worth speaking of—just the settlement, a clutch of sun-bleached shacks and a saloon with a warped piano that played only in minor keys. It wasn't the sort of place outlaws bothered with—until they did.

Aaron Casey wasn't a sheriff—he was a butcher with a bloodstained apron and a Remington behind the counter for cutting down wolves. But when riders in dusters the color of old bruises began circling the settlement like vultures, the dozen-odd souls left in town looked at him sideways. "Someone's got to." the widow Jessup said, thrusting a tin star into his hand. It left a greenish smear on his palm.

The riders didn't thunder into town—they arrived at dusk, hooves kicking up ghostly plumes of red dust. Seven men, their faces wrapped in faded bandanas. Their leader dismounted at the dry water trough, his boots crunching on locust carcasses. He had a voice like gravel in a tin cup. "Looking for a man," he said. "Got a name stitched on his shirt. Levi."

Aaron knew the name, everyone did. Levi Holt had dragged himself into the settlement three nights before. He was feverish and missing two fingers on his left hand. He'd collapsed in the livery, muttering about a gambler's debt and a stolen lockbox. "They'll come," he'd rasped before passing out. "Tell 'em I'm dead."

The riders weren't here for water or whiskey. Aaron wiped his hands on his apron—still flecked with the morning's lamb slaughter and stepped into the street. The leader peeled down his bandana, revealing a face that looked chewed up and spat out—a face Aaron had seen before, sketched in the margins of a ledger tossed into a sheriff's fire years ago. A scar split his lips into a permanent snarl. "You the law here?"

"Meat's the only law," Aaron said. The Remington hung heavy in his apron pocket.

The scarred man smiled. "Then let's negotiate."

They called the leader Harrow. No first name, no history—just a reputation for leaving settlements quieter than he found them. Aaron's "posse" consisted of a seventeen-year-old stable hand named Lot who could shoot a coyote at 200 yards, a consumptive schoolmarm named Cora who carried a derringer in her bustle, and Levi himself, sweating through a threadbare shirt in the saloon's back room.

"They'll burn the place down for him," Cora said, thumbing cartridges into her tiny pistol. "We could hand him over."

Lot spat tobacco into a spittoon. "Hand him over, and they'll still burn it. For fun."

Levi mopped his brow with a blood-crusted sleeve. "The lockbox," he wheezed. "It's not money. It's bones."

No one asked.

Harrow gave them until moonrise. Aaron spent the hours sharpening knives, the rhythmic scrape of steel filling the slaughterhouse. He'd never shot a man, but he knew how bodies came apart—the give of sinew, the pop of joint from socket. When Lot appeared in the doorway, backlit by the dying sun, he didn't look up.

"They're moving," she said. "Three flanking the east ridge. Two in the gully."

"And Harrow?"

"Sitting on the saloon steps. Whittling."

Aaron tested a blade's edge with his thumb. "What's he carving?"

"Something small. Maybe a doll."

The moon climbed, bone-white. The settlement held its breath.

It started with a lie—Aaron walked into the street, hands raised, and told Harrow that Levi had coughed his last at sundown. "Buried him out past the graveyard," he said. "Take the lockbox and go."

Harrow stood, pocketing his whittling—a tiny wooden snake, polished smooth. "You're a terrible liar, butcher." He drew a Colt with a mother-of-pearl grip.

Aaron's first shot took Harrow in the shoulder. The second went wide as the gully erupted in gunfire.

Harrow's left arm hang stiffly where Aaron's bullet had struck. "But I'll take the box anyway."

What followed wasn't a battle—battles have rhythm, a give-and-take. This was a fever dream—muzzle flashes lit the dark like hellfire, gunpowder thick as sin, Lot's curses as she picked off shadows from the church bell tower. Cora dragged Levi into the saloon, her derringer clicking empty. But when Aaron's cry echoed through the gunfire, she ran back outside, clutching a rusted cleaver. She made it three steps into the street before the bullet found her—a red bloom unfurling as she fell beside the burning stable.

Aaron crouched behind a rain barrel, reloading with hands that wouldn't steady.

Harrow's men fought like they'd done this a hundred times. Because they had—maybe more.

The lockbox had sat under Aaron's butcher block until Harrow's men shattered the shop doors. Aaron heard the splintering wood as he fired toward the gully—too late. By the time he lunged inside, the box was gone, leaving only sawdust and hoofprints. Now, crouched in the smoke, he spotted Harrow's horse tethered near the saloon. The saddlebag gaped open. Inside, the lockbox glared back, its edges rusted like old blood.

Bones, yes—but not human. They were delicate, charred things, strung on a wire—a bird's skeleton, maybe—or a child's mobile. A folded slip of paper fluttered out: Forgive me. The handwriting matched the ledger entries Harrow had burned years ago—entries that named names, debts, graves. Mercy, Aaron was learning, was just another forgotten word that didn't mean much this far west.

By midnight, the stable was ablaze, painting the canyon in hellish light. Lot's rifle had gone silent—whether by blood or bullets, no one could say. Cora lay in the dirt. Harrow grabbed Levi by the collar—ripping his shirt—took him to the porch and slammed him hard into the wood. He stood over Levi, his boot on the man's throat. "Where is it?"

Levi grinned, teeth pink. "Inside you. Always has been."

Harrow pulled the trigger. The shot echoed through the gorge, shaking loose a landslide of stones that buried the saloon's porch—and Harrow—under a tomb of debris. Aaron found the lockbox in the saddlebag of Harrow's horse, the beast still hitched to a post, eyes white with terror but unharmed. Stolen during the chaos when Harrow's men had raided the butcher shop, splintering the block where it lay hidden. Harrow, too consumed with Levi to notice the theft, had died without ever opening it. Inside, the bones rattled like teeth. He left the box on the saloon's splintered bar and walked east, following the dry riverbed.

The settlement didn't die—ghost towns never do. They linger, weathered and whispering, waiting for the next Levi, the next Harrow, the next butcher handed a star.

Some say Aaron made it to the next territory. Others swear they've seen him in the canyon's shadowed folds, sharpening his knives, the tin star still green on his palm.

As for the lockbox—crack it open on a moonless night, and you'll hear them—the bones, singing a lullaby in a key no living throat can replicate.

Forgive me. Forgive me. Forgive me.

The gorge endures—the riders return. The piano—still warped— still playing only minor keys.

Some standoffs aren't meant to be won.

The Forgotten

The man woke in the desert dust, his head pounding. No name came—only a worn pistol and a raw thirst. He stumbled into Dry Creek. People shrank back, whispering. He saw a wanted poster nailed to the saloon door. The face was his. *"Wade Garrett,"* it said. *"Wanted Dead. Murder."*

He rode out fast, but a lone rider tracked him across the badlands. They faced each other on a high ridge. The lawman drew slow. "You killed my wife, Wade," he said, voice flat. "Remember now?"

The outlaw stared—he saw only the stranger's grief. His finger tightened on the trigger. He fired first—the lawman fell. As the outlaw walked closer, he saw the dead man's eyes. They looked just like his own. His brother's name surfaced then, lost years flooding back. He dropped his gun, the truth hit him like a bullet in his gut.

Three Feet from Justice

The sun pinned Morgan and Dawes to the dusty street. Silence pressed down hard, broken only by the nervous shuffle of a horse at the hitching rail. Storefronts stood shuttered, faces hidden behind cracked boards. Dawes shifted—sweat tracing lines through the grit on his face. His hand hovered near his holster. "Should've stayed gone, Morgan."

Morgan stood utterly still—his gaze never left Dawes. "Came to settle it. Face to face." His own hand rested easy near his gun. The glare off the false-front buildings was blinding. A tumbleweed scraped across the packed earth between them. Dawes twitched. His eyes darted, then locked back. "You drew first last time."

"Didn't," Morgan stated flatly. His voice cut the thick air. "You know it."

Dawes' jaw clenched—his fingers flexed. "Liar!" The word cracked like a whip. His hand dropped. Morgan reacted, a single fluid motion. His gun cleared leather, roared. The shot echoed off the empty buildings. Dawes staggered back, surprise widening his eyes. He clutched his chest, then slumped to his knees. He stumbled forward, face down in the dirt.

Morgan lowered his smoking gun and stared at the body. Then he saw it. Dawes' holster was empty. The man's gun lay in the dust three feet away, unfired. Dawes had drawn nothing but air. Morgan hadn't won the draw. He'd shot an unarmed man. The street stayed silent—Morgan stood frozen, the gun heavy in his hand.

The Crossing

The wind moved steady across the mesa, brushing dry sage and yellow wildflowers. Two riders came out of the brush at sunrise, the sky behind them torn open by clouds thick as cotton bales. The first rider wore a yellow shirt stained from trail dust and blood that had dried dark at the hem. His red bandana clung to his neck like a warning. He rode a chestnut mare that moved with purpose, her breath steady despite the miles behind her. The second rider followed a few lengths back on a black horse, leaner, jumpier, eyes wide with the tension of its rider.

They hadn't spoken since leaving San Pablo.

The man in yellow, called Rook, knew silence was safer. They had run too far, too fast, and someone was bound to be close behind. The boy trailing him was young, maybe seventeen, hard to tell beneath the hat brim and dust. He hadn't said his name and Rook hadn't asked.

They were heading east, away from the massacre.

Three days earlier, in the canyon below the burned-out church, Rook had watched three men take a bullet each before the boy drew on the sheriff. Shot him clean through the chest. Rook fired the second shot, not to help, but because there was no way out otherwise—now there was a bounty on them both.

They crossed into a flatland broken by rabbitbrush and stunted pines. The sun hammered down hard, its intense heat baking the already scorched earth. Rook slowed his horse—sweat trickled through the grime on his neck. The boy came up beside him, his hand resting near his holster.

"You see anyone?" the boy asked, his voice tight.

Rook scanned the shimmering distance. He shook his head. "They'll be watching the water crossings. We head for the dry trail east of Devil's Mouth."

"You sure?"

"No."

The boy said nothing more—his eyes stayed sharp, flicking over the rocks and brush. He checked their rear every few minutes, twisting in the saddle. His knuckles held tight on the reins.

They rode on—the land dipped into shallow gullies choked with gravel. Rook guided them down one, seeking the scant shade of crumbling walls. The mare picked her way carefully—the black horse snorted, skittering sideways on loose stones.

"Hold him steady," Rook said without turning.

"Trying." The boy fought the reins. The black horse tossed its head.

They climbed out the other side onto higher ground. A dust devil spun across the flats ahead, a twisting column of grit. Rook watched it— dust devils meant wind shifts and nothing more. But movement caught his eye—he kept low.

By noon, the heat pressed down like a weight. Rook pulled a canteen and took a sip. He passed it back—the boy drank greedily, water spilling down his chin. Rook took the canteen back. "Easy. That's got to last."

"How far to water?"

"Two days. Maybe three." Rook corked the canteen. "Less if we push."

The boy wiped his mouth. "Then push."

They pushed—the horses' heads drooped and flies buzzed around their eyes. Rook kept them angled toward a distant notch in the hills, the start of Devil's Mouth. They passed a scatter of bleached bones—coyote— maybe deer. The boy stared at them.

Near sunset, they found a seep. Not exactly water, just damp earth under a ledge. Rook dismounted and scraped at the mud with his knife. The horses strained at their bits, smelling moisture. He let them nuzzle the mud, sucking what little they could. The boy knelt and scooped mud into his hands, he pressed it to his face.

"Save some for them," Rook said. The boy dropped his hands.

They moved on as the light failed, finding a ravine thick with juniper for camp. Rook took first watch—he sat with his rifle across his lap, his back against rough bark. The air cooled fast—the boy lay on his side, blanket pulled up, but Rook saw his eyes glint in the starlight. He didn't sleep—his fingers worked constantly, plucking at the blanket, tracing patterns in the dirt. Rook kept quiet—he didn't trust the boy's calm, the way his stillness felt like a coiled spring.

The night sounds started: the rustle of something small in the brush, the far-off yip of a coyote. Rook's ears strained for anything else—the crunch of a boot, the jingle of a bridle. There was nothing—just the wind sighing through the junipers.

Near dawn, Rook walked out of camp to piss. The sky paled in the east. When he came back, the boy sat cross-legged by the cold ashes, staring into nothing.

"You kill before San Pablo?" Rook asked, the question sharp in the quiet.

The boy didn't startle. He nodded slowly. "A couple. First was my brother."

Rook studied his young face, shadowed under the hat. "Why?"

"'Cause he hit my mother." The boy's voice held no tremor. He looked straight at Rook. "Second was the man who said she asked for it."

Rook met his gaze—the boy's eyes were like dark stones. Rook didn't reply—he tossed a few dry juniper twigs onto the ashes, then walked off again, heading further up the ravine. He climbed a short way and found a perch overlooking their back trail. He watched the light grow, searching for movement. Nothing stirred but the quiet felt heavy—watched. He stayed longer than needed.

They saddled up in silence. The boy avoided Rook's eye. They rode out as the sun cleared the horizon, painting the rocks blood-red. The trail climbed steadily towards the notch. The air thinned—the horses labored. Rook kept the rifle loose in his hand.

They reached the notch mid-morning. Devil's Mouth was a narrow cut through dark rock. Wind whistled through it. Rook stopped the mare and scanned the high walls. It was a perfect place for an ambush.

"We walk the horses through," he said. "Single file. Stay close to the wall."

He dismounted and led the mare in. The boy followed. The canyon floor was littered with fallen rock. Their boots scraped loud in the confined space. The wind whistled a light breeze through the canyon. Rook's shoulders tensed—he expected a shot with every step. Sunlight only reached the canyon floor in narrow slashes—shadows pooled deep.

Halfway through, the black horse shied, snorting. A rock clattered down from above. Rook froze, rifle coming up. He peered at the rim, seventy feet up but nothing moved except a lizard on a hot stone. The boy cursed softly, calming the horse.

"Keep moving," Rook whispered.

They cleared the canyon without incident. The land opened up again, sloping down into a wide valley dotted with greasewood. Buzzards circled high over the far end. Rook stopped—he pulled out a spyglass and extended it. He scanned the trail behind them, the valley floor and the distant ridges. He saw nothing move but the birds.

"They're out there," he said, collapsing the glass.

The boy adjusted his hat, sweat staining the band. "Let 'em come."

They kept close to a long rock wall where the sun gave little relief—the rock radiated heat. Around noon, they passed a cattle camp long abandoned. Ashes lay scattered inside a rusted fire ring, bleached bones nearby. A child's shoe, small and scuffed, sat half-buried in dust near a collapsed lean-to. The boy stared at the shoe—he kicked a stone, sending it skittering into the silence. Rook said nothing. They rode on.

The thirst grew—Rook rationed the water strictly. The boy's lips were dry and cracked, he licked them constantly. His eyes grew harder—they saw mirages—shimmering pools that vanished as they neared. The black horse stumbled once, catching itself—the boy swore at it.

That night, they found a shallow cave high in a bluff. Rook set no fire—the cold seeped from the rock. The boy spread his blanket near the entrance, his hand never far from his pistol. Rook stayed deeper in the gloom, his back against the cold stone. He kept one eye on the boy's silhouette blocking the stars.

The desert night pressed in, vast and silent. At some point, the boy spoke, his voice low. "What'd you do before this?"

"Rode with the army." Rook's voice sounded rough. "Down south."

"You shoot folks then?"

"Mostly." Rook paused. The dark hid his face. "Not always the right ones."

The boy said nothing after that—Rook didn't sleep. They just sat in the silence. He listened to the boy's breathing, listened to the night. The wind picked up, whining over the cave mouth. Rook shifted his weight. His leg ached from an old wound.

Dawn came gray and cold. They ate bread and jerky in silence. The boy's movements were stiff. They followed a dry wash snaking down from the bluffs toward a distant ridgeline. The wash deepened, walls rising steep on either side. The footing was treacherous, shale and loose rock shifting under the horses' hooves. Rook kept the rifle ready across his lap. The boy had his hand near his revolver, his eyes scanning the rim above them.

They climbed out of the wash near midday from the ridgeline, Rook pulled the mare up. Below, miles off, lay the green shimmer of cottonwood trees and the river—a day's hard ride. Rook didn't smile—the river meant crossing and crossing meant ambush—the trees offered cover for men waiting.

"Stay off the main trail," he said, pointing east along the ridge. "Follow this line. Drop down where it breaks."

"Thought that was your plan," the boy said, his voice flat.

"It still is."

They followed the ridgeline. The sun beat down—relentless. The green line in the distance taunted them. The boy swayed slightly in his saddle, Rook passed him the canteen. The boy took a single swallow and handed it back—his eyes looked sunken.

They dropped into another gulch later that afternoon, it was steeper than the last. Their horses worked hard, sliding on loose stones in the sand. Rook dismounted, leading the mare—the boy followed suit. Their progress slowed to a crawl. Rocks clattered down the slope ahead of them. Rook stopped often, listening. The gulch twisted, hiding what lay ahead.

Just before dusk, as they rounded a bend, Rook froze, he threw up a hand—the boy stopped. Ahead, maybe thirty yards, a thin column of smoke rose straight into the still air against the darkening sky. It was controlled—deliberate.

Rook motioned sharply for silence. He pointed back the way they'd come. They retreated around the bend, out of sight. They tied the horses to a tough clump of brush, reins knotted short. Rook crept forward on foot, staying low against the gulch wall. He moved like a shadow, placing each step with care. The boy followed, a few paces behind.

Rook reached a vantage point behind a boulder and peered around its edge. The fire sat near a flat rock—a man stood over it, turning meat on a stick. Another man squatted nearby, rolling a cigarette. A third sat with his back against the rock, methodically cleaning a rifle. None of them looked young. Their faces were hard and lined. All wore trail dust and long coats, despite the heat. Holsters held heavy revolvers, lever-action rifles leaned against the rock within easy reach.

Bounty hunters. Professionals.

Rook signaled the boy back with a sharp chop of his hand. They retreated to the horses. The boy's breathing came fast. "How many?" he whispered.

"Three."

"We go around?"

Rook shook his head. "They'll hear the horses in this rock. We wait 'til they sleep. Take them quiet."

The boy nodded. He started to move toward his horse, but Rook grabbed his arm, hard, the boy flinched.

"No shooting unless I say," Rook hissed. "Quiet. Knife work. Understand?"

The boy's eyes flickered. He pulled his arm free. "I know."

He stepped away, rubbing his arm. He checked his pistol, then slid a long skinning knife from his boot. He tested the edge against his thumb. Rook watched him—the boy's hands didn't shake.

They waited through the slow fall of night. The sky slowly turned black and the stars pricked through. The coyotes started again—closer now. The fire flickered down to a bed of glowing coals. The man who'd been cooking walked a slow perimeter, scanning the gulch walls—he paused, looking their way. Rook held his breath—he man moved on, disappearing into the dark beyond the firelight. The other two rolled into blankets.

Silence settled, thick and waiting—the coals pulsed faintly. The guard returned, stamped his feet near the fire, then settled against the rock near the sleeping men, his rifle across his lap. His head nodded as he drifted in and out of sleep.

Rook waited another hour. The guard's head slumped forward, his breathing deepened. Rook touched the boy's shoulder—a silent signal. They moved fast and silently.

Rook led, a shadow among shadows. The boy followed, his knife held low. They crept to the edge of the camp. The guard sat slumped, chin on chest—the others slept soundly. Rook pointed to the guard, then to himself. He pointed to the two sleepers, then to the boy. The boy nodded once, his face a pale smudge in the dark.

Rook moved like smoke—he covered the last few yards to the guard in utter silence. He clamped a hand over the man's mouth, yanked his head back—the knife flashed once, deep across the throat. The guard stiffened, gurgled, then went limp. Rook lowered him silently to the dirt.

He looked up—the boy stood frozen over one of the sleepers, knife raised. The man stirred and mumbled—the boy hesitated. The man's eyes flew open. He saw the knife, saw the boy. He opened his mouth to yell.

Rook lunged toward him, but he was too far. The boy stabbed down. The blade punched into the man's chest. The man gasped, a wet, choking sound. The other sleeper woke, scrambling for his rifle. The boy ripped his knife free and plunged it again, frantic—the man thrashed.

Rook reached the second sleeper as the man grabbed his rifle. He kicked the rifle away and drove his own knife into the man's side, up under the ribs. The man choked and clawed at Rook. Rook twisted the blade, hard—the man went still.

The silence crashed back—the only sounds were the soft crackle of the dying coals and the boy's ragged breathing. He stood over the man he'd killed, his knife dripping. He stared at the body, his chest heaving.

Rook wiped his blade clean on the dead man's coat. He scanned the gulch walls. There was no movement—no sound but the wind and the boy's breathing. "Take what you need," Rook said, his voice low. "Food. Water. Ammo. Quick."

The boy blinked, seeming to come back to himself. He knelt beside the man he'd killed, avoiding the staring eyes. He pulled a canteen, almost full. He found a sack of jerky. He yanked a saddlebag from near the fire, rummaged inside and pulled out boxes of cartridges. He stuffed everything into his own gear.

Rook took the guard's rifle, a newer model, and his cartridge belt. He found a nearly full flask of whiskey and pocketed it. He took the jerky sack the boy had missed. He checked the bodies quickly—there were no papers—no names. They were just hired guns.

They moved fast after that, leading the horses back down the gulch, away from the camp. They didn't mount until they were well clear. The moon rose, casting sharp shadows. They rode hard, putting distance between them and the dead men. The boy rode hunched over, clutching the saddle horn—he didn't look back.

The stolen water revived them. The horses picked up speed—they rode through the night, guided by the stars. The boy stayed silent. Rook watched him. The frantic stabbing played in his mind. Hesitation costs lives but the boy learned—or did he?

By midday, the air changed, it grew heavier, carrying the smell of mud and damp vegetation. They saw the river, it was muddy and slow. The water was thick with reeds and buzzing mosquitoes. There was no bridge. The cottonwoods offered dense cover on both banks—too dense.

Rook reined in well back from the bank. He pulled out the spyglass and scanned the trees, the far bank, the bends upstream and down. The water flowed sluggish and brown. Sandbars broke the surface. There were no obvious tracks on the near bank, but the mud looked churned.

"Something's off," Rook murmured.

"I don't see tracks," the boy said, squinting.

"Doesn't mean they're not watching. Too quiet. No birds."

They dismounted and Rook pointed downstream. "There. That bend. Water's shallower. Reeds give some cover on the other side."

"Looks deep in the middle."

"It is. We lead the horses. Stay low. Move fast."

They walked the horses down the bank, sliding on mud. The horses smelled the water, strained toward it. Rook held the mare back. "Easy, girl. Easy." The boy struggled with his horse, which tossed its head, eager to drink.

They stepped into the river—cold water soaked Rook's boots instantly and climbed his legs. Mud sucked at his feet—the chestnut mare pushed forward, snorting. Rook kept a firm grip on the reins, his rifle held high. The boy followed, the black horse plunging in, water surging to its belly.

Midway across, the current tugged harder. The water reached Rook's waist and the mare's saddle. The bottom dropped away—the black horse balked, stopped dead. The water swirled around its chest. It whinnied, high and scared. The boy cursed, yanked its reins. "Move! Damn you, move!"

"Keep him moving!" Rook shouted, fighting the current and the mud. "Don't let him turn!"

The boy hauled on the reins, slapped the horse's neck. "Go! Go on!" The black horse reared slightly, panicked, hooves churning muddy water. It lurched forward, stumbled, then found footing and surged ahead.

They scrambled up the far bank, dripping and gasping. The slope was steep sand, Rook hauled himself and the mare up. He turned immediately, dripping, scanning the ridge above the cottonwoods. The boy dragged the black horse up the bank, coughing.

A rifle cracked—sharp—close.

The black horse screamed, it dropped, legs kicking. Blood spread in the muddy water at its flank.

The boy dove sideways behind a boulder, drawing his pistol. Rook spotted the muzzle flash—two of them, firing from a dense stand of mesquite further up the bank, maybe forty yards away. He dropped behind a rotting stump, brought his rifle up and fired once. The shot kicked dirt near the mesquite—he missed. Bullets snapped past his head and thudded into the stump, splinters flew around him.

"You run!" he roared at the boy. "Get to those trees! Keep east!"

"I ain't leaving you!" The boy fired blindly around the boulder. His shot went wide.

"Move! Now!" Rook levered a fresh round. He rose and fired twice at the mesquite. One of the shooters ducked—the other fired back. Rook saw the puff of smoke and felt the wind of the bullet. He dropped back.

He saw the boy break from the boulder, sprinting low and fast towards the thicker brush further east. Rook rose again, laid down rapid fire, levering and shooting, levering and shooting—brass casings flew. He drove the shooters down.

The boy vanished into the brush.

Rook fired again—one of the shooters staggered out from the mesquite, clutching his arm. Rook shot him center mass. The man crumpled and fell back into the tree, blood spreading through his shirt.

The second shooter fired. Rook felt a hammer blow to his left shoulder—it spun him. He hit the sand and rolled—pain exploded, hot and deep. His left arm went numb, useless. He fumbled the rifle, levered it one-handed and propped it on the stump. He fired towards the mesquite, sand kicked up near the hidden shooter.

Another shot—fire seared Rook's thigh. He cried out and dropped behind the stump again. Blood soaked his shirt, warm and sticky. It ran down his leg, mixing with the river mud. He gasped, trying to lever the rifle, his fingers slipped on the lever. He saw the boy disappear over a low rise further east. He was safe—for now.

Rook smiled, a grim twist of his lips. Then he gritted his teeth hard and crawled out from behind the stump, dragging his rifle. He used his good arm to prop himself up. He aimed at the mesquite thicket, waiting for movement. A shape shifted—he fired—the shape jerked, then slumped. After his last shot echoed out, only silence remained.

He lay there, bleeding into the sand. The sun burned down on his face. Flies found him. The world swam in a dizzy haze of shimmering heat around him. He heard the river, the buzzing flies and the harsh rasp of his own breath.

The sound of boots came later. They were slow and careful steps crunching on gravel approaching from the east—not from the river. Rook turned his head, it was agony. The pain blurred his vision.

The boy stood over him. He held his revolver—his face was blank, streaked with dirt and sweat. His chest heaved from hard breathing.

Rook blinked, trying to clear his sight. "You came back."

The boy nodded slowly. He looked down at the pistol in his hand— then at Rook.

"Why?" Rook breathed. The word tasted like blood.

The boy looked at the pistol. He looked at Rook's bleeding shoulder and his ruined leg. He looked at the dead men by the mesquite and at his own dead horse. His jaw tightened, then he raised the pistol. It was steady now.

Rook's eyes widened. Understanding dawned—it was a cold and final understanding.

"You're worth more dead than I am," the boy said. His voice was flat and empty.

The shot echoed once across the river. It was a sharp and final crack that broke through the silence. Then again—a second shot, insurance.

The boy stood still for a long time. He looked down at Rook, he looked at the river. He looked back the way he'd run. Then he holstered his pistol.

He bent down and took Rook's hat, placing it on his own head. He picked up Rook's rifle and slung it over his shoulder. He walked to the chestnut mare, still standing where Rook had left her, head down. He gathered her reins and checked the saddlebags, adding Rook's canteen and the stolen jerky to his own haul. He mounted.

He sat for a moment, looking down at the bodies—Rook's, the bounty hunters' and the black horse. He touched his heels to the mare's sides. He rode east, towards the trees, not looking back. The mare carried him steadily away from the river, away from the dead. The sun glinted on the rifle slung across his back.

The Ghost of John Wilkes Booth

Part I

Chapter 1

Ford's Theatre smelled of gaslight and sweat—packed bodies—heavy velvet curtains. Dust moved aimlessly in the light beams.

John Wilkes Booth stood in the shadows—backstage right—stagehand territory. He knew this place, he knew its rhythms. His hand rested inside his coat. His fingers closed around cold wood and metal.

He watched the box. The Presidential box.

Abraham Lincoln sat inside—a tall figure, leaning forward, watching the play—his wife beside him. Soldiers flanked the door below. They seemed relaxed, off duty. They were laughing at the stage.

Booth checked the Derringer in his palm. It was a single shot, loaded—ready. He pulled his coat tighter, concealed the weapon. His heart beat hard inside his chest. He was steady, controlled, like waiting for a cue.

He moved, smooth and silent. Down the narrow passage behind the boxes. The guard's chair outside Lincoln's door stood empty. Booth smiled, tight, without warmth. Luck favored him—or fate.

He opened the outer door to the vestibule, softly. He stepped inside, closed it behind him. Wood scraped faintly on wood, the sound died in the laughter from the stage. He faced the inner door. The door to the box itself was a simple wooden panel. He peered through a tiny hole drilled earlier. He saw Lincoln's profile. It was clear, close.

Booth drew the Derringer. He raised it and took a breath. He held it, then exhaled slowly.

He pushed the door open.

The play's dialogue filled the air—a comic line. The audience roared with laughter. Lincoln leaned back, chuckling. His eyes on the actors below.

Booth stepped into the box. He took two strides and leveled the pistol. His arm extended—point-blank range.

The crack split the laughter.

A sharp, shocking sound. Like a plank snapping.

Smoke curled from the barrel. It was acrid yet familiar.

Lincoln's head jerked sideways. A spray of dark matter bloomed against the crimson wallpaper. His body slumped, he folded into the rocking chair. Mary Lincoln screamed—a High, piercing scream.

Major Rathbone lunged from his seat and grabbed for Booth. Booth dropped the Derringer. He pulled a knife from his belt, a long Bowie blade. The silver flashed in the gaslight.

Rathbone gripped Booth's coat. Booth twisted and slashed down. The knife bit deep into Rathbone's arm. Rathbone cried out in pain. He released his hold. Blood soaked his sleeve—dark red—spreading fast.

Booth turned and faced the railing. The stage lay ten feet below. It was a long, hard drop but there was no other way. This was his only chance of escape. The actors stared up. They were frozen mid-scene, distracted by the commotion from above. They stood, mouths open—confusion on their faces.

Booth put a boot on the red velvet cushion and pushed off. He vaulted over the rail.

He flew, for a second—suspended above the stage. A dark shape against the bright footlights. Then gravity pulled him down—hard.

He landed hard. His left foot landed first, his right leg buckled under him. A sickening crunch came from his ankle. Pain exploded deep within his foot. It was white hot, unbearable pain, shooting up his leg. He stumbled. He fell forward onto the stage boards, his breath knocked out. He gasped, trying to catch his breath—trying to escape.

Gasps filled the theater. Shouts rose. "Stop that man!" "Murder!" "The President!"

Booth scrambled up. He ignored the fire in his ankle. He limped badly, dragged his left leg. He raised the bloody knife high and shouted into the sudden chaos.

"Sic semper tyrannis!"

The cry echoed—Raw—Defiant.

He ran, a limp-shuffle-run across the stage. He ran past the frozen actors, towards the stage right wing. The painted backdrop of a street scene blurred past. Faces stared—Stagehands—Actors—Wide-eyed, he shoved his way past them all.

Backstage, was darker, cluttered with ropes and flats. He knew the way. He had rehearsed it with the same rigor he used in preparing for a role. He made his way down the narrow corridor, past the dressing rooms. The smells of greasepaint and sweat were stronger here.

A stagehand blocked the exit door. He was a big man, his arms spread wide. "Hold there!"

Booth didn't slow down, he ran—a limp-shuffle-run. He lowered his shoulder, rammed into the man. He sent him crashing into a stack of scenery, canvas tore, wood clattered. Booth hit the door release bar, he burst out into the alley—his ankle swollen, throbbing. The pain was almost more than he could bear.

The cool night air hit his face. It was sharp, a relief after the theater's heat. His horse waited, still tethered in the shadows. A bay mare, saddled—ready. Booth had left her there himself, hours ago.

He grabbed the reins. Pain shot through his ankle again, he gritted his teeth. He hopped on his good leg, fumbled for the stirrup. He heard shouts behind him. They were coming from inside the theater—getting louder—closer.

He hauled himself up into the saddle. Agony spread through his leg. He gasped, grabbed the pommel, steadied himself. He kicked the mare hard—once—twice.

She leapt forward. Hooves clattered on the cobblestones, loud in the alley.

He guided her left, towards the back streets—away from 10th Street—away from Pennsylvania Avenue—away from the main lights. The darkness swallowed them. The narrow lanes and boarded-up shops. Puddles reflected slivers of moonlight.

He pushed the horse, faster. He leaned low over her neck. Wind whipped his face, his ankle throbbed. A steady, deep pulse of pain vibrated through his leg, he ignored it. He was focused on the next turn—the next shadow.

Shouts erupted ahead. Figures spilled from a tavern doorway. They were curious, drawn out by the distant noise. They saw the rider charging towards them.

"Who goes there?" A rough voice called.

Booth didn't answer. He urged the mare straight at them. They scattered, jumped back. Murmurs and curses followed him.

He turned right and headed down another alley. It was dank, smelling of garbage. A dog barked furiously from a yard.

He reached the edge of the city. The streets were wider now. Still dark, fewer lamps. The Capitol dome loomed black against the sky behind him. He didn't look back.

He needed the Navy Yard Bridge. South, out of the city—into Maryland.

He heard new sounds. No longer just shouts, hooves, multiple sets. Hard—purposeful. Behind him—getting closer.

He risked a glance back. The shapes moved in the gloom. Horsemen, two, three, maybe more. They were coming fast—uniformed?— hard to tell.

They shouted. Their words were torn away by the wind and the pounding hooves. They were demanding he halt.

Booth kicked the mare again and bent lower. Pain screamed from his ankle up his spine. He clenched his jaw and breathed through his nose. The mare stretched out and flew over the road.

The bridge was getting closer. It was a dark span over the Anacostia River. The sentry box stood at the near end. A single soldier, Seargeant Silas Cobb of the 3rd Massachusetts Heavy Artillery stood guard. He was alert now, rifle held ready—hearing the commotion.

Booth slowed the mare, just a fraction. He forced himself upright and masked the pain. He projected calm—authority.

"Halt!" The sentry challenged, his rifle raised. "Who passes?"

Booth kept his voice level, confident. "A friend."

"Name?"

Booth gave a name—not his own—a common one. "Smith. John Smith."

The sentry peered, hesitant. The horsemen behind Booth were closing in fast. Their shouts distinct now. "Stop him! Assassin!"

The sentry lowered his rifle slightly, confused. "Advance, friend, and give the countersign."

Booth nudged the mare forward. He walked her past the sentry, onto the bridge planking, hooves echoed hollowly.

"Hey!" The sentry yelled after him—unsure.

Booth didn't look back. He kicked the mare hard the moment he cleared the sentry box. She surged forward, galloped across the bridge. The dark water flowed silently below.

He reached the Maryland shore and didn't slow down. He plunged into the network of country roads. The trees closed in, they were thick, black, covered in darkness.

The pursuit reached the bridge. He heard the sentry shouting, explaining. The clatter of hooves stopped. The distant voices were angry, shouting, getting harder to hear as he moved farther away. Then the hooves started again. They were crossing the bridge, following him.

Booth pushed deeper into the Maryland night. The trees offered cover. The roads were poor, unlit. He relied on the mare's sight, his own night vision was fading. Every jolt sent pain rocketing up his leg. He felt sweat slick on his back. He was cold, despite the exertion.

He needed distance—he needed to find shelter—a place to hide. He needed to bind his leg—to think.

He knew the first safe house, a farm—south. It's run by a sympathizer—Samuel Mudd. He had to reach it, before dawn. Before the news spread like wildfire. Before the entire countryside knew his name—his face.

Behind him, the sounds of pursuit faded. Distance and the winding roads swallowed them—for now. But they wouldn't stop—he knew that— they would never stop hunting him.

They would fan out, double back, check every shadow—question everyone. Telegraph wires would get the message out. Roads would be watched, bridges blocked and rivers patrolled.

He was the most wanted man in the country.

He rode, the mare's breath came in labored puffs. His own breath rasped. The pain in his leg was a constant companion. It felt like a white-hot brand below his knee. He focused on the next bend, the next mile marker— the next hour.

The dark road stretched out ahead of him. It was empty, for now.

He touched the knife still tucked in his belt. The pistol was gone. Left on the stage floor. Only the knife remained—and his will.

He rode south, into the deeper darkness. He rode towards the first uncertain refuge.

The hunt had begun.

Chapter 2

The mare stumbled, Booth jerked in the saddle—pain ripped through his leg. He bit down hard on his lip, he tasted blood. He pulled the reins hard, slowed the animal to a walk. They needed rest, both of them. The road was empty, pitch black. Trees pressed close together on either side. He was in unknown territory. He listened. He heard only the mare's heavy breathing—the creak of leather—the throb in his ankle. No hoofbeats followed, not yet. He hoped the winding roads confused his pursuers, bought him more time.

Dawn approached—it was a gray smear in the east. He needed shelter before full light. His face was known—his leg screamed for attention. He remembered the name—a doctor, Samuel Mudd he had first met the previous year at St. Mary's. His farm was south of here, near Bryantown—he was a sympathizer. He hoped the information was good. Hope was all he had.

He guided the mare off the main road, onto a smaller track. There would be less chance of patrols. The going was a lot slower but it was safer. There were muddy ruts and overhanging branches. He ducked low to avoid them—sweat stung his eyes. His injured foot hung useless in the stirrup—every jolt was agony.

He saw a farmhouse ahead, it was set back from the track. A single light in a window, an early riser. Booth hesitated—he weighed the risk versus necessity. He knew he was close but he needed directions, confirmation. He approached the farmhouse cautiously. He dismounted. When he hit the ground, pain shot up his leg. He leaned heavily against the mare. He took a few deep breaths, trying to ignore the pain ravaging his leg. Then, he hobbled to the door and knocked—firm—authoritative.

A man answered, he squinted in the dim light—suspicion on his face. Booth kept his voice low, steady. "Good morning. Apologies for the hour. I'm seeking Doctor Samuel Mudd. Near Bryantown. Can you point the way?"

The farmer studied him. He saw the mud-splattered clothes, the fine boots, the obvious pain. "Doctor Mudd? Yonder. Five miles south. Take the fork left after the creek crossing. Big white house. Oak trees." He paused. "You hurt, mister?"

"Fell from my horse," Booth said quickly. "Last night. Dark road. Need the doctor's attention."

The farmer nodded slowly. "Rough night for travel. Heard noises. Shouting. Down towards the city." His eyes lingered on Booth's face.

"Unruly drunks, likely," Booth dismissed. "My thanks for the directions." He turned and limped back to his horse. He mounted with difficulty. He felt the farmer's eyes on his back until he rounded a bend.

The gray light grew, getting brighter as the sun peeked over the horizon. He passed the creek, took the left fork. He saw the white house. It was large, imposing—framed by oak trees. He rode up the lane, the pain in his leg sharp—excruciating. Dogs barked—a man emerged onto the porch. He was tall, thin, wearing spectacles—Samuel Mudd.

Booth reined in and dismounted, his leg buckled as he landed. He caught the saddle horn to balance himself. "Doctor Mudd?"

"I am. And you are?"

"Booth. David Booth." The lie came easily. He'd only met Doctor Mudd once, a year earlier. He didn't expect the doctor would remember. He needed trust first. "I've had an accident. My horse fell. My leg..." He gestured down.

Mudd stepped closer and examined him. He noticed the fine quality of the coat, the riding boots and the pallor of pain. "Bring him inside, John," Mudd called over his shoulder. A younger man appeared. He helped Booth hobble into the house, into a small room off the hall—a surgery.

Booth sank onto a table, he felt a sense of relief but the tension was still there. Mudd cut away the boot, Booth hissed. The ankle was swollen, purple, painful. Mudd probed it gently, Booth clenched his fists. "Broken," Mudd stated. "Fibula. Clean break. Needs setting. Splinting." He looked up. "You rode far on this?"

"Several hours," Booth admitted. "Needed help."

Mudd began work, setting the bone. Booth gritted his teeth—sweat poured down his face—he made no sound. Mudd fashioned splints from pieces of a bandbox. He bound the leg tightly with bandages and gave Booth a pair of crude crutches cut from timber. "Rest is crucial. Weeks of it. No weight."

"Rest is a luxury I lack, Doctor," Booth said. He tested the crutches. His movement was awkward, painful but mobile. "I must travel south. Urgently."

Mudd frowned. "Impossible. You'll ruin the leg. Cause permanent damage."

"Permanent damage is preferable to capture," Booth said flatly. He met Mudd's eyes. Time slowed, the moment seemed to last forever. The name 'Booth'. The urgency. The broken leg from a fall. Mudd was no fool. The news would be spreading—fast.

A shadow crossed Mudd's face, understanding—perhaps fear—perhaps both. He stepped back. "John," he called again. "Help Mr. Booth outside. To the stable. See to his horse." He avoided Booth's gaze. "I can offer no further aid. You must go. Now."

Booth understood. His sanctuary had been withdrawn—the risk was too great. He nodded. "My thanks for the leg, Doctor." He hobbled out on the crutches and John helped him mount the waiting mare. The pain of swinging his leg over was excruciating. He settled in the saddle and gripped the reins. He looked down at Mudd. "Which way to the Potomac? To Virginia?"

Mudd pointed south. "Piney Church. Ask for Oswell Swann. He knows the river. He…facilitates crossings." The words were careful. "Go quickly."

Booth nudged the mare. He headed south, he didn't look back. He knew Mudd would talk, eventually. When soldiers came asking questions—the clock was ticking louder.

He rode through the day, the crutches tied awkwardly to the saddle. The splinted leg was a dead weight—the pain was a constant fire. He avoided towns, stuck to woods and fields. He saw smoke in the distance. He heard bells tolling but not church bells—alarm bells.

He found Oswell Swann's cabin near dusk, it was a rough place by a swamp. Swann was a waterman—he was a grizzled, wary man. Booth gave the same name he had given to Mudd. "David Booth." He asked for passage across the Potomac, to Virginia.

Swann spat tobacco juice. He looked at the splinted leg, the exhausted horse. "Crossing's watched. Soldiers. Gunboats. Risky business."

"I can pay," Booth said. He pulled out a roll of greenbacks and Confederate bills. They were worthless to some but gold to others.

Swann's eyes narrowed. He took the money, counted it. He nodded. "Tonight. Late. Meet me at Dent's Meadow. Moonrise. Bring your horse. Stay hidden 'til then."

Booth hid in a thicket near the meadow. He watched the river. He saw the dark shapes of gunboats patrolling the river. Lanterns glowed on the Maryland shore, soldiers patrolling the shore. He shivered—not from the cold, his body burned with fever. The leg felt like a log—maybe infected. He drank from a canteen, ate bread and waited.

Moonrise came—the silvery light reflected on the water. Swann appeared like a ghost—poling a small flat-bottomed skiff. "Quiet now," he whispered. "Get the horse in. Easy."

It took effort—the pain was constant. Booth coaxed the nervous mare into the shallow draft boat. She stood trembling, Booth crouched beside her. Swann pushed off and he poled silently into the current. The river was wide here, black water. It was silent except for the lap of waves and the distant chug of a gunboat engine.

They drifted—Swann used the pole sparingly. He let the current carry them south. Booth glanced around the shores, he saw campfires on the Maryland side. He heard a shout, carried over the water. His hand went to the knife at his belt.

Minutes seemed long—the Virginia shore remained dark—distant. The gunboat sound grew louder. A lantern light illuminated the darkness, its light reflecting across the water's surface. Booth held his breath, the mare shifted. The boat rocked gently just out of reach of the light. Swann froze as the light passed—the darkness returned.

The skiff scraped bottom on the Virginia shore. It settled into mud and reeds. Swann jumped out. He pulled the boat further up. "Out," he hissed. "Quick."

Booth led the mare onto Virginia soil—Confederate soil. He felt a surge of grim triumph. It was short-lived, he was still hunted—still broken. He paid Swann extra. "My thanks."

Swann nodded and pushed the skiff back into the current. He vanished into the night. Booth was alone again—on the run, in a new state. The fever burned brighter—he needed shelter—he needed medical help, again.

He rode inland, away from the river. He found a farmhouse—it was smaller than Mudd's. He knocked, a woman answered with fear in her eyes. Booth used a different name. "James Boyd. Confederate courier. Wounded. Need shelter. Just for the night." He leaned heavily on the crutches, he played the part.

The woman hesitated. She looked past him into the dark. "My husband…he's not here…"

"Please, ma'am," Booth rasped. The exhaustion was real, the pain was real—he swayed.

She relented. "The barn. You can sleep in the hay. I'll bring water. Food. No more."

He spent a fitful night in the barn. Fever dreams haunted him. Lincoln's face—Rathbone's scream—The crack of the Derringer—The crunch of his own bone as he hit the stage. He woke drenched in sweat, shivering. His leg pulsed, hot and tight.

At dawn, the woman brought cornbread and water. Her husband had returned. He stood in the barn door—he was big and stern—he studied Booth. "Courier, huh? Where from? Where to?"

"Richmond," Booth lied. "Carrying dispatches. Ambushed near the river. Lost my papers. Horse fell." He gestured to his leg.

The man grunted. "Heard about the trouble. Up north. Big trouble. Lincoln." He watched Booth's face—Booth kept it still, blank. "Soldiers everywhere. Asking questions. Looking for a man. On a horse. Hurt leg." He paused. "You best move on. Today. We can't have trouble here."

Booth ate the cornbread, drank the water. He knew the man wouldn't help further. The man had to take care of his family and he was a risk. He saddled the mare, mounted with difficulty. The farmer pointed south. "Port Royal. Down the road. Ten miles. Ask for Captain Jett. Willie Jett. Stays at the hotel sometimes. He…knows people. Might help a stranded soldier."

Booth rode hard. The fever affected his vision, landmarks blurred. He focused on staying upright, staying conscious. Port Royal was a small riverside town. He saw blue uniforms—Union soldiers—questioning people near the dock. He avoided the main street. He found the small hotel, dismounted behind it and hobbled inside.

The lobby was empty. A clerk looked up, bored. "Help you?"

"Willie Jett," Booth said. His voice sounded thick, hoarse. "Captain Jett. Is he here?"

The clerk jerked his head towards a closed door. "In there. With friends."

Booth pushed the door open. It was a small sitting room. Four young men looked up, startled. They wore Confederate gray, faded, unofficial. Willie Jett was the one in the middle. He had a boyish face with curly hair. He frowned. "Who're you?"

Booth closed the door and leaned on his crutches. He was weak—exhausted. The room seemed to tilt. "John Wilkes Booth," he said, quietly, firmly.

Silence—absolute silence. Four pairs of eyes widened. They stared. The name hung in the air—heavy—dangerous.

"You're…" one breathed. "The one who…"

"Yes," Booth cut in. "Lincoln. I did it. For the South. I'm hunted. My leg is broken. I need to cross the Rappahannock. Get further south. To safety. I need horses. Guides. Help."

Jett exchanged looks with the others. Ruggles and Bainbridge stood close to Jett like bodyguards. David Herold sat silently at the table, studying a map. Booth saw calculation in their eyes. Fear—excitement—sympathy.

"Federal cavalry is thick as fleas," Jett said slowly. "Roads watched. Ferries guarded."

"I know," Booth said. "I need men who know the back ways. Swamps. Who aren't afraid."

Jett stood up and paced, thinking. "It's death if we're caught helping you."

"It's death if I'm caught regardless," Booth countered. "Help me reach the Carolinas. I have money. Gold." He pulled out a heavy coin purse and let it clink.

The sound decided for them. Jett nodded. "Alright. We help. But we move fast. Now. You look like hell. Can you ride?"

"I can ride," Booth said. The fever spiked—the barn walls seemed to pulse. "Get the horses." He needed to reach Garrett's farm. The next name on his list—a safe haven. He needed to get there before his body gave out, before the soldiers closed the final gap. The barn seemed far away—safety seemed farther. The gold bought him guides but time was running out. The road south stretched ahead, harder now. The hunters were closing in. He was the hunted.

Chapter 3

The Garrett farmhouse stood dark against the moonlit Virginia fields. Its white paint peeling, porch sagging. Booth swayed in the saddle. The fever burned. His leg felt like a stone column holding him down. It was heavy and hot—the pain was sharp and constant. Willie Jett rode ahead—Bainbridge and Ruggles flanked Booth. David Herold trailed behind, his nervous eyes scanning the dark.

Jett dismounted and knocked hard on the farmhouse door. A long minute passed, then a lamp glowed inside, the door creaked open. An old man peered out. It was Richard Garrett, suspicion etched deep in his face. "Willie Jett? What brings you out this hour? Who's with you?"

"Evening, Mr. Garrett," Jett said, friendly, easy. "These are friends. Confederate soldiers. Just escaped Yankee prison. Need a place to rest a night or two. Harmless. We vouch for them."

Garrett's gaze swept over Booth on his horse. The splinted leg visible, the pain in his face. Herold's fidgeting. "Soldiers? Names?"

"James Boyd," Booth rasped. The alias felt thick on his tongue. "This is David Herold." He gestured weakly. "We're bound for home. Can hardly ride. Need shelter."

Garrett hesitated, he looked past them into the night. "Heard there's trouble. Manhunt. Lincoln's killer loose. Soldiers crawling everywhere."

"Not us, sir," Jett insisted. "Just weary men. A barn floor would suffice. We'll be gone by morning light."

Garrett sighed, reluctant. "Barn's yonder. You can bed down there. But no fires. No noise. You leave at first light. Understood?"

"Understood," Jett said quickly. "Our thanks, Mr. Garrett."

They led the horses to the tobacco barn. It was a large, shadowy structure smelling of dried leaves and earth. They helped Booth dismount and he collapsed onto a pile of burlap sacks. Pain roared through him, he bit back a groan. Herold spread blankets, his hands shook.

Jett crouched beside Booth. "We ride on. Stay here risks us all. Garrett's jumpy." He handed Booth a small flask. "Brandy. For the pain."

Booth took it and nodded. "Your help won't be forgotten."

Jett, Ruggles, and Bainbridge mounted their horses. "Good luck," Jett muttered. They vanished into the darkness towards Port Royal. Booth and Herold were left alone in the vast, quiet barn.

Silence pressed in as the night wore on—crickets chirped, an owl hooted somewhere nearby. Booth sipped the brandy, it felt like fire down his dry throat. It was little relief for the pain vibrating through his leg. Herold paced nervously. "They'll find us. Jett talks. He drinks. He'll brag."

"Quiet," Booth hissed. "We rest. We move at dawn. South. To the Carolinas." He tried to sound certain but the plan felt thin—brittle. The brandy fogged his mind. He saw Lincoln's face again—clear—close. He shook his head, tried to focus.

They slept fitfully—Booth woke often, stiff and cold. The pain was constant. Herold snored beside him, twitching. Dawn came gray and damp—mist clung to the fields. Booth struggled up on his crutches and peered out a crack in the barn wall. The farmhouse door opened and John

Garrett walked towards them. His sons, Jack and William, followed. Their faces grim, looked like trouble coming.

Garrett stopped outside the barn door. "Boyd? Herold? Time you moved on. Sun's up."

Booth pulled the door open. He leaned heavily, trying to keep balance. "Mr. Garrett. My leg...it's worse. Fever. We need another day. Just one. To rest the horse. To gather strength."

Garrett's eyes narrowed. "You said gone by morning. Soldiers came through last night. Asking about strangers. About a man with a broken leg." He looked pointedly at Booth's splints. "Who are you really?"

"Confederate soldiers," Booth repeated, his voice tight. "Escaped prisoners. Harmless."

"You look familiar, Boyd," young Jack Garrett said—staring hard. "Real familiar."

Booth met his gaze, it was steady—defiant. "You mistake me for another." Inside, alarm bells rang—louder.

Garrett shook his head. "No. You leave. Now. We want no trouble here. Pack your things."

Booth saw the resolve—arguing risked more. "Very well. We need food. Can you spare any? We pay." He pulled out coins.

Garrett took the money and nodded curtly. "My boy Jack will bring you something. Then you go." He turned and walked back to the house with William—Jack lingered, watching.

Herold started saddling the horses, his hands clumsy. "They know. Or suspect. We have to run."

"Where?" Booth snapped. "I can barely stand. We ride into a patrol?" He lowered his voice. "We wait. See what Jack brings. See what he says."

Jack Garrett returned, he was carrying a rough cloth bundle with bread and cold bacon. He handed it to Herold but his eyes never left Booth.

"My Pa sent me to town. Port Royal. Heard soldiers are thick there. Setting up a camp."

Booth forced calm. "Is that so? Best avoid it then."

Jack shifted. "Yeah. They got a description. The man they want. Plays actor. Famous. Name's Booth." He watched Booth's face. Booth kept it still like stone—emotionless. "They say he killed the President. Got a busted leg. Jumped off a stage."

There was a brief awkward silence. Herold stopped moving, he was tense. Booth leaned on his crutch and met Jack's stare. "A terrible thing. Killing a President. Even a tyrant. But what's that to do with us?"

Jack shrugged—he didn't look convinced. "Just saying. Be careful on the road. He looks like you." He turned and walked back towards the house, slowly. He only looked back once.

Herold exploded the moment Jack was out of earshot. "He knows! He'll tell! We have to go now!" He fumbled with the saddle girth.

"Stop," Booth commanded, cold. "We don't run blindly. We need a plan. We wait until dark. Slip away then." He felt the trap closing, the walls of the barn felt closer. He hobbled to a crack facing the road, he scanned the horizon—nothing—yet. "Eat. Rest. We move tonight."

The day crawled—an eternity. Booth watched the road, his leg throbbed in time with his heartbeat. Herold paced and chewed his nails, muttered prayers. Booth ignored him, he was focused outward. Every bird call sounded like a signal, every rustle of wind like approaching riders.

Late afternoon, Booth saw dust. It was far down the road, moving fast toward them. He took a deep breath and squinted through the crack. There were horsemen, a dozen or more. Their blue coats glinting in the low sun heading straight for the farm.

"Herold!" Booth hissed. "Soldiers! Coming here!"

Herold scrambled to the wall and peered out. Fear overtook him, he went pale. "Oh God. They found us! What do we do?"

"Into the loft," Booth ordered, quick, decisive. "Hide. Be silent. They might pass. Or Garrett might send them away." Hope was a thin thread, he knew it was fraying.

They scrambled toward the loft. Herold helped Booth climb the rough ladder to the tobacco loft. Hay dust filled the air, it tickled their throats. They burrowed deep into the dry, prickly stacks. They concealed themselves, weapons ready just in case. Booth's knife—Herold's pistol—Below, the barn door stood slightly ajar.

They heard the horsemen arrive. Their voices were harsh and loud—horses snorting. Booth held his breath and peered through a gap in the floorboards. They were Union cavalry, grim-faced. They were led by two men in civilian clothes—detectives—Luther Baker and Everton Conger. Booth recognized the type—they were hunters.

Richard Garrett stood on the porch. His hands raised, trying to calm the situation. "Gentlemen? How can I help?"

One detective spoke, he was loud—authoritative. "We track two fugitives. John Wilkes Booth. David Herold. They came this way. Last night. With Willie Jett. We know they stopped here. Where are they?"

Garrett stammered. "Men...men were here. Called themselves Boyd and Herold. Left this morning. Early. Headed south. Towards Guinea Station."

"Did they?" The detective sounded skeptical. "Search the house. The outbuildings. Now!" The soldiers dismounted, they stormed the farmhouse, doors banged—women cried out inside.

Another soldier approached the barn. He was tall, thin—a strange intensity in his eyes. Booth felt a chill, he recognized Boston Corbett. The name surfaced—he was known, a zealot. Corbett peered into the barn's dim interior. He walked inside and looked around. His boots crunched on the dirt floor. He glanced around the empty stalls and the ladder to the loft.

Booth froze—he didn't breathe—didn't move. Herold trembled beside him. A small whimper escaped Herold's lips. Booth clamped a hand over his mouth, hard. His eyes warning silence.

Corbett stopped and looked up at the loft. He listened—he heard nothing but the wind whistling through the barn. Then he turned and walked back out. "Barn's clear, Capatain. Just old hay."

Relief washed over Booth, weak—temporary. He released Herold. Herold gasped for air.

Outside, the detective questioned Garrett again. "You sure they left? On horses?"

Garrett hesitated, he glanced towards the barn. Jack Garrett stepped forward. He was young, earnest—defiant. "They ain't gone, sir. They lied. They're hiding. In the barn. Right now. In the loft. Booth's the one with the busted leg."

It was betrayal, sharp and cold. Booth cursed silently. Herold whimpered again.

"Jack!" Old Garrett hissed, too late.

The detective's voice turned hard. "Booth! Herold! We know you're in there! Surrender! Come on out with your hands up! You're surrounded!"

Silence from the loft. It was heavy—final.

"Last chance!" the detective shouted. "Come out peacefully!"

Booth gripped his knife, his knuckles white on its handle. He looked at Herold. He saw terror—saw surrender in his eyes. "No," Booth whispered, fiercely. "We fight. To the end."

Herold shook his head violently. "No! They'll kill us! Booth, please! I can't!" Tears streaked his dirty face.

"Then be silent!" Booth snarled.

The detective spoke again—to his men. "Set it up. We wait them out. They won't last the night." Orders were barked—the soldiers moved. Booth heard the sounds—men taking positions, rifles cocking. The soft thud of bodies lying prone in the dirt. They were circling the barn—a cordon of steel and blue cloth. Lanterns were lit, casting long, shifting shadows across the barn walls.

The trap was set—the barn was a cage. Booth and Herold were the prey. They were exhausted but filled with adrenaline. Their pain mixed with fear, the air in the loft grew thick and stale. Booth watched the ring of light tighten around the barn through the cracks. He watched the shadowy figures settle in, they were waiting. Corbett stood near the front—he was quiet and still, watchful—like a hawk.

The night deepened—the soldiers didn't move, they didn't speak. A terrible, patient silence settled over the farm. It was broken only by the crackle of the lanterns and the frantic beat of Herold's breathing. Booth shifted. He tried to ease the agony in his leg—it was futile. Escape seemed impossible—surrender meant the gallows—a public spectacle.

He thought of the stage, of applause, the leap, the crunch of bone in his leg—Lincoln falling. This was the final act—there would be no encore—only, the curtains closing forever. There would be no more applause, only the eternal darkness of an empty theater. He wouldn't give them the satisfaction of capture. He wouldn't beg. He would make them come in. He would make it cost them.

"Herold," Booth whispered. "When they come...we take some with us. Aim true."

Herold didn't answer. He was afraid, even the thought terrified him. He just stared into the dark loft, his eyes wide with dread. The weight of the waiting pressed down on him, heavy—suffocating. Outside, a soldier coughed. The sound was loud in the stillness. Time seemed to slow down— stretched into this one moment, thin, tight—ready to snap. Booth listened to the night. He listened for the signal, for the rush—for the end to begin. The barn walls felt like they were breathing. In—Out—Tightening. Closing in on them.

Chapter 4

The barn held its breath—Booth listened. Below, soldiers shifted, leather creaked, metal clicked and clacked. A low murmur passed between men. The detective's voice cut the quiet—it was Luther Baker, he yelled toward the barn. "Booth! Send Herold out! Now! He surrenders, he lives! Booth stays! Your choice!"

Herold jerked beside Booth, a choked sound escaped him. "They mean it," he whispered, desperate. "They'll kill us both if we don't..."

"Quiet," Booth hissed. His knuckles whitened on the knife handle. Surrender was death, slow, public—the gallows. He wouldn't give them that. He glanced around the dim loft. The hay bales, old tools, the ladder down. The thick plank walls, a rear wall. Less guarded? He couldn't see. "We fight. Or we burn."

"Burn?" Herold's voice cracked. "No...no fire…"

Baker shouted again, impatient. "Last chance! Herold comes out! Or we smoke you out! Decide!"

Silence answered him—it was heavy and defiant.

"Alright!" Baker yelled. "Have it your way!" His voice hardened. "Conger! Get that straw! Light it up! Under the front wall!"

There was movement below, scraping sounds—hay rustled. Booth heard the scratch of a match—a hiss. A small flare of light visible through the floor cracks. Then the distinct crackle of dry straw catching. Smoke began to curl upwards—thin wisps at first. It was acrid mixing with the stale barn air—hard to breathe.

Herold whimpered. "Fire! They set fire!"

"Stay low!" Booth commanded. He pulled his neckerchief over his nose and mouth. The smoke thickened fast, stinging his eyes, burning his throat. He crawled towards the loft edge facing the rear wall. He peered through gaps, he saw soldiers crouched behind trees and fences. Their rifles aimed, focused on the front. The fire grew louder, hungrier. The flames licked the base of the front wall. Orange light flickered through the barn, shadows danced wildly.

Heat washed over them—it was intense and suffocating. The crackle became a roar. Thick black smoke billowed, filling the loft. Herold coughed violently. "Can't breathe! Booth! We have to go out! Now!"

"Not the front!" Booth yelled over the fire's noise. He pointed towards the back. "The rear wall! Less light! Less men! We go through it! Kick it out!" He scrambled towards the back wall, ignoring the searing pain in his leg. He braced his good leg against a heavy roof support beam. He kicked hard at the planks near the bottom. The wood creaked, resisted, didn't yield. He kicked again—agony shot through his broken leg. The fire roared behind him, heat seared his back—smoke choked him. He kicked again and again. A plank splintered, a small gap—not enough.

Herold stared at the solid planks. He shook his head, panic seizing him. "No time! Too strong! Fire! The door! They said surrender!" He scrambled towards the ladder, ignoring Booth's command. "I'm coming out! Don't shoot! I surrender! David Herold! I surrender!"

"Herold! No!" Booth lunged, he missed, grabbed air. Herold was already clambering down the ladder, disappearing into the thickening smoke below.

Cursing, Booth turned back to the rear wall. He kicked again, pouring every ounce of strength and desperation into the blows against the splintering wood. *Crack!* Another plank yielded. *Crack!* The hole widened. Flames licked closer, greedily consuming the dry timber near him. He kicked one last time. A gap large enough opened. He saw darkness beyond—open ground—trees.

Below, he heard Herold stumble, coughing. "Hands up! Hands up! I surrender! Don't shoot!" Herold's voice was shrill with terror.

"Come out slow! Hands high!" Baker ordered.

The firelight outside, in the front blazed brighter, illuminating the barn door. A figure stumbled through the smoke—his hands raised high. He was silhouetted against the inferno consuming the front wall. David Herold stood in the opening of the barn door, framed by the hot orange flames.

A single shot cracked—it was sharp and distinct over the fire's roar. Booth saw Herold jerk violently. His hands dropped, he crumpled forward. He fell face down just outside the burning doorway—motionless. Flames from the barn door licked hungrily at his boots and legs.

Boston Corbett lowered his smoking carbine and stood rigid. "Providence directed my hand," he stated, flat and certain.

Chaos erupted—shouts. "You shot him!" "He was surrendering!" "Is that Booth?" Soldiers surged forward towards the fallen figure—drawn to the firelight. They were focused on the front, clustering around Herold's body, some trying to drag him back from the flames engulfing the barn entrance.

Booth saw his chance. The distraction, the blinding smoke—the roaring flames, the soldiers crowding towards Herold. He pushed his crutches through the hole, then his head and shoulders. He wiggled his way through, it was tight. He scraped his back, his broken leg snagged. Fire licked at his boots, the heat was intense. He pulled hard, tore his leg free—a scream tore from his throat, lost in the fire's roar. He tumbled out of the barn, the flames reaching out for him before being pulled back into the fire. He fell onto cool, damp grass. It was a welcome relief from the heat inside. Behind him, the barn was a roaring pyre. Flames shot through the roof, sparks filled the night sky—the heat was immense.

He grabbed his crutches, pulled himself up. He glanced back, soldiers milled around Herold's body near the front. They were silhouetted against the flames, shouting and pointing. Herold's legs were ablaze now, the fire from the doorway consuming him. No one looked towards the back. The fire and smoke were his shield. He turned and limped as fast as he could away from the blinding light. He pressed his boots into the soft earth near the barn wall and then across the open ground, leaving deep, unmistakable impressions. He disappeared into the deep shadows at the edge of the field towards the treeline. Every step sent jagged pain through his leg. His lungs burned, he gasped for clean air.

He heard voices behind him. They were louder now—angry—confused.

"Herold! That's David Herold! Pull him back!"

"Fire's got him! Help me!"

"Where's Booth?"

"Still inside! Burn him out!"

"Fire's too hot! No one could be alive in there!"

"Check the body! Is it Booth? Before it burns!"

Booth reached the trees. He stumbled into the undergrowth and collapsed behind a thick oak trunk. He lay panting, trying to catch his breath, watching the inferno. The barn was fully engulfed. It was a column of flame against the night. Figures moved in the hellish glow. The soldiers finally dragged Herold's burning body further from the flames, beating out the fire on his clothes. They huddled around it. The front of his coat was dark with blood from Corbett's shot, his face momentarily visible before the smoke and milling soldiers obscured it.

He saw Detective Baker kneel, examine the face—shake his head—stand up. "It's Herold! Just Herold! Booth's still inside! Trapped!" Baker's voice carried over the roar.

Captain Edward Doherty yelled orders. "Keep the perimeter! He might try to run! Watch the flanks!" The soldiers fanned out, rifles ready. Their eyes scanned the fields away from the barn, *away* from the trees where Booth lay and the rear wall he'd breached. The intense heat forced them back. The roar of the fire drowned quieter sounds.

Booth pushed himself up and leaned against the tree. He had to move, put distance between himself and the light. He needed to move before they widened the search, before dawn revealed the trail he'd left. He looked down at his leg—the splint was charred, bandages blackened. Pain radiated like a furnace—but he was alive—free. He looked back at the burning barn. The soldiers were silhouetted against the flames, still focused on the front, believing him caged within the inferno. Herold's body, damaged by the shot and the fire, lay as a grim decoy.

A grim thought formed—cold—calculating. They thought he was inside—trapped—burning. Herold was dead—shot and scorched. They needed Booth. Dead or alive, preferably dead—to end the hunt—to show victory. Herold's body, burned and broken, might serve...if they believed the fire did its work.

He saw Baker and Conger conferring urgently, gesturing at the inferno, then down at Herold's body. Baker looked up at the flames, shielding his face. He shook his head slowly. Booth read it in his posture—a realization dawning, but not the one Booth had escaped. They believed he was in there, being consumed. They *needed* him to be in there.

He turned away from the light. He faced the dark woods, south. He took a step, then another. His crutches biting into the soft earth. Each movement was agony but he moved. He moved away from the fire. He moved away from the soldiers. He moved away from the man the world would soon believe had died screaming in the Garrett barn.

He disappeared into the woods. The roar of the fire faded behind him. It was replaced by the rustle of leaves, the chirp of insects, the pounding of his own heart. The hunt wasn't over, but the hunters thought it was—for now. That was his only advantage. He needed distance—shelter—a new skin. He limped deeper into the Virginia night. A ghost leaving a borrowed corpse behind.

Chapter 5

The Garrett barn groaned like a dying beast—timbers shrieked. Then, with a final, shuddering crash, it collapsed inward. A volcano of sparks erupted skyward. The flames roared higher—hungry—consuming everything within their grasp. The intense heat forced the soldiers further back—forming a grim, soot-streaked circle around the inferno—the blinding light and choking smoke masking the rear of the ruin.

David Herold's body lay on the grass, twenty feet from the burning wreckage. The front of his coat was dark with blood from Corbett's shot. His trousers were charred and blackened where the flames had caught him. His boots were scorched, his face smudged with soot and blistered from the intense heat near the doorway. Detective Luther Baker stood over him, hands on hips, face grim. Everton Conger joined him. They stared at the body, then at the roaring, collapsing structure. The heat pressed hard against their faces.

"He *has* to be in there," Conger said, raising his voice over the fire's roar. "No way out. Front was blocked. Sides and back covered. He burned." He wiped sweat and ash from his forehead, squinting against the glare.

Baker crouched and examined Herold again. The young face, slack in death, marked by fire. "This one talked. Briefly. Gasped it out before he died. Said Booth was upstairs. Armed. Defiant." He looked back at the barn, a seething mass of flame. "Booth wouldn't surrender. He'd die first. He died in there."

Boston Corbett approached. His face was blank, his eyes fixed on the flames as if seeing a divine judgment. "Providence guided my shot. The tyrant's accomplice is judged. The President's killer faces divine fire." He made no move towards Herold's body.

Captain Edward Doherty joined the group, his expression strained. "We need confirmation, gentlemen. Booth's body. Proof." He scanned the blazing ruin, the heat making his eyes water. "No one retrieves anything from that until it cools. Hours. Maybe dawn."

Baker stood up. He looked from Herold's fire-damaged body to the consuming inferno. A thought formed—cold—practical. Desperate. "Proof," he repeated slowly. He looked at Conger, then meaningfully at Herold. A silent communication passed between them. Years of hunting men, understanding necessities, the crushing weight of public expectation. "The fire...it will do its work. Inside. On whatever remains."

Conger's eyes narrowed, then widened slightly as he grasped Baker's implication. He gave a curt, almost imperceptible nod. "Unrecognizable. Utterly."

Baker stepped closer to Doherty, lowering his voice, forcing the Captain to lean in against the fire's roar. "Captain. Think. The nation *needs* this. Needs it ended. *Tonight*. Lincoln's killer dead. Justice served. The public needs certainty. Closure." He gestured towards the roaring fire. "That," he pointed, "*is* John Wilkes Booth. Trapped. Burned to nothing. Destroyed by his own defiance. By the consequences of his heinous act." He paused, letting the heat and the horror emphasize his point. "The body inside...it will be ash. Bone. Utterly destroyed. Fitting for a monster. But we know it's him. We saw Herold come out alone. We heard Booth defy us. The structure was surrounded. He didn't escape. He died in there." His gaze flickered towards Herold's body. "We have *one* body. Herold. Burned somewhat by the doorway fire before we pulled him clear. Badly enough..."

Doherty frowned, following Baker's gaze to Herold's scorched form. "But this one...he's Herold. They'll know his face, or what's left of it..."

"The fire inside that barn," Baker pressed, his voice urgent, "is far hotter than the flames that licked Herold. What comes out will be...less. Much less. Unrecognizable. Charred beyond *any* knowing. And found *inside* Booth's last stand." He leaned closer. "We place Herold's body *inside* the ruins. Before the fire cools. Where the loft collapsed. We say we found Booth's remains there. Along with his possessions. Things that survive the flames. Things we *can* identify." He looked meaningfully at Conger. "We have Booth's diary. His compass. Found earlier. We place them near the body in the ash."

Conger stepped in, his voice low and persuasive. "It's the clean end, Captain. The only end possible tonight. The hunt is over. We announce Booth is dead. Killed resisting capture. Burned in the barn. Herold shot trying to escape. The country exhales. Order is restored. Stanton gets his victory." He paused, his eyes hard. "The alternative? Admitting Booth might have escaped a surrounded barn? With every man watching? Admitting failure? The manhunt continuing indefinitely? The chaos? The doubt?"

Doherty hesitated. He looked at Corbett. The sergeant stared into the fire, unreadable, lost in his providence. Doherty thought of the telegrams that would fly. The relief in Washington. The end of the manhunt that had consumed the capital and the nation. He thought of Secretary Stanton's iron will demanding a corpse. He thought of the burned, anonymous thing Herold's body would become if placed deep within the hottest ashes. The impossibility of proving it *wasn't* Booth. The sheer, overwhelming *need* for it to be Booth.

"Alright," Doherty said finally, the word heavy with the weight of conspiracy. "We proceed on that understanding. Booth perished in the fire. Herold was shot fleeing. Secure the scene. *Absolutely* secure it." He looked at Baker and Conger with intense gravity. "Manage the…recovery. And the identification. Make it conclusive. For the record. Only we," his gaze swept over Baker, Conger, and Corbett, "know the full truth. The hunt for Booth continues. But silently. Secretly. For as long as it takes. Is that clear?"

Baker nodded sharply. "Understood, Captain. Conclusive." He turned, barking orders with new authority. "Sergeant! Post guards! No one approaches the barn until I say! *No one*! That includes civilians!" He gestured fiercely towards the Garretts huddled on their porch. "Keep them back. Way back! This area is sealed!"

The soldiers formed a tighter ring, facing outward, their rifles ready. They formed a human barrier against the growing crowd of locals and late-arriving cavalry drawn by the blaze. The fire raged unchecked, consuming wood—hay—David Herold's identity—and time.

As the flames finally began to subside towards dawn, the barn was a blackened, smoldering skeleton. Deep piles of ash and debris filled its footprint. Wisps of smoke rose into the cool morning air. The stench of burnt wood, hay, and flesh hung heavy in the smoke filled air.

Baker, Conger, and Doherty approached the ruins cautiously, their boots crunching on hot cinders. Soldiers followed with shovels. Baker directed them towards the center, where the loft had collapsed. "Search there. Carefully." He and Conger exchanged a look. While the soldiers began sifting ash near the center, Baker subtly gestured Conger towards the rear wall, partially collapsed but still standing in sections. They moved along the perimeter, away from the main search.

Near the back, partially obscured by fallen, charred timbers, Baker spotted it. A section of plank wall, low down, near the foundation, it had been kicked out from the inside. The wood splintered, a hole just large enough for a man to squeeze through. He crouched, ignoring the heat still radiating from the timbers. He pointed. Conger joined him, his eyes widening.

"Look," Baker whispered harshly. He pointed not just at the hole, but at the ground immediately outside. Clear, deep impressions in the soft earth. The distinct mark of boot heels and the rounded ends of crutch tips. Leading away from the barn, straight across the open ground towards the treeline. "He kicked his way out. Here. While we were distracted with Herold."

Conger stared at the prints, then back at the hole, a cold dread settling over him. "He escaped. Booth escaped."

Baker stood, his face like stone. He looked towards the woods, then back to where the soldiers were carefully uncovering something in the center of the ruins. "Yes," he said flatly. "He did. But the nation cannot know. Not now. Not ever, if we can help it." He kicked loose dirt over the clearest boot print near the wall. "Cover these. All of them. Now. Before anyone else sees." He grabbed a fallen, half-burned plank and tossed it carelessly near the hole, partially obscuring it. Conger quickly scuffed the remaining visible prints with his boot, then scattered debris over the area.

They turned and walked back towards the center, where the soldiers had uncovered a charred, twisted shape half-buried in the deepest ash. It was horrific, shrunken by heat, charcoal black, limbs drawn up—utterly unrecognizable. Nearby, Conger, following the silent plan, *found* items in the ash: Booth's little red leather diary, slightly scorched but intact, and his metal compass, blackened but undamaged. Baker himself carefully placed Booth's distinctive initials ring, "J.W.B.", recovered earlier, near the blackened claw of a hand.

"Here! Booth's effects!" Conger announced loudly, holding up the diary and compass for Doherty and nearby soldiers to see. "Found near the body!"

Baker crouched by the ghastly remains and used a stick to move debris. He saw fragments of clothing fused to the burnt mass—leather—a belt buckle. He made a show of examining the skull—mere fragments of charred bone, the face completely gone. "Severe burns," he declared, his voice carrying. "Utter consumption by the fire. Consistent with death at the heart of the inferno." He stood and looked at Doherty, then at the surrounding soldiers. "John Wilkes Booth. Positively identified by personal possessions found directly on his person. Deceased." He pointed at the remains. "Handle *that* carefully. It goes in the box."

Doherty nodded. "Record it." He turned to his aide, his voice firm, burying the secret deep. "Draft the telegram to Washington. Highest priority. 'We tracked Booth and Herold to Garrett's farm near Port Royal, Virginia. Barn surrounded. Herold surrendered, was shot attempting escape. Booth refused surrender. Barn set ablaze. Booth perished in fire. Body recovered. Possessions including diary and ring confirm identity conclusively. Manhunt ended.' Send it now."

The aide scribbled furiously and rushed off.

Baker supervised the grim task. Soldiers used blankets to lift the charred remains—David Herold's body, placed in the hottest ashes hours before. Handled with distaste, they placed them into a spare ammunition box. The real Herold's body, the one shot by Corbett, would vanish into an unmarked grave, his role erased. The diary, the compass, the ring—sealed as irrefutable evidence of Booth's demise.

Corbett watched silently as the box was sealed. His face remained impassive. He looked once at the scorched fragments visible within, he looked away, and murmured, "God's will be done."

News traveled at the speed of electricity. The telegraph clicked the message north to War Secretary Edwin Stanton. Stanton read the telegram. He let out a sigh of relief. "Conclusive? The body?"

"The telegram states possessions confirm identity beyond doubt, sir. Diary Ring. Body burned beyond recognition. Captain Doherty and Detectives Baker and Conger are certain."

Stanton nodded slowly, the need for closure outweighing doubt. "Very well. Release the news. To all papers. Booth is dead. Justice is served." He needed the symbol destroyed, the chapter closed.

The newspapers screamed the next day in bold black type.

"BOOTH DEAD!"

"ASSASSIN PERISHES IN FLAMES!"

"DIARY AND RING CONFIRM IDENTITY - HEROLD SHOT!"

The details were dramatic—final. The barn fire—the defiance—the charred remains identified by intimate possessions. The nation celebrated. Sighed with profound relief. The monster was gone, reduced to ashes.

A wagon rolled north towards Washington, escorted by cavalry. Inside the ammunition box, the charred bones of David Herold rested on a bed of straw. The evidence—the diary, the compass, the ring—traveled under guard. The official story was set—immutable. Deep in the Virginia woods, miles south, a man read a discarded newspaper announcing his own fiery death. John Wilkes Booth, the ghost, limped westward, the secret hunt for him already begun by the three men who knew the truth, even as the nation rejoiced at his demise.

Part II

Chapter 1

The stagecoach jolted forward—slowly. Dust coated James Trent's face, grit filled his mouth. He squinted against the glare. The endless prairie stretched under a hard blue sky. Wyoming Territory—far from Virginia— far from the barn—far from the fire.

He paid the driver and collected his single bag. He stood on the boardwalk of a raw settlement—False Creek. Timber buildings lined both sides of the mud street. A few horses were tethered to the hitching post. Men in rough clothes moved with purpose. He scanned the faces, they looked at him, the stranger in town. There was no recognition. He was blending in— playing the part—years of work on the stage had prepared him. His left leg ached. It was a dull, familiar throb. The jump from the balcony—the escape from the barn—the long journey west. It never fully healed. He carried it, like the name, James Trent—laborer—drifter.

He found work at a ranch outside town. He built and maintained fences. It was hard labor but it suited him. It required focus and strength. It left little room for thought. He kept his head down. He spoke little and answered questions with grunts or single words whenever possible. He avoided crowds—avoided talk of the East—avoided newspapers. Newspapers carried danger and memory—he needed neither.

Weeks passed—the ranch owner paid him in cash. He saved most of it. He avoided the saloon, he avoided town. But supplies ran low—he needed tobacco, flour and cartridges for the worn Colt he carried. He hitched a ride into False Creek on a supply wagon. It was midday, the sun was high, the dust hung thick in the air.

He entered the general store. The ceilings were low. The stale air inside was filled with smells of leather, coffee and dried apples. He gathered his items. He avoided the counter where men clustered were talking. He heard snippets of their conversation. They spoke of cattle prices—a broken axle. Then, a different tone.

"...whole country breathin' easier," one man said with a thick accent. "Devil's gone. Burned to ash. Justice served."

James Trent froze. His hand hovering over a tin of peaches. He didn't turn—he just listened.

"Read it myself," another voice chimed in. "In the Cheyenne paper. Booth. John Wilkes Booth. Cornered in a barn down Virginia way. Shot his partner. Refused to come out. They lit 'er up. Burned him alive. Found his bones. His pistol. Done." The man slapped the counter. "Good riddance. Lincoln was a good man."

James Trent picked up the tin—his hand was steady. He moved to the counter. He placed his items down. Tobacco—flour—cartridges—tin of peaches. The store owner tallied the cost. James paid, coins clinked as he placed them on the counter.

"Paper still here?" James asked, his voice low, rough. Like a man unused to talking.

The owner nodded towards a stool by the cold stove. "Over there. Yesterday's. From Cheyenne."

James walked slowly over to the table. His limp reminded him of the theater, the president, the barn fire, the escape. It remnded him of Booth, the man he left behind in the ashes. He picked it up, the *Cheyenne Leader*. It was folded neatly on a table with other papers. He opened it—the newsprint smudged his fingers. He scanned the front page. There were stories about cattle auctions, land disputes—then he saw it in the bottom right corner.

"BOOTH MEETS FIERY END!"

"Lincoln's Assassin Perishes in Virginia Blaze!"

He read it, standing by the cold stove. The sunlight slanted through the dirty window.

The report was brief, dramatic. Garrett's farm—Barn surrounded—Herold shot escaping—Booth defiant—Barn set ablaze—Booth perished—Body recovered—Charred—Possessions confirmed identity—Derringer—Photographs—Manhunt concluded—Nation relieved—Justice served.

Then he read it again, slowly. He focused on each word. *Charred. Possessions confirmed identity. Perished. Concluded.*

The store owner called out. "Need anything else, Trent?"

James folded the paper tight and neat. "This. How much?"

"Penny."

James paid the penny. He tucked the folded paper inside his coat against his chest. He picked up his sack of supplies and walked out. The sunlight felt too bright—the street noises seemed loud and jarring.

He walked, past the smithy, past the small hotel—towards the edge of town. A saloon stood there—the Lone Star. It was held together by rough boards. Piano music drifted out into the street. He needed a drink, not water, something stronger—to mark the moment. He pushed the saloon doors open, they swung shut behind him.

The saloon was filled with smoke and the smell of stale beer. A few men sat at tables, two at the bar. He walked to the far end, away from the others and leaned his sack against the bar. The bartender approached, he was a big man with a stained apron.

"Whiskey." James placed a coin on the bar.

The bartender poured a heavy glass of amber liquid. James picked it up. He looked at it and raised it slightly—a silent toast. To his death—to his resurrection—to his freedom. He drank it down, fast. It burned like fire in his throat. The warmth spreading in his gut. He tapped the glass and the bartender refilled it.

He drank the second glass slower. He stared at the smudged glass. The words from the newspaper echoed in his head—*Charred. Possessions confirmed identity. Perished. Concluded.* A strange feeling washed over him. It wasn't fear or triumph. It was a profound emptiness, a finality he hadn't expected. The world had buried John Wilkes Booth. Dug the grave, lowered the coffin, thrown the dirt. The ceremony was complete— Officially—Irrevocably. John Wilkes Booth was dead.

He felt a pressure lift, an immense weight he hadn't fully acknowledged. The constant looking over his shoulder—the dread of recognition—the fear of the rope. It eased, not gone completely but lessened. The hunters had called off the dogs—they believed their prey was dead—he was a officially a ghost.

Relief came, cold and deep. Then, something else, a new feeling— isolation, profound and absolute. He was truly alone now. He never thought about it before but now it seemed more real. He was cut off, not just from family, friends and his old life, he was cut off from his own history—from his very name. John Wilkes Booth was a corpse in an official report. A villain in a story told in saloons and newspapers. He was James Trent, a man with no past, only a painful leg and a future built on silence.

A dark amusement flickered. They had his derringer, his photographs—his bones?—Herold's bones, or some poor soul caught in the blaze—charred beyond recognition. Identified by *his* possessions planted near the body. Baker and Conger were clever and efficient. They gave the nation its closure. They gave him his freedom—the irony tasted bitter like the whiskey dregs.

He finished the second drink then pushed the glass away. He paid the bartender, picked up his sack and walked out of the saloon. The afternoon sun slanted lower, shadows lengthened. He walked past the last buildings onto the dirt track leading back towards the ranch.

He stopped and looked back at False Creek. It seemed small, temporary. He looked west. The land seemed to roll away. It was vast, empty, mountains blue in the distance. The future—James Trent's future.

He reached inside his coat and pulled out the folded newspaper. He looked at the headline one last time. ***"BOOTH MEETS FIERY END!"*** He crumpled the paper tight. He crumpled it into a hard ball and drew back his arm, he threw it far into the scrub brush beside the track. It vanished into the dry grass.

He adjusted the sack on his shoulder. He felt the worn grip of the Colt at his hip. The ache in his leg was a constant reminder of his past. The name James Trent settled on him—not a disguise—an identity. The only identity left. He was a ghost, walking, breathing, needing work. Needing to vanish deeper into the vastness.

He started walking. He walked away from False Creek towards the ranch—for now. But the West was wide, he needed to keep moving. He needed to stay ahead of the memory, to stay dead. James Trent turned his face towards the setting sun. He walked, leaving the crumpled lie of his death in the weeds behind him. He was a ghost on the long road west.

Chapter 2

The Wyoming ranch faded behind James Trent. He walked west. His savings bought a worn saddle and a tired horse. He called the horse 'Dust'. Dust carried him away from False Creek, away from Wyoming. He headed south towards Colorado.

He kept the mountains on his left. He avoided established trails, followed dry creek beds. He camped alone. He built small fires he could douse quickly. He woke often, listening—always listening. The Colt always near his hand.

He needed a new name. James Trent felt thin and temporary. He needed a new identity, he needed to blend in wherever he went. He saw a stagecoach station, a cluster of buildings. He approached cautiously—a sign creaked in the breeze 'Pine Gulch'. He needed supplies and information. He tied Dust to a hitching post out front. He adjusted his hat and pulled it low. He walked into the station store. His shoulders hunched slightly, he took on a laborer's stoop, his natural limp helped sell the performance.

The storekeeper eyed him as he walked in. "Help ya?"

"Flour. Coffee. Beans." James kept his voice flat—Midwestern—neutral. Not the trained cadence of the stage. He paid the storekeeper. "Road west clear?"

"Clear enough," the storekeeper said. "Stage to Denver leaves tomorrow. You riding?"

"Walking," James said. He scooped his purchases into his sack. He heard a commotion outside—shouts from a wagon that rolled in—men jumped down. They were loud, boisterous miners. They crowded into the small store. James pressed himself against a shelf. He made himself small, unnoticeable.

One miner bumped him. Hard. "Watch it, friend."

James ducked his head. "Sorry." His voice was a mumble. The miner laughed. He turned away and James slipped out unseen. He rode Dust west before the miners finished their business.

He practiced the stoop, the flat voice. James Trent became quieter, slower, less certain. He grew a thick beard, untrimmed. It itched—it changed the shape of his face—it hid the line of his jaw. He let his hair grow longer, shaggy. He kept it covered with a wide-brimmed hat. The hat was old, sweat-stained. The transformation was almost complete. His new costume was a perfect fit.

He crossed into Colorado—the land changed. It was higher and drier. The towns were farther apart. He found work where he could. A week digging irrigation ditches—two weeks cutting timber—he took cash. He never stayed long. He listened, learned the rhythms of work talk—the complaints about weather—pay—women. He added nothing—he only nodded and grunted—he was just another drifter, unremarkable.

He saw his picture once. In a Denver newspaper blowing down a street. It was a wanted poster, a crude drawing—John Wilkes Booth—the face looked nothing like the man in the mirror now. The beard, the weathered skin—the eyes, dulled by constant watchfulness. He kicked the paper into the gutter and walked on.

He pushed south to New Mexico Territory—the air smelled different. He entered a larger town, Las Vegas. It was busy, a lot busier than he wanted. He felt exposed, there were too many eyes but he needed supplies. He entered a general store. He heard arguing near the counter. There were two men with loud voices having a dispute over credit.

The store owner, red-faced, pointed at one man. "Pay what you owe, Sanders, or get out! No more credit!"

Sanders, a big man, leaned over the counter. "I'll pay when I get paid, Henderson! You know that!"

James moved quietly past them. He focused on the shelves, sugar, salt. He felt Sanders' anger. He was volatile, dangerous. He kept his back turned and remained quiet. He made himself part of the wall and blended in.

Sanders slammed a fist on the counter. "You calling me a liar?"

Henderson flinched but stood his ground. "I'm calling you broke, Sanders. Now leave."

Sanders grabbed Henderson's shirt. He hauled him halfway across the counter. "Why you little—"

James acted—instinct took over, not thought. He stepped forward. He was on stage again. The sunlight from the window cut through the dust and stale air like a spotlight. His voice cut the air. It was clear and commanding. The cadence of the stage he usually tried to avoid. The voice of Marcus Brutus, the voice of Pescara. "Release him!" The word rang out—it was sharp and authoritative.

Sanders froze—he turned and saw James. He was smaller, bearded but the eyes held him—steady—unflinching. The voice held unexpected power.

"Who the hell are you?" Sanders growled. His grip loosened slightly.

James held his gaze—he didn't blink. He dropped the laborer's stoop. He stood straighter. For a fraction of a second, John Wilkes Booth looked out. "Someone who dislikes bullies. Release him. Walk away." The voice tolerated no argument. It was theatrical, dangerous—it was John Wilkes Booth.

Sanders hesitated—he was confused by the transformation, by the sudden authority in the ragged drifter. He looked from James to Henderson. Shoved Henderson back. "This ain't over, Henderson." He spat on the floor. He shouldered past James and stomped out.

Silence filled the store. Henderson straightened his shirt, breathing hard. He looked at James. A new appraisal. "Mister...I...thank you. That could've turned ugly."

James felt the heat on his neck. He quickly slumped his shoulders again. His voice dropped back to the flat Midwestern drone. "Just passing through. Didn't like his manner." He grabbed his sack of sugar. "How much for this and the salt?"

He paid Henderson and hurried out. His heart hammered hard in his chest. That voice, that posture, it had felt good—natural and terrifying. He couldn't risk it, not ever. John Wilkes Booth was dead and must stay buried.

He rode hard out of Las Vegas. He didn't stop until the town was a smudge on the horizon. He camped under a rocky outcrop. He had no fire— he just chewed jerky and stared into the dark. The incident replayed in his mind—the surge of power—the terrifying ease of the performance. He had to be better, more controlled. James Trent couldn't command a room. James Trent faded into the background. James Trent needed to be a nobody, an unremarkable drifter.

He needed a name with less weight. James Trent felt like a costume he'd worn too long. He thought of the storekeeper, Henderson. It was a common name but not unremarkable. Then it came to him. Brown. John Brown. The name surfaced. It was simple, forgettable. It was unremarkable, like the man he needed to be. John Brown—laborer—drifter—nobody. It was perfect.

He practiced the name—whispering it to Dust. "John Brown." He tried it with the flat voice. "Name's John Brown." It fit the stoop, the limp, the worn clothes, the quiet demeanor. He buried the memory of commanding Sanders, hopefully his last performance—he buried the actor deep.

He crossed into Arizona Territory—the desert stretched forever. It was harsh and beautiful. He found work with a survey crew, mapping land for a railroad. The crew boss was named Murphy. He was a hard man but fair. He looked at James's leg, the limp.

"Can you walk the line, Brown?"

"Can walk," John Brown said. His voice low and rough. "Limp don't stop me."

Murphy shrugged. "Alright, Brown. You handle the marker stakes. Follow Peters. Do what he says."

John Brown did as he was told. He carried stakes. He hammered them in where Peters pointed. He walked miles each day. The leg ached but he ignored it. He spoke only when spoken to and offered nothing. He was reliable—silent—invisible. The crew accepted him—he was just another broken man seeking wages.

At night, around the campfire, the men talked. They boasted and argued. Told stories of women, fights, gold strikes. John Brown sat apart. He mended a harness, cleaned his Colt and listened. He learned the rhythms of their speech—their slang—he absorbed it—filed it away—tools for the performance.

One night, a new man joined the crew. He was talkative with sharp eyes. He scanned their faces. His gaze landed on John Brown. "You're quiet, friend. Where you hail from?"

John Brown didn't look up from the leather strap he was oiling. "Back east." His answer was purposefully vague. "Ohio."

"Ohio?" The man pressed. "Whereabouts? I got kin near Cincinnati."

John Brown kept oiling the strap, slow, methodical. "North. Farm country." He offered no details. He made it sound dull and unimportant.

The man studied him. "You look familiar. Ever work the riverboats? St. Louis?"

John Brown shook his head. "Never been." He kept his face angled away from the firelight. "Just farm work. Then timber. Now this." He gestured vaguely at the desert.

The man lost interest. He turned back to the louder talk. John Brown exhaled slowly. He felt the man's gaze linger once more. He finished the harness, then slipped away from the fire into the dark. He stood looking at the stars. The cold distant points of light, the vast indifference of the desert.

He was John Brown—only John Brown—he had to believe it—every moment.

The survey job ended—Murphy paid him cash. "Good worker, Brown. Steady. Need a hand further south? Tucson way?"

John Brown shook his head. "Moving on. Thanks." He packed his gear. He saddled Dust and rode south but not towards Tucson. He cut west towards California. The coast, new country, farther from the past.

He passed through small settlements, Socorro, Yuma. He avoided towns when possible. He traded with isolated ranchers. He worked a few days for food and rest for Dust. He was always John Brown—quiet—competent—unmemorable. He bought a better coat and sturdier boots. He looked like a hundred other men drifting through the territories.

He reached the California border—the air changed again—it was cooler, carrying the scent of the sea. He found a valley—it was green and fertile—it was filled with orchards and vineyards. He stopped at a farmhouse and asked for work. The farmer needed help clearing a field. Removing rocks and stumps.

"Name's Brown. John Brown," he said. The words were automatic now. The stoop was part of him. The flat voice felt natural. "Need work. Can swing an axe,"

The farmer looked him over. He saw the strength, the worn hands, the quiet way he stood. "Pay's a dollar a day. Meals. Barn loft to sleep. Start tomorrow."

John Brown nodded. "Suits me." He led Dust to the barn. He unpacked his gear. He looked around the valley. It was peaceful, isolated, he liked it. He could stay here a while. He could work, save, be John Brown. The actor rested—the performance became routine—he almost believed it.

He washed his face at the farm pump. The water was cold. He looked at his reflection in the metal basin. A stranger looked back, bearded, long hair, eyes guarded with lines etched by sun and wind. He *was* John Brown—farmer—laborer—a ghost in plain sight. The road stretched behind him. It was a long performance, he was tired now. The road ahead seemed calmer, quieter—for now. He picked up the axe and tested its weight.

Tomorrow, he would clear rocks and stumps like any other man. The past was buried deep and he needed it to be. He turned away from the reflection. The ghost walked towards the barn, ready for work—ready for silence—ready for the next act of disappearance.

Chapter 3

The stagecoach rolled into Oak Creek just before sundown. John Brown watched from the window. The dust settled on a single main street. The town was the usual wooden buildings with false fronts, a church steeple, livery stable, a saloon and one general store. 'Peterson's Mercantile'. The hills rose steeply around the town. Pine forests thick and dark—isolated. The air smelled clean. Pine tar—earth—distance.

This place felt different, not a place to pass through. This was a place to stop, a place to vanish into. The stage driver called out stops. The hotel. The saloon. Peterson's. John Brown grabbed his single bag and stepped down. The stage rolled on. He stood on the boardwalk, alone. The town was quiet. A few people moved but no one looked at him twice. He was just another arrival—unremarkable.

He walked into Peterson's Mercantile. When he opened the door, bells jingled. He was hit with the smells of dry goods, leather and coffee. A man stood behind the counter. He was in his late fifties wearing steel-rimmed spectacles with sharp eyes. He looked up, assessed John Brown.

"Help you?"

"Need supplies," John Brown said. His voice was the flat drone he'd been rehearsing. It was automatic now. "Flour. Coffee. Sugar. Cartridges. Forty-four." He placed his list on the counter. His handwriting was careful, blocky, uneducated. It fit the part, it *was* John Brown's handwriting.

The man—Peterson—picked up the list. He looked it over. "New in town?" He began gathering items.

"Passing through," John Brown said. He looked around the store. The shelves were neatly stocked—barrels of pickles—nails—tools. It felt solid and permanent. "Looking for work. Know anyone hiring?"

Peterson paused. He looked him over. He saw the worn but serviceable clothes, the strong hands, the quiet way he stood. "What kind of work?"

"Anything. Labor. Stock. Loading. Honest work." John Brown kept his gaze level, unthreatening.

Peterson finished packing the order. He tallied it. "Need help here. Part-time. Stocking shelves. Unloading shipments. Odd jobs. Pays a dollar a day. Cash weekly." He waited, watching.

John Brown considered the offer. Inside the store, sheltered. Watching people come and go, learning the town. This would be safer than ranching, less visible. "Suits me," he said. "When do I start?"

"Tomorrow. Seven sharp." John Brown nodded. He paid for his supplies. "Name's Brown. John Brown."

"Peterson," the store owner said. "See you tomorrow, Brown."

John Brown walked out, his bag was heavier. He needed a room. He saw a sign. 'Rooms to Let. Mrs. Henderson. Next to Church.' He walked slowly down the street, limping. He found the house. It was small, neat with a white picket fence. He knocked.

A woman answered. She was short with glasses, her gray hair pinned up. Her eyes were calm. "Yes?"

"Saw the sign. Room to let?"

"For one? No trouble?" Mrs. Henderson asked, practical.

"Just me. John Brown. Work at Peterson's store. Quiet. Pay weekly." He kept it simple.

She stepped back. "I'll show you the room." The room was small, in the back of the house. It had a bed, a washstand, a chair and a window overlooking a small garden. It was private and clean. It had everything he needed "Two dollars a week. Includes breakfast. Dinner extra."

"Suits me," John Brown said. He paid the first week and took the key. He unpacked his bag, a few clothes, his Colt, a spare knife and the worn wallet holding his savings. He placed the knife under the thin mattress. He hung his spare shirt on a nail and sat on the bed, the springs creaked. Silence pressed in—it was different from the desert—it was a contained silence. He listened to Mrs. Henderson move in the kitchen, dishes clinking—normal sounds. Sounds he hadn't heard in a while.

The next morning, he was at Peterson's at seven. Peterson showed him the stockroom, the layout. "Sweep first. Then check stock on these shelves. Note what's low. When the wagon comes, unload. Crates go here. Barrels there. Keep things tidy. Help customers if I'm busy. Simple questions only. Send anything complicated to me."

John Brown nodded. "Understood." He picked up the broom and started sweeping—methodical—thorough. He noted the stock as instructed. The flour sacks were low, coffee beans half gone, sugar barrel near empty. He wrote it in block letters on a slate Peterson provided. He was careful to use John Brown's handwriting. He avoided the counter unless Peterson signaled.

Customers came—farmers—ranchers—townsfolk. John Brown fetched items from high shelves. He carried heavy sacks to wagons. He spoke little. "Yes, ma'am." "Over here, sir." "That'll be two bits." He kept his head down. His hat often shading his face. He listened and learned names—Henry Miller, the blacksmith—Joe Sutton, who ran the livery— Mary Clark, the schoolteacher—He filed them away.

Weeks passed—routine settled, sweep, stock, unload, carry. He ate breakfast with Mrs. Henderson—eggs—bacon—biscuits. He ate dinner at the small table in his room—bread—cheese—canned meat. He saved his wages. He added it to the wallet under the mattress. He walked the town after work. He learned its edges. The creek behind the livery. The path up into the pines.

Peterson grunted approval one day. "You're reliable, Brown. Keep things moving. Think I'll keep you on full-time. Dollar twenty-five a day. Still cash weekly."

"Thank you, Mr. Peterson." John Brown felt a flicker, something like satisfaction. He had steady work, steady pay, anonymity.

He started staying for dinner at Mrs. Henderson's table. It was an extra dollar-fifty a week but it was easier than cooking in his room. She was a good cook and quiet company. She talked about the town—the new preacher—the schoolhouse roof needing repair. She didn't pry and he offered nothing. They ate in comfortable silence mostly.

He met Henry Miller properly when the blacksmith needed nails. The crates were heavy, John Brown delivered them to the smithy. It was hot and loud. The smell of coal and iron filled the air.

"Appreciate it, Brown," Henry boomed, wiping sweat. "Strong back. Peterson's lucky." He was a big man, friendly. "Join us sometime? Saloon. Saturday nights. Few of us share a bottle. Talk." He gestured towards the street.

John Brown hesitated. He didn't like crowds, noise or risk but refusing might seem strange and standoffish. He needed to blend in. "Maybe. Saturday."

He went to the saloon that Saturday. He stood at the end of the bar. Henry waved him over to a table. Joe Sutton was there and Tom Evans, the barber. They welcomed him and offered a glass. "Brown! Sit!"

He sat and took the offered whiskey. He sipped and mostly listened. The talk was about cattle, weather, a broken wagon axle, the new mine opening east of town. Henry dominated the conversation with loud stories. John Brown smiled when others smiled. He nodded, said little. "That so?" "Rough break." His flat voice didn't stand out, he was just Brown. The quiet one from the store. They accepted him as part of the background.

Months passed—Fall came with cool air and the leaves changing on the lower slopes. John Brown felt a rhythm—work—dinner with Mrs. Henderson—saloon on Saturdays—walks by the creek. He bought a better coat and thicker boots for winter. He felt the wallet under his mattress grow heavier.

Peterson trusted him more. He left him alone in the store for short periods. "Mind the place, Brown. Back in an hour." John Brown handled simple sales. He made change, kept the ledger for small transactions. He wrote numbers, block letters with no flourishes. He stacked shelves precisely, swept the floor spotless. It was his domain—orderly—predictable.

He rented the room from Mrs. Henderson for another month. He paid in advance. She smiled. "You're a good tenant, Mr. Brown. Quiet. Pays on time." He almost smiled back—almost.

He bought a book, second-hand. A history of the West. He read it in his room at night by lamplight, slowly. The words were a comfort, a connection to something beyond Oak Creek, safe. He didn't read plays—never.

Walking home one evening, Mary Clark passed him. The schoolteacher. She carried books. "Evening, Mr. Brown."

"Evening, Miss Clark." He touched his hat brim but kept walking.

"You're settling in well," she called after him. She was pleasant, observant.

He paused and looked back. "Oak Creek's a good place." He kept moving. Her gaze felt sharper than Henry's. He avoided walking that way again when school let out.

Winter came—snow dusted the hills. The store stayed busy. Townsfolk stocking up on winter supplies. John Brown worked longer hours, he didn't mind. The store was warm, the routine was solid. He bought a small stove for his room. Mrs. Henderson helped him set it up. "Keep you warm, Mr. Brown." He felt a pang, almost like belonging.

One Saturday at the saloon, Henry clapped him on the shoulder. "Been here near six months, ain't ya, Brown? Feels like you always been here. Solid." He refilled John Brown's glass. "You're part of things now."

John Brown looked around the table—Joe Sutton nodded—Tom Evans raised his glass. "To Brown. Quietest man in Oak Creek. But reliable."

They drank. John Brown drank with them. The warmth of the whiskey spread but the warmth of the words spread deeper. *Part of things now*. He looked at the fire in the saloon stove, the faces of the men. Henry's booming laugh, the smell of tobacco and beer. He felt the ache in his leg—it was a distant thing, a painful memory. The fear was a shadow—it was fainter. The watchfulness was a habit now, not a necessity.

He walked home later—snow crunched under his boots. The cold air bit his face. The stars were sharp and bright, he looked up at them. For a moment, just a moment, the weight lifted completely. John Brown, store clerk, tenant, quiet man. That was all, that was enough. Oak Creek was his home now. The past was a buried thing—a ghost story from another life— the future stretched ahead and it was calm, ordinary and safe.

He reached his small room and lit the lamp. The book lay on the chair. His spare clothes hung neatly, the bed was made. This was his space, his life. The small stove warmed the room. He checked the lock on the door, it was habit. He sat on the bed and took off his boots. The silence of the house wrapped around him. Mrs. Henderson slept downstairs. The town slept. He lay down and pulled the blanket up. The bedsprings creaked their familiar sound.

He closed his eyes. The face of Lincoln didn't come. The crack of the Derringer was silent. The roar of the barn fire was just wind in the pines outside. He breathed in the quiet, he breathed out the tension. John Brown slept, the ghost rested—the performance felt real—the curtain stayed down. Life was simple—life was good. He let himself believe it, just for the night—just for now. The quiet of Oak Creek held him. The watchfulness slept—John Brown slept. The road behind him seemed very far away. The road ahead seemed settled. He slept.

Chapter 4

The stagecoach arrived Tuesday afternoon. The horses kicked up dust and snorted as they came to a stop. John Brown was stacking flour sacks near the Mercantile window, he watched idly. Peterson handled arrivals. He sold tickets and took deliveries. One passenger stepped down with a single leather bag. A man of medium height, slim build wearing a dark suit. City clothes, dusty but not worn. A hat shaded his face.

The man looked up and down the street. He assessed the town. His gaze swept past the Mercantile window. John Brown kept stacking heavy sacks—methodical. The man paid the driver and picked up his bag. He walked towards the hotel. He moved with purpose—not a drifter—not a settler.

John Brown finished with the sacks. He wiped his hands on his apron and went back behind the counter. Peterson returned from the stage. "New fellow. Name's Davies. Arthur Davies. Says he's a land assessor. Looking over parcels east of town. Might be a week." Peterson sorted mail. "Need nails from Miller. Can you fetch them after closing?"

"Yes, Mr. Peterson," John Brown said.

He saw Arthur Davies later. He was standing outside the hotel, smoking a thin cigar—watching people pass. His eyes tracked Joe Sutton leading a horse to the livery. They moved to Mrs. Henderson chatting with Mary Clark. Then they landed on John Brown sweeping the boardwalk outside the Mercantile.

Davies watched him sweep. Not casually, he was studying him. John Brown felt the gaze like a physical touch. He ignored it and kept sweeping. Slow methodical strokes, his head down. The man finished his cigar, stubbed it out and went inside the hotel.

John Brown finished his sweeping and went inside. He closed up with Peterson. He walked towards Miller's smithy. He felt a tingle between his shoulder blades. He stopped and looked back. Davies stood in the hotel doorway watching him walk away. John Brown turned the corner. The gaze abruptly cut off.

He collected the nails from Miller. The crate was heavy, he carried it back to the Mercantile storage. On his way back, Davies was not visible. John Brown walked home. He ate dinner with Mrs. Henderson. She talked about the new preacher's sermon. John Brown nodded. His ears strained for sounds outside. He checked his door lock twice that night.

Wednesday, Davies entered the Mercantile mid-morning. He browsed, tobacco, shaving soap, writing paper. He moved slowly, examining items—taking his time. His eyes kept drifting to John Brown stocking shelves. John Brown kept his back turned. He was focused on arranging tins.

"Need some pipe tobacco," Davies said approaching the counter. Peterson was weighing sugar for Mary Clark. John Brown turned. He kept his face neutral. "What kind?"

Davies studied the jars behind the counter. "Virginia blend. If you have it." His voice was educated—Eastern—not loud but firm.

John Brown took down a jar. He measured out two ounces and wrapped it in brown paper. He tied it with string. "Ten cents."

Davies paid. He took the package but didn't leave. He looked directly at John Brown. A small frown creased his forehead. "Forgive me… do I know you? You look remarkably familiar."

John Brown's gut tightened. He kept his expression blank. Slightly puzzled. He shook his head slowly. "Don't think so, mister. Name's Brown. John Brown." He turned away and started rearranging the tobacco jars. It was pointless but it gave him something to do.

Davies persisted. "Brown? Hmm. Perhaps not. But the resemblance is striking. You have the look of a man I saw perform. Years ago. Back East. In the theatre." He paused. "Ever been on stage, Mr. Brown?"

John Brown kept his back to Davies. His hands steady on the jar. "Stage? No, sir. Never been east of Kansas." His voice was flat—uninterested. "Farm work. Timber. Store work now." He moved further down the counter.

"Ah. My mistake then," Davies said lightly. But John Brown felt the man's eyes still on him. "Must be a coincidence. Though a strong one. The man was quite famous in his day. John Wilkes Booth. Ever hear of him?"

The name hung in the air like a dropped pin. John Brown forced himself to turn. He looked Davies in the eye—blank. "Booth? Think I heard the name. Killed the President, didn't he? Got burned up." He shrugged. "Long time ago. Far away." He picked up a rag and wiped the counter, a spot near Davies' hand. "Anything else today?"

Davies watched him wipe. The frown deepened slightly, then it smoothed away. "No. No, thank you, Mr. Brown." He picked up his tobacco. He nodded politely and left the store.

John Brown kept wiping the counter long after the spot was gone. His knuckles were white on the rag. Peterson glanced over. "Everything alright, Brown? Davies bothering you?"

"No," John Brown said quickly, too quickly. He forced his grip to loosen. "Just talkative. Wondered if I was someone else. Guess I look familiar"

Peterson grunted. "City folk. Always looking for something." He went back to his ledger.

John Brown finished his shift. He walked home. He took a different route—past the church—down the alley. He stopped and leaned against the cool brick wall. He took a deep breath. *The look of a man I saw perform. John Wilkes Booth.* Davies knew or suspected—deeply. The casual mention was a probe—testing.

Thursday, Davies came in again. He bought writing paper and ink. He asked John Brown about local trails. "Heard there's good land east. Past Miller's Creek. You know it?"

John Brown kept stacking canned peaches. "Don't go out that way much. Miller or Sutton could tell you." He didn't turn around.

"Perhaps you could point it out on a map?" Davies suggested. "Peterson said you handle maps."

John Brown stopped stacking. He turned slowly. "Maps are behind the counter. Peterson handles sales." He walked to the back, into the stockroom. He stayed there, sorting sacks until he heard Davies leave.

Friday, John Brown avoided the main street. He worked in the back room all morning, unpacking a shipment. Peterson handled the front. He heard voices—Davies' voice—then Peterson calling, "Brown? Need you up front a moment."

John Brown wiped his hands. He pushed through the curtain. Davies stood there. Peterson looked slightly flustered. "Mr. Davies needs directions to Henderson's Ridge. For his assessing. You helped old man Henderson haul timber up there last fall. Remember the way?"

John Brown met Davies' gaze. The man's eyes were sharp, curious. "Rough trail," John Brown said. "Need a horse. Steep in parts."

"I have a horse," Davies said. "Could you sketch it? Roughly?" He pushed a piece of paper and a pencil across the counter.

John Brown stared at the paper. He picked up the pencil. His hand felt clumsy. He drew lines—blocky—simple. He drew a creek, a split rock and the ridge line. He pushed the paper back. "Like that. Follow the creek bed. Look for the split rock. Turn left. Up the ridge." His voice was flat.

Davies studied the crude map. Then he looked up at John Brown, a long look. "Thank you, Mr. Brown. This is most helpful." He folded the paper and tucked it away. He didn't leave immediately, he lingered, examining a display of pocket knives. His presence filled the small space.

Saturday was saloon night. John Brown almost didn't go. The risk felt higher. The crowds, Davies might be there but not going might seem strange—suspicious. Henry expected him so he went, late. The table was full—Henry—Joe—Tom—Two miners—and Arthur Davies.

Henry waved. "Brown! Over here! Meet Mr. Davies. Land assessor. Mr. Davies, this here's John Brown. Peterson's strong right arm."

Davies smiled. Extended a hand. "Mr. Brown. We've met. At the Mercantile."

John Brown shook the hand, brief but firm. "Mr. Davies." He took the last chair, farthest from Davies. He ordered a beer and sipped it slowly.

Talk flowed, the usual—cattle prices—weather—the new mine. Davies listened. H asked intelligent questions. He seemed knowledgeable about land and minerals. He fit in easily—too easily. He turned to John Brown. "You've been here a while, Mr. Brown? Oak Creek seems like a solid little town."

"About eight months," John Brown said staring into his beer.

"Find it to your liking? After…Kansas, was it?" Davies asked. Casual.

"Wyoming," John Brown corrected. He immediately wished he hadn't. Davies' eyes noted the correction. "It suits me. Quiet."

"Quiet is good," Davies agreed. He took a sip of whiskey. "Reminds me of a place back East. Maryland, actually. Near the water. Peaceful. Until things…erupted." He paused. Looked directly at John Brown. "Ever been to Maryland, Mr. Brown?"

The table noise faded for John Brown. He saw the barn fire again. He felt the heat, heard the roar. He gripped his beer mug. "No," he said. The word felt thick. "Never."

"Ah. Different world," Davies said. He leaned back and smiled faintly. "Different lives entirely. Though people can change places. Change names. Start fresh. Fascinating, isn't it?" He addressed the table, but his eyes stayed on John Brown.

Henry laughed. "Ain't that the truth! Why, my cousin Bill changed his name three times! Debt collectors!" The table laughed. John Brown forced a tight smile. He finished his beer fast. Stood up. "Early morning. Stock day tomorrow. Good night." He nodded at the table. Avoided Davies's eyes.

He walked out. The cold air hit him hard. He took a deep breath. His heart hammered. *Change names. Start fresh. Fascinating, isn't it?* Davies knew. He was circling. Tightening the net.

Sunday, John Brown stayed in his room. He read his book, listened to Mrs. Henderson go to church. The town was quiet. He felt exposed—trapped. He cleaned his Colt methodically. The weight of it was familiar—comforting. He checked his savings. He had enough to run. But where would he go? How far could he go? Davies would follow or telegraph ahead. He felt a sharp pain in his leg again—it was always there as a reminder. He ignored it.

Monday morning, the Mercantile opened. John Brown swept the boardwalk early. He saw Davies leave the hotel. Davies saw him and crossed the street directly, purposeful.

"Morning, Mr. Brown," Davies said. He stopped close—too close for strangers. He held a folded newspaper.

"Morning," John Brown mumbled. He kept sweeping.

Davies didn't move. "I was reading this old newspaper last night. Found it in the hotel lobby." He unfolded it. Showed John Brown a page. Not the front. An inside page, advertisements, theater listings. Davies pointed. "Look here. Ford's Theatre. Washington. Playing this week, April 1865. 'The Apostate'. Starring Mr. John Wilkes Booth." Davies tapped the name. His eyes locked onto John Brown's. They were sharp, unblinking. "I saw him perform that. Twice. Extraordinary presence. Commanded the stage. A unique talent."

John Brown stared at the newsprint—the date—the name—the play. A cold wave washed over him. He kept his face still. It was a mask he felt slipping. "Looks fancy," he said. His voice sounded distant. "Don't know much about plays."

Davies folded the paper slowly. "Remarkable resemblance, Mr. Brown. Truly. The eyes. The jawline. Especially when you're concentrating." He tilted his head. Studying John Brown's profile. "Even the way you stand sometimes. Like you're waiting for a cue."

John Brown gripped the broom handle hard. "Must be your imagination, mister. Like I said. Never been east. Never been on stage." He started sweeping again, vigorously. The dust flew across the boardwalk.

Davies smiled. It was a thin, knowing smile. "Of course. My imagination. Apologies for troubling you." He didn't sound apologetic. He sounded satisfied. "Good day, Mr. Brown." He walked away. Towards the livery.

John Brown watched him go. Davies walked with a slight spring in his step. He was confident—he vanished around the corner. John Brown stopped sweeping and leaned on the broom—his leg throbbed. The peaceful rhythm of Oak Creek was shattered. The ghost was seen, the past was here standing in the street—smiling—holding a newspaper clipping like a warrant. The trap was sprung. The performance wasn't enough anymore. Davies wouldn't stop. The quiet life was over—John Brown stood on the boardwalk, the dust settled around his boots. The sun felt cold, he needed a new plan. Silence wouldn't work, not now. He looked towards the livery stable where Davies had gone. Then he looked down at his hands—strong hands—capable hands. They knew other work besides stacking sacks— hard—final work. The Colt rested heavy against his hip under his apron. The ghost had no choice. He had to fight back. He had to make Davies disappear.

Chapter 5

The confrontation came Tuesday morning. It was early when John Brown unlocked the Mercantile. He slid the heavy wooden bar aside and pushed the door open. The cool air rushed out with smells of leather and dust. He stepped inside and walked towards the counter to fetch the broom.

A shadow filled the doorway—Arthur Davies stood there. His hat in his hand, his face was serious—intent. He stepped inside and closed the door behind him. The latch clicked—a final sound.

Davies walked towards the counter. He stopped a few feet from John Brown. No smile now, his eyes were direct, unwavering. "Good morning, Mr. Brown. Or should I say...Mr. Booth?"

John Brown stopped moving. His back stiffened. He kept his face still, blank. "Name's Brown. Like I told you." His voice was flat—empty.

Davies shook his head slowly. "No. It isn't. I know who you are. John Wilkes Booth. I saw you perform in Washington. Twice. 'he Robbers'. 'The Apostate'. You commanded the stage. Unforgettable." He took a half-step closer. "You're supposed to be dead. Burned in a barn in Virginia. But here you stand. Alive. John Brown of Oak Creek."

John Brown met his gaze. He didn't blink. "You're mistaken, mister. Dead men don't run stores." He turned away. He reached for the broom behind the counter, a normal movement. His heart pounding in his chest—hard—loud. He felt the weight of the Colt under his apron, high on his hip.

"I'm not mistaken," Davies said—firm—certain. His voice dropped lower. "The eyes. The jaw. The way you hold yourself when you think no one sees. It's you. I knew it the moment I saw you sweeping that boardwalk." He paused. "Why are you here, Booth? Playing shopkeeper? Living this...small life?"

John Brown gripped the broom handle tight, knuckles white. "My name is John Brown. You need supplies? Buy them. Otherwise, leave. I got work." He started sweeping vigorously. The dust swirled around them.

Davies didn't move. He watched the sweeping. "Deny it all you want. I know the truth. You can't hide from that." He let the words hang heavy—threatening. "A man like you...secrets have a way of surfacing. Especially valuable secrets."

John Brown stopped sweeping. He looked at him. "What do you want?"

Davies smiled. It was a thin smie. "Just...understanding. For now. We'll talk again, Mr. Brown. Soon." He turned and opened the door. The sunlight flooded in. He stepped out onto the boardwalk. He didn't look back.

John Brown stood frozen, broom in hand. Davies knew. He absolutely knew. He wasn't just guessing. He wasn't going away. He would talk again, soon. *Valuable secrets*. Davies wanted something—leverage— reward. It didn't matter. The threat was clear—exposure—capture—death.

He finished sweeping, mechanically. He stocked shelves, served customers. His mind worked, cold and clear. Davies was a pest. A buzzing fly that wouldn't leave. He needed elimination—permanent silence. It was the only way. The only security.

He observed Davies closely. The man stayed in town. He walked the streets. He spoke to people—Henry Miller—Joe Sutton. He asked questions. John Brown watched from the store window. Davies pointed towards the Mercantile once while he talked to Sutton. Sutton shrugged and laughed. He shook his head. Davies moved on, persistent.

Davies always returned to the hotel by dusk. He ate dinner at the small hotel dining room, alone. Afterwards, he often took a walk. A short one, down Main Street past the Mercantile. Sometimes turning down the alley that ran behind the buildings towards the creek path. He smoked a cigar, looked at the stars. He was a creature of habit.

John Brown planned. He needed privacy, quiet. No witnesses. The alley behind the Mercantile was best. It ws dark at night, sheltered by the high backs of the buildings. It was empty after sundown. Davies walked it. He could be intercepted there, easily.

He needed tools—no gunshots, too loud, too much attention. He thought of the heavy Colt—the grip—solid steel. A blow to the head might do it—then silence. He thought of rope—it was strong, quiet, final. He had rope in the Mercantile storage—a good rope. He used it for bundling—he selected a length—three feet. It was sturdy, he coiled it tight and hid it under his mattress with the knife alongside the savings wallet—tools for the job.

He planned the timing—tomorrow night, Wednesday. Stock day was Thursday. Peterson always left early on stock day. John Brown opened alone. He could arrive early, before dawn. Dispose of anything... inconvenient...before the town woke. The alley was perfect. It was hidden and close to the store. He could use the store itself, briefly, if needed.

He thought of Davies. The man's confidence. His probing questions. His satisfaction at cornering his prey. Davies thought he held the power. He didn't understand the hunted animal, the desperation. The willingness to do anything. *Anything* to survive.

John Brown ate dinner with Mrs. Henderson. She served chicken stew and bread. He listened to her talk and nodded when appropriate, said little. His mind was elsewhere. On the alley—on the rope—on the heavy weight of the pistol grip—on Davies' face. The moment of recognition turning to shock, then nothing.

He went to his room early. He told Mrs. Henderson he felt tired. She nodded, concerned. "Long day, Mr. Brown. Rest well." He locked his door. He took out the coiled rope. He ran it through his hands. It was rough, strong. He checked the Colt, the cylinder was full. He wouldn't need the bullets, just the weight.

He sat on the bed. The small stove glowed—warm. He looked around the room. It was *his* room, his quiet life and Davies threatened it. He threatened everything. The peace—the safety—the fragile sense of being John Brown. The ghost couldn't afford a witness.

He lay down but didn't sleep—his mind raced. He listened to the town, it was quiet—the distant bark of a dog—the wind in the pines. He rehearsed it, step by step just like preparing for a play. He'd wait in the alley shadows behind the water barrel. When Davies walks past the short route he always takes he'd step out—fast—silent. The heavy Colt grip swinging upward. Aim for the base of the skull—hard—once—maybe twice. Davies falls—no cry—no sound. Then the rope around his neck, tight. Pull until it's done. He'd drag the body under the Mercantile's back porch. It'd be concealed by the lattice. Then he'd wait until the deepest dark. Before dawn he'd take the body far out past the creek. He'd bury it deep. Then he'd scrub the alley, burn the rope. He'd be at the store in time to open, sweeping at seven. Normal.

It's simple—necessary—pest control.

The hours passed, slow. He watched the moonlight move across the floor. He thought of the barn fire, the escape. He thought of the long ride west, the years of silence. All threatened by one man. One persistent, knowing man. Davies had to go, tonight—no choice—no regret.

He rose before dawn. He dressed in dark trousers and a dark shirt. He strapped on the Colt, felt its familiar weight. He tucked the coiled rope into his coat pocket. It formed a heavy bulge. He unlocked his door silently, slipped out. Mrs. Henderson's door was closed. The house was quiet.

The street was empty filled with a gray pre-dawn light—cold— silent. He moved quickly into the alley behind the buildings. The shadows clung deep. He found his spot behind the large water barrel near the Mercantile's back steps. He crouched, pulled his coat collar up. He melted into the gloom. He waited, motionless, breathing slow. The Colt was in his hand, grip forward, ready.

He heard footsteps on the boardwalk turning into the alley. They were crisp, measured steps. Davies was walking his usual evening path. He was a little late, returning to the hotel. He was smoking, the tip of his cigar glowed red in the dimness.

John Brown watched him approach. He was getting closer—ten feet—five. Davies hummed softly, unaware.

John Brown moved—he was a shadow detaching from deeper shadows. He was fast and silent. He took two long strides and raised the Colt, gripped tight. He swung hard, a downward arc aimed perfectly. The heavy steel grip connected with the base of Davies' skull. It was a solid, meaty thunk.

Davies grunted, a short, choked sound. His legs buckled underneath. The cigar dropped, the glowing ember in the dirt. He collapsed forward—face down—motionless. He was a dark shape on the alley floor.

John Brown stood over him. He was breathing hard, adrenaline sharp in his veins. He listened. There were no other sounds, no shouts. The alley remained silent. The town slept. He knelt and rolled Davies onto his back. The man's eyes were open but unfocused. A trickle of blood darkened his hairline. He breathed. It was a shallow, ragged breath. He was unconscious, not dead.

John Brown pulled the rope from his pocket. He uncoiled it. He looped one end and slipped it over Davies' head. He tightened the noose around the neck. He braced his boot against Davies' shoulder. He gripped the other end of the rope with both hands and pulled—steady—relentless. Putting his full weight into it.

Davies jerked, a gurgling sound escaped his lips. His hands fluttered weakly. His feet scraped the dirt. John Brown pulled harder. The rope bit deep into Davies' neck. Davies' struggles weakened—slowed—stopped. His body went limp, completely still.

John Brown held the tension. He counted to sixty, slow. He released the rope. Davies didn't move, he didn't breathe. John Brown felt for a pulse at the neck. There was nothing, only silence.

He worked fast—he dragged the body by the arms. It was heavy, dead weight. He pulled it to the back of the Mercantile under the low porch, behind the latticework. It was hidden from casual view. He arranged the body face down and covered it loosely with an old burlap sack he kept for trash. It was invisible now.

He picked up the cigar stub and crushed it into the dirt. He scanned the alley—there was no sign of struggle, just scuff marks near the water barrel. He kicked dirt over them, smoothed the ground. He coiled the rope and stuffed it back in his pocket. The Colt went into his belt hidden again by his coat.

He listened—it was still quiet. The sky was lightening in the east, pink streaks started showing through the distant haze. He had time, an hour maybe—before the town stirred—before Peterson arrived. He unlocked the Mercantile's back door and slipped inside. He relocked it and stood in the dark stockroom. He leaned against the door. He took a deep breath, steadying himself. The smell of hemp rope and gun oil clung to him.

He moved through the store, it was familiar in the gloom. He went out the front and unlocked the main door. He picked up the broom and started sweeping the boardwalk—it was his normal routine. The first rays of sun touched the false fronts across the street. He swept—methodical—calm. Inside, his thoughts raced. Davies was gone—the threat was silenced. Oak Creek was safe again. John Brown was safe—John Wilkes Booth was still dead.

He finished sweeping and went inside. He started arranging goods on the shelves—waiting for Peterson—waiting for the day. The body under the porch felt like a stone in his gut but it was done. It was necessary. He focused on the cans, straightening the labels in perfect rows. Order was restored. The ghost had protected its peace. The performance could resume. He almost believed it.

A rider approached the hotel down the street. He was dusty but official-looking. He dismounted and looked around the town. He carried a leather satchel and went inside. John Brown watched from the store window. A minute later, the rider came out. He mounted and rode off towards the livery. The hotel door opened again, the clerk stepped out. He looked around and saw John Brown sweeping inside the Mercantile. He hurried across the street.

"Mr. Brown? Telegram just came. For your...guest. Mr. Davies. You seen him this morning? Usually up by now."

John Brown kept sweeping, slow strokes. "Haven't seen him," he said, his voice flat, calm. "Maybe sleeping late. He didn't look up.

The clerk hesitated. "Odd. He's usually punctual. Well, if you see him...tell him it's here." He turned and went back to the hotel.

John Brown swept. He watched the hotel door. The telegram sat inside for Arthur Davies. A man who wouldn't be collecting it. He wondered who sent it, what it said. It didn't matter. Davies was gone, handled. Oak Creek belonged to John Brown again. He swept the dust into the street—a clean boardwalk—a clean slate. He pushed the pile over the edge. The breeze caught some dust and carried it away. It was gone like Davies. He went inside, ready for the day—ready for Peterson—ready for the quiet life to resume. The incident was closed. The ghost had won. He locked the door behind him. The store felt safe, silent. The only sound was his own breathing and the faint, imagined buzz of a fly, silenced.

Part III

Chapter 1

The heavy door clicked shut. John Brown stood inside the Mercantile. The familiar smells of leather, dust and dry goods wrapped around him. Outside, the town of Oak Creek was waking—a wagon rattled past—voices called greetings. It was the normal sounds of early morning in Oak Creek. He leaned his back against the door, the solid wood felt real. The broom handle was smooth in his hand. He had swept the boardwalk clean just like every morning, it was his normal routine.

The body was under the porch. Arthur Davies—cold—still—hidden by burlap and lattice. John Brown took a deep breath, he exhaled slowly. His heart pounding against his chest—steady—hard. It was done. It was necessary pest control. He pushed away from the door and walked behind the counter. He placed the broom in its corner. His movements were precise, routine. He picked up a rag and began wiping the counter with long, slow strokes. The wood grain emerged under the damp cloth, clean.

Peterson would arrive soon. It was stock day. John Brown focused on the counter, he wiped every inch. He avoided looking towards the back room, towards the door leading outside—the porch—the thing under it. The rag moved—back and forth—back and forth. The silence inside the store became noticeable. He heard his own breathing. He heard the distant sounds of the town. He did not hear Davies. Davies was silent—gone.

The front door opened. Peterson walked in, his usual cheerful self. "Morning, Brown. Ready for the wagon?" His eyes were bright, unknowing.

John Brown nodded. He put the rag down. "Ready. Out back." His voice sounded normal, flat, calm—like always. He led the way through the store, past the shelves, into the stockroom. The air was cooler here. Dust particles moved in the light from the high window. He unlocked the heavy back door and pushed it open. The alley stretched behind the buildings, sunlight reached only the tops of the walls. The ground below was still in deep shadow. His eyes flickered towards the porch, the burlap sack looked like discarded trash—nothing more.

Peterson followed him out. "Looks like rain later. Hope we get the flour in before it hits." He walked towards the loading area, not glancing at the porch. John Brown moved with him. They worked. They unloaded sacks of flour, crates of canned goods, bolts of cloth. John Brown lifted, carried, stacked. His muscles worked, sweat dampened his shirt. He focused on the weight of the sacks. The rough grain of the wood crates. The smell of new fabric. Not the other smell he imagined. The smell of damp earth and death under the porch. Peterson talked about his wife, about the price of sugar. John Brown grunted in response when needed. He kept his eyes on the task. On the alley mouth. On the back door of the hotel. He was expecting trouble at any time—no one came.

They finished unloading. Peterson wiped his brow. "Good haul. Need to get these inside before that rain." He grabbed a sack of flour. John Brown took another. They carried them into the stockroom and stacked them neatly. John Brown closed and locked the back door. The click was loud in the sudden quiet of the stockroom. The alley was shut out—the porch was shut out—Davies was shut out.

The day passed, customers came. They bought nails and cloth and coffee. They talked about the weather, the new preacher coming Sunday and Joe Sutton's lame horse. John Brown served them. He took money and made change. He wrapped purchases in brown paper. His hands were steady and calm. His answers were short, polite. His eyes watched faces. Did Mrs. Gable look at him longer than usual? Did Henry Miller seem curious when he asked if Davies had bought tobacco? John Brown answered simply. "Haven't seen him today." He kept his tone neutral—unconcerned.

At noon, the hotel clerk came in. He looked worried. "Mr. Brown? Still no sign of Mr. Davies. His room's untouched. Bed not slept in. And that telegram..." He trailed off, looking at John Brown expectantly.

John Brown was arranging cans of peaches on a shelf. He turned one so the label faced front. "Is that so?" He picked up another can and adjusted its position. "Maybe he took a walk. Got turned around."

"Without his bag? His coat?" The clerk shifted his weight. "It's strange. Very strange. He paid through Friday."

John Brown placed the can on the shelf. He turned to face the clerk. "People do strange things." He held the clerk's gaze. "If he comes back, I'll tell him about the telegram." He turned back to the cans. The clerk stood for a moment, then sighed. "Alright. Thanks, Mr. Brown." He left the store. John Brown listened to the bell jingle on the door. He picked up another can. His fingers were cold.

Rumors started that afternoon—whispers. John Brown heard them from customers. Davies was missing. He hadn't been seen since last night. Some thought he'd skipped town without paying. Others wondered if he'd met with trouble on the creek path. Joe Sutton came in, his face serious. "Heard about that fella stayin' at the hotel? Davies? Vanished. Clean gone. Sheriff's asking around."

John Brown nodded. He was counting nails into a small paper bag. "Heard." He folded the top of the bag neatly. "Seems sudden."

"Sure does," Sutton agreed. "Talked to him just yesterday. Right outside. Asked about you, actually." Sutton watched him. John Brown met his look. His face was blank. "Oh?"

"Yeah. Wanted to know how long you'd run the Mercantile. Seemed...interested." Sutton paused. "You know him from somewhere?"

John Brown handed Sutton the bag of nails. "Never met him before he walked in here." It wasn't a lie. John Brown was used to only answering the question asked without offering additional information. "A dollar twenty." Sutton paid. He lingered. "Just odd, is all. Him asking. Him disappearing." He pocketed his change. "Well. Hope he turns up. Or hope he don't cause trouble." He left the store.

John Brown watched him go. Sutton's words echoed. *Asked about you. Interested.* Davies had been talking—probing—planting seeds. The seeds were still there, lying dormant in the dirt, waiting. He felt a tingle on the back of his neck. He turned but no one was there. There were just rows of shelves—the bolts of cloth—the quiet store. He walked to the front window. He looked out at the street, people moved about their business. It was normal, routine, nothing out of place. He saw the sheriff talking to the hotel clerk outside the hotel entrance. The clerk gestured, talking fast. The sheriff nodded, taking notes. John Brown stepped back from the window. He went behind the counter and pretended to check the ledger. His hand gripped the pen, tight, too tight.

Closing time came and Peterson left. "See you tomorrow, Brown." John Brown locked the door behind him and turned the sign to 'Closed'. The silence was relaxing—he stood still, listening. The town outside was settling down. A dog barked—a door slammed. He walked through the store and checked the back door, locked it. He went to the front window again and looked out, the street was emptying. Lamplight glowed in windows. The sheriff was gone. The hotel looked quiet.

He went into the stockroom and stood before the back door. His hand rested on the cold metal lock. Davies was out there under the porch— waiting. He needed to move the body, tonight. He needed to bury it, deep and far away. He needed to do it before a dog caught the scent—before the sheriff looked harder. He had planned this—he'd take the body past the creek to a place where the ground was soft, where trees grew thick.

He waited—hours passed. He sat on a crate in the dark stockroom. He didn't light a lamp. He just sat in the dark and listened to the town sleep. The wind picked up, it whistled faintly around the building corners. The rain started. It was just a soft patter on the roof, then harder—drumming hard against the building. The rain was good, an unknowing accomplice. It would wash the alley, cover tracks. He waited until the sounds were only rain and wind in the deep night.

He unlocked the back door. He opened it slowly. The alley was a black pit. The rain slanted down in silver lines in the faint light from a distant window. He stepped out. The rain soaked his shirt immediately. It was cold against his skin. He closed the door quietly behind him. He moved to the porch and crouched. He pulled aside the lattice. The burlap sack was dark with rain. He grasped the rough fabric and pulled. The body slid out. It was heavy, limp—a dead weight in the mud. He grabbed Davies under the arms and dragged him. The body left a dark groove in the wet earth. He dragged it down the alley, away from the street, towards the open land behind the buildings, towards the creek. The rain plastered his hair to his head. Water ran into his eyes, he blinked it away. He pulled, slowly, step by step. The mud sucked at his boots, his leg ached. He ignored it and continued to pull—through the rain—through the mud—through the pain. The creek roared ahead, swollen with rain.

He reached the bank. The water churned below, brown and fast. He stopped, breathing hard—almost out of breath. He looked down at Davies. The face was pale in the gloom. His eyes were closed now, mouth slack. The rope mark was a dark line on the neck. John Brown felt nothing—no remorse—no fear—just a cold necessity. He needed to bury him, deep. But the creek was high. The current was strong, it pulled at the bank. He looked at the water. Then back at the body. An idea formed. Something simpler, faster. The creek would take it, carry it far away. There would be no grave to dig—no place to be found. The rain would hide the drag marks to the bank and the creek would dispose of the body.

He dragged Davies to the edge, the mud was slippery. He positioned the body and gave it one hard shove with his boot. Davies rolled and slid down the bank. He hit the water with a splash. The current caught him. It pulled him under, then pushed him up. The body turned, limbs loose. It was swept downstream, into the darkness. It was gone, swallowed by the rain and the roaring water.

John Brown stood on the bank. He watched the spot where Davies disappeared. The creek flowed on, unconcerned. The rain beat down on him. He was soaked through, cold, shivering but a weight lifted. The evidence was gone. It was washed away. He turned and walked back through the rain, up the alley. He kicked mud over the drag marks as he went. He reached the Mercantile porch and replaced the lattice. He went inside the stockroom. He locked the door and leaned against it. He was dripping wet, water pooled at his feet. He was cold—wet—exhausted but it was over—truly over. Davies was erased, taken by the creek. He was gone forever. There was no body, no proof. Just a missing man—a mystery that Oak Creek would forget. He stripped off his wet clothes and rubbed himself dry with a sack. He dressed in clean, dry clothes from the store stock. He bundled the wet things. He would burn them later. He sat again on the crate and waited for dawn. He felt clean—purged. The stain was washed away—by rain—by water.

The next day was Thursday. Stock day leftovers. John Brown opened the store. He swept the boardwalk as usual. The rain had stopped. The air was fresh. Everything was washed clean. The town was buzzing about Davies. The sheriff made inquiries. He came into the Mercantile. "Morning, Brown. You hear about that fella Davies? Vanished."

John Brown nodded. He was dusting shelves. "Heard. Strange business."

"Any idea where he might've gone? He talk to you much?"

"Bought tobacco once." John Brown kept dusting. "Paid cash. Didn't say much. Seemed like a private man." He moved a jar of pickles. "Maybe he just left. Had business elsewhere."

"Without his things?" The sheriff watched him. "His bag's still at the hotel. Clothes. Everything."

John Brown shrugged. He met the sheriff's gaze. "Like I said. Strange. Maybe he had reasons." He turned back to the shelf. "Hard to know another man's mind." His voice was flat, uninvolved.

The sheriff asked a few more questions. John Brown answered simply. Truthfully, where he could. He hadn't seen Davies leave. He didn't know where he went. He offered nothing. The sheriff finally nodded. "Alright. Thanks, Brown. You see anything unusual, let me know." He left.

John Brown watched him go. The sheriff was thorough but he had nothing. There was no body, no sign of struggle—just a missing man. The town would talk for a week then it would fade. Davies would become a story, a footnote. John Brown felt a flicker of satisfaction. He had handled it. He had protected himself—protected Oak Creek—his home.

He served customers. He ordered new stock. He ate dinner with Mrs. Henderson. She talked about the missing man. "Gives me a fright, Mr. Brown. Right here in Oak Creek! Where could he have gone?" John Brown chewed his food. "Hard to say. Maybe he fell in the creek. Water's high." He said it casually, like it was a possibility, not a confession.

He went to his room and locked the door. He sat on the bed. The small stove warmed the room. He looked at his hands. They were clean, no visible stain but he felt it. It was a deep, cold spot inside. The act—the dragging—the shove into the water. He saw Davies' face in the rain. It was pale and empty. He closed his eyes and took a deep breath. He pushed the image away. He told himself that it was necessary. Davies knew, he threatened everything—the peace—the safety. He threatened the life John Brown had built. The ghost couldn't afford a witness. The ghost had survived—again.

He thought about running. The idea surfaced. It was strong, insistent. It was the old reflex, the only way he knew for years. When danger came, you ran. You became someone new, started over. He could go somewhere else—California—Oregon—Further north. He could pack tonight. Take his savings and disappear into the night. He could leave Oak Creek behind, leave John Brown behind. He could become...someone else— Smith—Jones—another name—another face—another empty room.

The thought was tempting. Just make a clean break, absolute safety. No sheriff asking questions. No chance of Davies' body washing up downstream. No lingering looks from Joe Sutton. No fear in Mrs. Henderson's eyes if she ever guessed. He could vanish, again, he knew how. He was good at it—an actor changing roles. Just a quick costume change and a new stage with a new cast of supporting characters.

He stood up and walked to the window. He looked out at Oak Creek. Main Street was dark and quiet. A single lamp glowed outside the saloon. He saw the shape of the Mercantile across the street—his store. He saw the roof of Mrs. Henderson's house. He thought of Peterson, of Henry Miller nodding hello—the rhythm of the days. He thought of sweeping the boardwalk and stocking shelves—the smell of leather and coffee—the solid weight of the counter under his hands.

Running meant leaving this. Leaving the first place that felt like a home since...before—since everything. It meant rootlessness again, suspicion in every new town. The constant watchfulness, the loneliness. The fear of recognition, always. He was tired—bone-deep tired—tired of running—tired of hiding—tired of being no one.

Oak Creek was his, he had built this. He became John Brown— respected, reliable. He became a part of the town, he belonged here. He had friends, not close—but present. He had a place. He had earned it. Davies was gone, handled. The creek had taken him. The rain had washed the alley. There was no evidence. Only whispers that would fade. Running now would be weakness. It would be letting Davies win from beyond the grave. It would mean Davies had succeeded in destroying John Brown.

He turned from the window and faced the room—his room—his things—his quiet life. He would not run, not this time. This was his ground, he would stand on it. He would be John Brown. He would live his small life and sweep his boardwalk. He would run his store and eat Mrs. Henderson's stew. He would face the sheriff's questions if they came again. He would act the part. The part of the innocent shopkeeper. The part he knew now, deep in his bones.

He made the decision. It was firm and final. He was not running anymore. Oak Creek was his home. He would stay. He would protect it. Protect the ghost inhabiting John Brown. He blew out the lamp and lay down on the bed. The darkness was complete. He listened to the silence as the town slept. He closed his eyes and breathed in the quiet air of his room—his home. He would sleep. Tomorrow, he would open the Mercantile. He would sweep the boardwalk. He would be John Brown. The ghost was safe—for now.

A sharp knock sounded on the door, downstairs. It was loud—insistent—breaking the deep silence of the night. Mrs. Henderson's voice, muffled but alarmed, called out. "Mr. Brown? Mr. Brown, are you awake?" Heavy boots thumped on the stairs outside his room, coming closer. The knock came again, right on his door. It was hard—authoritative. "John Brown? Open up. Sheriff."

Chapter 2

The pounding on the door stopped John Brown cold. He was lying flat, eyes open in the dark. Mrs. Henderson's voice rose again, thin with alarm. "Mr. Brown! Sheriff needs you!" The heavy boots shifted on the landing outside his room. The knock hammered the wood once more. "Brown. Open the door."

John Brown pushed himself up. He moved deliberately. He struck a match and lit the lamp on his bedside table. The yellow light pushed back the shadows. He pulled on his trousers over his long johns and buttoned his shirt. He took his time. He needed the moments—to think—to prepare. He needed time to become John Brown, shopkeeper, disturbed from sleep.

He unlocked the door and opened it. Sheriff Pike stood there, hat in hand. His face was set. Mrs. Henderson hovered behind him on the stairs, a shawl pulled tight over her nightdress, her eyes wide.

"Sheriff," John Brown said. His voice was rough, sleep-thickened. He rubbed his eyes. "What's wrong? Something happened?"

"Need to talk to you, Brown," Pike said. His gaze swept past John Brown into the small room. "Downstairs. Now."

John Brown nodded. He grabbed his coat from the hook behind the door and followed Pike down the narrow stairs. Mrs. Henderson retreated into her parlor, leaving the door slightly ajar. John Brown felt her watching.

Pike stopped in the small hallway by the front door. He turned. "Davies," he said, blunt.

"What about him?" John Brown asked. He kept his face slack, confused. He yawned.

"Still missing," Pike stated. "No sign. Hotel clerk's worried sick. Man's belongings are still there. Paid for the week." He paused, watching John Brown. "You were the last person known to see him. Yesterday. Before he vanished."

John Brown frowned and ran a hand through his hair. "Last person? I sold him tobacco day before yesterday. Didn't see him yesterday. Not that I recall." He kept his tone mild, puzzled. "Peterson was with me most of the day. Stock unloading. Customers."

"Joe Sutton says he talked to Davies yesterday afternoon. Right outside your store. Davies was asking about you. Again." Pike's eyes were steady. "Sutton mentioned it earlier. Just came to see me about it. Said it struck him as odd. Davies seemed…focused on you."

John Brown shrugged. He met the sheriff's look. "Like I told Sutton. Never met the man before he came in here. Bought tobacco. That's it. Maybe he heard I was from back east. Maybe he knew someone I knew. Who knows?" He let a note of weary irritation creep in. "Why's this about me? Man disappears, you come banging on my door in the middle of the night?"

"Because it's strange, Brown!" Pike's voice hardened slightly. "A stranger shows up, asks pointed questions about you, then vanishes without a trace? Right after talking about you? You don't find that worth looking into?"

"I find it inconvenient," John Brown said flatly. "I got a store to open in a few hours. I need sleep. Davies isn't my problem. I didn't know him. I didn't make him disappear." He held Pike's gaze. "You think I did something? Search the store. Search my room. Search the alley. You won't find him. Or anything else." The challenge was calm—defiant.

Pike stared at him for a long moment. John Brown didn't blink. He was John Brown—innocent—annoyed—tired.

Finally, Pike let out a breath. He put his hat back on. "Alright, Brown. Alright. Just doing my job. Checking lines. Man disappears, you look at the last people he talked to." He adjusted the hat brim. "You see anything, hear anything, you come straight to me. Understand?"

"Of course, Sheriff," John Brown said. His voice was level again, cooperative.

Pike nodded. He opened the front door. The cool night air rushed in. He stepped out onto the porch. "Get some sleep," he said, not looking back. He walked down the path to the street.

John Brown closed the door and locked it. He leaned against the wood. His heart beat hard against his chest. He listened to Pike's boots on the boardwalk fade away. He waited. Mrs. Henderson's parlor door clicked shut. Silence settled over the house again.

He climbed the stairs slowly and went back into his room. He closed the door and locked it. He didn't sit, he stood by the window, looking out at the dark street. The sheriff's visit was a warning, a sign the seeds Davies planted hadn't been washed away. With Sutton talking and Pike digging—it wasn't over—not yet.

He thought of the creek—the rushing water. Davies' body turning in the current. Where was it now? Miles downstream? Caught on a snag? Found by a farmer? He pushed the thought down. If there's no body, there's no proof. Pike had nothing, just questions without answers. He had handled the sheriff. He could handle more questions. He would stay calm—he would stay John Brown.

He blew out the lamp and lay down. Sleep wouldn't come. He stared at the ceiling. The sheriff's knock echoed in his mind. The suspicion in Pike's eyes. The fear in Mrs. Henderson's voice. He had built a life here—brick by brick. Davies had tried to knock it down. He had stopped him. But the cracks were showing. The ghost felt exposed. The performance felt harder. He breathed—in—out. He would hold on. He would not run.

Two days before John Brown pushed Arthur Davies into the swollen Oak Creek, a telegraph key clicked rapidly in a small Western Union office in Oak Creek. The operator, a young man named Finley, transcribed the dots and dashes onto a flimsy yellow form. The message was brief, coded—meaningless to him. He stamped the time and date. He placed it in the wire basket for the hotel. It was addressed to A. Davies.

Arthur Davies had sent one late Tuesday afternoon before his evening walk—before his meeting in the alley. He had written the coded words carefully on the form. He paid with coins and watched Finley send it. He seemed satisfied—purposeful. He left without another word. Now the reply sits waiting for Davies at the hotel.

The telegram traveled east along buzzing wires. Over mountains and plains. It reached a nondescript brick building in Washington. A different operator received it. This operator recognized the code sequence. He didn't transcribe it. He carried the flimsy yellow paper upstairs and knocked on a heavy oak door.

"Enter."

The man inside the office sat behind a large, plain desk. He was thin. His hair was long, lank, and graying. His eyes were pale and intense. They held a strange, burning light. He wore a dark suit, impeccably clean but slightly outdated. His hands rested on the desk. They were still—calm. He looked up as the operator entered.

"Coded message, sir," the operator said. "From Oak Creek, New Mexico Territory. Sent by Davies."

The man took the paper. He didn't look at it immediately. He dismissed the operator with a small nod. The door closed, silence filled the room. Only the ticking of a clock on the mantelpiece broke it.

The man unfolded the telegram. His eyes scanned the coded groups. He didn't need a cipher book. He knew this code—he had designed it. He deciphered it in his mind, letter by letter.

F-O-U-N-D-J-W-B-I-N-O-A-K-C-R-E-E-K.
G-O-E-S-B-Y-J-O-H-N-B-R-O-W-N.

His pale eyes didn't change. No muscle moved in his face but the air in the room seemed to thicken. The stillness deepened, he read the words again. Slowly.

Found JWB in Oak Creek. Goes by John Brown.

JWB. John Wilkes Booth.

The man leaned back in his chair very slightly. His gaze fixed on a point beyond the wall—beyond the city—westward. He had waited years for this. He had known, deep in his bones, he had known. The barn fire, the charred body. It had never been right. It was too convenient, too final for a man like Booth—a performer—an escape artist.

He had pursued the whispers—the shadows. The rumors of a man who moved like Booth, a man who vanished into thin air. He had sent others, good men. They found nothing or they stopped reporting. Davies was the latest. He was a careful man, a persistent man—he had found him.

Oak Creek. John Brown.

The man stood up and walked to the window. He looked out over the rooftops of Washington. The city where Booth had killed Lincoln. Where he, Boston Corbett, had become famous—infamous. The man who shot the assassin in the burning barn—the avenging angel—the madman.

They called him mad. He didn't care. He had done God's work. He had stopped the serpent or so he thought. The doubt had gnawed—the possibility. Now it was confirmed—the serpent lived—hidden. He was playing shopkeeper in some dusty New Mexico town.

He felt no anger, only a cold, righteous purpose. A task unfinished—a duty unfulfilled. Booth had escaped God's judgment once. He would not escape it again.

He turned from the window and went back to his desk. He pulled a sheet of paper towards him. He dipped a pen in ink. His handwriting was precise, sharp.

Assemble team. Immediate departure. New Mexico Territory. Oak Creek settlement. Target confirmed: JWB. Using alias John Brown. Proprietor, Mercantile store. Extreme caution. Target dangerous. Armed. Resourceful. Priority: Capture alive if possible. Elimination authorized if necessary. Use code designation: RECKONING.

He signed it with a single initial: *C.*

He rang a small brass bell on his desk. A man entered almost instantly. He was broad-shouldered, impassive. He wore a dark suit like Corbett's, but it looked like it covered muscle built for action, not administration.

"Harker," Corbett said. His voice was soft, almost toneless. He handed the folded paper to the man. "This. To the duty officer. Full authorization. Team of four. Including us. Horses. Supplies. Travel light. Ready to ride in two hours."

Harker took the paper. He didn't open it. He nodded once. "Yes, sir." He turned and left.

Corbett sat down again. He closed his eyes. He saw the burning barn in Virginia—the smell of smoke and hay—the figure inside, wounded, desperate. He saw his own hand raise the pistol—the shot—the chaos that followed—the confusion—the charred remains they pulled out.

He opened his eyes. The image faded replaced by a name. *Oak Creek. John Brown.* A mercantile store—a hiding place—it ended now. The reckoning was due.

He stood and walked to a locked cabinet in the corner. He took a key from his pocket and opened it. Inside, laid carefully on a shelf, was a heavy, long-barreled Colt revolver. The metal was clean, oiled. He picked it up. The weight was familiar, comforting. He checked the cylinder. It was loaded. He holstered it under his coat and took a box of cartridges. He put them in his pocket.

He left the office and walked down the quiet corridor. His footsteps echoed as he descended the stairs. Outside, the Washington night was cool. Harker was already there, holding the reins of two saddled horses. Two other men stood nearby, checking their own mounts and saddlebags. They were like Harker—solid—quiet—efficient. Their faces were stern, professional. They knew the mission designation: *RECKONING*. They knew the target was high priority. They knew Corbett's reputation and they didn't ask questions.

Corbett mounted his horse. He adjusted his coat, settling it over the holster. He looked at the men. "We ride west," he said. His voice was still soft, but it carried. "No stopping. No delays. We reach Oak Creek as fast as horseflesh can carry us."

He didn't wait for acknowledgment, he nudged his horse forward. Harker and the other two fell in behind him. They rode out of the stable yard, turning onto the dark street. Hooves clattered on the cobblestones as they headed west, out of the city, towards the long road to New Mexico.

They rode hard, changing horses at relay stations, pushing the animals to their limits. They slept in short shifts, curled in blankets by the side of the road or in cheap stables. They ate cold food from their saddlebags. They spoke little. Corbett led them, he seemed tireless. His pale eyes scanned the road ahead. He was focused—utterly focused. The name echoed in his mind with every mile. *Oak Creek—John Brown.*

The landscape changed—cities gave way to towns—towns gave way to scattered farms—farms gave way to open prairie. The air grew drier, dust coated their clothes and faces. The sun beat down hard but they pushed on. Days blurred into nights. They crossed rivers—skirted settlements.

Corbett studied maps at stops. He questioned stationmasters about the territory west of Independence and settlements along the trails. He learned about Oak Creek—a small town—a stage stop—a mercantile store. He learned the name of its owner: Peterson and his one employee, a quiet man: John Brown. He kept to himself. Ran the store for Peterson for several years—well respected.

Respected. Corbett's lips thinned. It's a mask—a lie. The serpent hiding in plain sight. He's playing the humble shopkeeper. It's just another role, another character for the great actor. He's made Oak Creek his theater—his stage. It was an insult—to the nation—to the memory of Lincoln. Corbett was determined to make sure this was his final act.

Harker rode beside him sometimes. He reported on the horses, on supplies. He didn't ask about the target. He knew Corbett would speak when necessary. The other two men, Carter and Vance, followed. They watched the trail. They watched Corbett, they understood the gravity in his silence. One evening, camped by a shallow creek, Vance finally spoke. He was cleaning his rifle by the firelight. "This Brown," he said, not looking up. "He expecting company?"

Corbett poked the fire with a stick, sparks flew into the dark sky. "No," he said. The firelight flickered in his pale eyes. "He thinks he's safe. He thinks he's buried his past. He thinks John Wilkes Booth is dead." A ghost of something cold touched his expression. "We are here to correct that mistake."

No one spoke again that night. The only sounds were the crackle of the fire, the stamp of a horse and the distant cry of a coyote. The vast emptiness of the prairie pressed in around their small circle of light.

They rode into New Mexico Territory. The land flattened further. Dry desert sand stretched to the horizon. Towns were farther apart—the air tasted of dust. They pushed the horses harder. Time was running out, every hour Booth remained free was an insult.

Corbett felt the old certainty solidify. The righteousness—the purpose—this was his destiny. This was his chance to finish what he started in that barn—to bring the true reckoning. God's hand guided him. He was just the instrument.

Late on the eighth day, they topped a low rise. The sun was setting behind them, casting long shadows. Below, nestled in a shallow valley beside a winding creek, lay a cluster of buildings. Wooden structures with a single dusty street. A larger building with a false front stood near the center. Even from this distance, Corbett could make out the faded lettering painted on its side: *Mercantile*.

Harker reined in beside him. He pointed. "Oak Creek."

Corbett didn't move, his horse stood still. His pale eyes were fixed on the town—on the building. His hand rested on the butt of the Colt under his coat. The weight was reassuring.

John Wilkes Booth. He was down there behind those walls. Thinking of himself as John Brown—thinking he was safe.

The long ride was over. The hunt reached its end.

Corbett nudged his horse forward down the slope towards the sleeping town. Harker, Carter, and Vance followed, a silent line of shadows against the darkening prairie. The only sound was the steady beat of hooves on the hard-packed earth, carrying them into the valley towards Oak Creek—towards the reckoning.

Chapter 3

The four riders reached the edge of Oak Creek as the last light bled from the sky. Corbett reined in his horse just before the first buildings. The town felt quiet—too quiet. Lights glowed in a few windows. The saloon emitted a dull murmur. The mercantile stood dark and silent.

"Split up," Corbett said, his voice low. "Harker, Vance stable the horses. Carter, with me." He dismounted, handing his reins to Harker. The movement was stiff from days in the saddle, Carter followed suit.

Harker and Vance led the horses down the side street towards the livery stable. Corbett watched them go, then turned towards the main street. Carter fell in step beside him. They walked like men weary from travel, their boots scuffing the dusty boardwalk. Corbett kept his hat brim low. His pale eyes scanned everything—the closed shops—the darkened windows of the mercantile—the sheriff's office further down, a lamp burning inside.

They reached the Oak Creek Hotel. A sign creaked in the evening breeze. Corbett pushed the door open, a bell jangled. The lobby was small, cramped. A thin man with spectacles looked up from behind a counter and wiped his hands on a rag.

"Evening," the clerk said. "Need rooms?"

"Two," Corbett said. He kept his voice neutral. "My partners will be along."

"Got two left. Adjacent. Back of the house. Quieter." The clerk pulled a ledger forward. "Names?"

"Smith," Corbett said. "John Smith. My partner is Carter." He placed coins on the counter.

The clerk wrote slowly. "Smith. Carter. Two rooms. Paying by the night or week?"

"Night. For now." Corbett took the keys the clerk offered. "Long ride. Need a bath. Food?"

"Bathhouse next door. Opens at seven. Saloon does meals. Closes soon." The clerk pointed vaguely down the street.

Corbett nodded. "We'll manage. Town seems quiet."

"Usually is. 'Cept when the stage comes. Or trouble." The clerk adjusted his spectacles.

"Trouble?" Carter asked, leaning on the counter.

The clerk hesitated. "Well...had a man go missing few days back. Stranger. Davies. Stayed right here. Room four. Paid for the week. Just...vanished. Sheriff's lookin'." He lowered his voice. "Folks are jumpy. Sheriff questioned a few people. Including John Brown, down at the mercantile. Davies was asking about him, see."

"Brown?" Corbett asked, feigning mild interest.

"Runs the store for Peterson. Keeps to himself. Good man, runs a fair business. Sheriff didn't find nothin', of course. But strange, all the same." The clerk shook his head. "Nothin' like that happens here."

Corbett pocketed the keys. "Appreciate the information. We'll head up."

The rooms were small and plain. Corbett took one, Carter the next. Corbett placed his saddlebags on the narrow bed and walked to the window. It overlooked the alley behind the hotel and the rear of the buildings across the way, including the mercantile's loading door. Darkness pooled there. He stood watching, motionless, for a full minute. Then he turned and left the room, locking the door. Carter met him in the hallway.

"Saloon," Corbett said.

The Saloon was half-full, smoke hung thick in the air. Men hunched over tables or leaned against the bar. Conversations were low. Corbett and Carter took stools at the far end of the bar. The bartender, a burly man wiping a glass, approached.

"Whiskey. Two." Corbett laid coins down.

The whiskey was rough. Corbett sipped his, eyes sweeping the room. Carter sipped his, watching the door. Harker and Vance entered a few minutes later. They took a small table near the back wall, ordering beer. The team was dispersed, observing.

Corbett focused on the patrons. He listened to snatches of talk. It was the usual idle conversations, cattle prices, a broken wagon axle and the missing man. Davies' name surfaced at a nearby table.

"...looked everywhere, Pike says. Creek banks. Old mineshafts. Nothin'."

"Foul play, you reckon?"

"Coulda just lit out. Men do."

"Left all his gear? Paid his room? Don't figure."

"Sheriff questioned Brown again today. Brown didn't like it. Told Pike to stop botherin' him. Got sharp about it."

"Brown? Sharp? That ain't like him."

"Wasn't. Pike pushed. Said Davies was askin' everyone about him before he disappeared. Made Brown look bad."

"Brown ain't no killer. Man runs a store."

"Strange though. Why was Davies so set on him?"

"Who knows? Easterner. Prob'ly thought Brown owed him money or somethin'."

Corbett kept his expression blank. He signaled the bartender for another whiskey. He didn't drink it. He pushed it aside.

"Quiet town," he said to the bartender.

"Usually. Like I said." The bartender refilled another man's glass.

"Except for this missing fellow. Davies."

The bartender grunted. "Yeah. Bad business. Upsets folks."

"Heard he was asking about the storekeeper. Brown."

The bartender shrugged, wiping the bar. "Asked me too. Day before he vanished. Wanted to know how long Brown been here. Where he came from. What kind of man he was. Usual stranger curiosity, I thought. Didn't think much on it."

"What did you tell him?"

"Told him Brown's been here near five years. Runs the mercantile. Keeps to himself. Pays his bills. No trouble." The bartender paused. "Then he asked if Brown ever talked about the war. Or the East. That seemed odd."

"The war?"

"Asked if Brown ever mentioned serving. Or places back east. Gettysburg. Washington. Names like that." The bartender shook his head. "Told him Brown never talks about himself at all. Man's a blank slate. Davies seemed...disappointed. Finished his beer and left."

Corbett nodded slowly. "Strange questions for a stranger."

"Sure was. Made sense later, when he disappeared. Sheriff asked me the same things." The bartender moved away to serve another customer.

Corbett caught Carter's eye, he gave a slight nod. They had confirmation. Davies had been digging, he had found the right man. Corbett felt the weight of the Colt against his side. He could feel it, the reckoning was close. He hoped it was too close for Booth to sense.

Dawn broke with dim light and a cool breeze. Corbett was up before first light. He stood at his window, watching the alley. The town stirred slowly—a rooster crowed—a door slammed. Smoke began to rise from chimneys.

Across the alley, the rear door of the mercantile opened. A man stepped out, he wore a worn work shirt and trousers. He carried an empty crate and placed it beside others near the loading door. He stretched, rubbing his lower back. Then he turned and limped back inside. The limp was pronounced, a dragging hitch in the left leg. The door closed.

Corbett didn't move. He had seen it, the walk he remembered from descriptions shouted in the chaos after Ford's Theatre, from Garret's barn. The injury sustained jumping to the stage—John Wilkes Booth's limp. It was him—John Brown. Corbett's breath felt cold in his chest. He saw the serpent, fetching crates and he knew it was him.

He dressed quickly and left the hotel. He walked down the main street. The mercantile was still closed. He passed it, noting the windows, the door, the alley access. He walked to the end of the street, past the blacksmith's silent forge, past the church. He turned down a side lane leading towards the creek. The sound of rushing water grew louder.

He walked along the bank. The water was high, muddy, swirling around rocks and snags. He scanned the banks, looking for anything, a scrap of cloth caught on a branch, a disturbance in the mud. He saw nothing obvious. Davies was gone, swept away. Booth had covered his tracks—for now.

He walked back towards town. People were emerging. The town was coming to life. A woman swept her porch, a boy drove cows towards pasture. Corbett kept his head down. He saw Sheriff Pike emerge from his office, buckling his gun belt. Pike glanced at Corbett, a stranger, but didn't approach.

Corbett positioned himself on a bench outside the barber shop, two buildings down from the mercantile. He had a clear view of its front door. He took out a pipe, though he didn't smoke it. He pretended to clean it and waited.

The mercantile doors opened at seven. John Brown stood there, keys in hand. He looked out at the street. His gaze swept over Corbett on the bench, lingered for a fraction of a second, then moved on. He unlocked the door fully and went inside.

Corbett studied him—the man fit the description Davies sent. He was average height, lean build, dark hair, graying at the temples and a beard, neatly trimmed but hiding the jawline. The face was different from the wanted posters Corbett carried folded inside his coat—older, harder, the eyes wary but the bones were there—the shape of the skull and the eyes. Corbett had seen those eyes in nightmares—haunted—defiant. Now masked with shopkeeper's calm.

Brown moved behind the counter inside. He lit a lamp and began arranging items. His movements were precise, careful. Corbett watched the limp as Brown walked from counter to shelf—consistent—unmistakable. A performance of normalcy, but the flaw was written in his gait. The ghost couldn't hide that.

Customers arrived—a woman with a basket—an old man. Brown served them—polite—reserved. He smiled sometimes, but it didn't show in his eyes. Corbett noted the tension in his shoulders, the way he glanced towards the door too often. Booth was on edge—Pike's questions—the town's whispers—he felt the pressure.

Harker appeared, walking down the boardwalk. He stopped near Corbett's bench. He leaned against a post, rolling a cigarette. He didn't look at Corbett.

"Vance is at the livery," Harker murmured, pretending to search for a match. "Asked about Davies. Stableman remembers him. Rented a horse. Never brought it back. Horse showed up two days later, saddle empty, wandering near the west ford. Sheriff searched that area. Found nothing."

Corbett gave a small nod. Booth had been thorough. The creek was the key.

"Storekeeper?" Harker asked softly.

"Confirmed," Corbett said, his voice barely audible. He tapped his pipe stem against his own left leg. "Limp. Deep."

Harker lit his cigarette. He exhaled smoke. "Carter's checking the creek bank downstream. See if Davies washed up anywhere obvious." He pushed off the post. "Orders?"

"Observe," Corbett said. "The town. Him. His patterns. We move when we know the ground."

Harker walked away, towards the hotel. Corbett stayed on the bench. He watched John Brown weigh flour for a customer. The shopkeeper's hands were steady. But Corbett saw the slight tremor when he reached for the scoop. The ghost was rattled. The performance was costing him more than he expected.

The day passed slowly. Corbett moved around town. He bought tobacco at the mercantile, Brown served him. Corbett kept his face expressionless, his voice flat. "Two ounces. Shag cut." Brown measured it and wrapped it in paper. Brown's eyes met Corbett's for an instant. Corbett saw the wariness deepen—a stranger—another stranger. Brown took the coins. "Thank you." His voice was neutral. Corbett nodded and left. He felt the assassin's gaze on his back until he turned the corner.

He walked to the sheriff's office. He stood outside, looking at the noticeboard. Wanted posters. Livestock sales. A notice about Davies: *MISSING. Arthur Davies. Easterner. Last seen Tuesday. Reward for information.* Corbett memorized the details. He saw Pike inside, writing at his desk. Pike looked up. Corbett touched his hat brim and walked on.

He found Carter near the west ford of the creek. Carter shook his head. "Nothing. Banks are steep. Muddy. Current's strong. If he's down there..." He gestured downstream. "He's gone."

Corbett looked at the churning water. Booth had chosen well, nature was his accomplice. "Back to town. Watch the store."

The late afternoon sun slanted down Oak Creek's main street. Corbett stood in the shadows of the alley beside the mercantile. He watched the front door, Brown was closing up. He flipped the sign to 'Closed' and locked the door. He tested the handle, he turned and limped down the boardwalk, heading towards Mrs. Henderson's boarding house.

Corbett followed, keeping distance between them. He used the cover of other pedestrians and doorways. Brown walked steadily. He greeted a passing woman with a nod. "Mrs. Peterson." His voice carried back to Corbett. It was calm and ordinary. The limp was his only flaw—it was the only thing he couldn't hide or change, it betrayed his true identity.

Brown reached the boarding house and climbed the porch steps. He paused at the door, looking back down the street. His eyes scanned the boardwalk. Corbett stepped deeper into a recessed doorway. Brown's gaze passed over the spot. He seemed to stare right through the shadow where Corbett stood. Corbett remained still, breath held. Brown turned and went inside. The door closed.

Corbett waited. Five minutes—ten, there was no sign of Brown. Brown was in for the night.

He walked back towards the hotel. He saw Vance near the livery, talking to the stableman. Vance saw him and gave a small shake of his head. There was no new information. Harker leaned against the hotel porch rail. Carter was inside, watching from a window.

Corbett joined Harker on the porch. The street was quieter now. Lamplight glowed in windows.

"He knows something's wrong," Corbett said quietly, looking towards the boarding house. "Too many strangers. Pike pushing. He's careful. Alert."

"Can't stay that way forever," Harker said.

"He won't need to. If he feels the net closing..." Corbett left it hanging. Booth had run before. He would run again. "We need to know his ground. Inside that store. His room. The boarding house. Davies was asking questions. We need answers he didn't get."

"Tonight?" Harker asked.

Corbett watched a lamp go out in an upstairs window of the boarding house. John Brown's room? "Tonight," he confirmed. "The mercantile first. He locks it tight. We find a way in. Look for anything, papers, hiding places—Davies might have missed something or left something." He paused. "Then the boarding house. His room. While he sleeps,"

Harker nodded. "Carter's good with locks. Vance watches the street."

"Midnight," Corbett said. The town would be asleep. Booth would be asleep—thinking himself safe—thinking John Wilkes Booth was dead and buried. "We find what Davies found. We finish what he started." He turned and entered the hotel. The heavy Colt felt solid against his side. The reckoning would not wait for dawn.

Chapter 4

Midnight draped Oak Creek in a thick silence. Corbett stood in the alley beside the mercantile. The air was cool and still. Above, a sliver of moon offered little light. Harker and Carter materialized from deeper shadows. Vance remained near the alley mouth, a watchful shape against the darker street.

"He's asleep," Harker whispered. "Light went out hours ago. Boarding house is dark."

Corbett nodded. He pointed to the mercantile's back door. Carter stepped forward and pulled tools from his pocket. He knelt at the door. His metal instruments scraped softly against the lock. Corbett watched the boarding house windows. There was no movement—no light.

There was a click from the door behind Corbett. Carter pushed the door open, it swung inward without a sound. The smell of dry goods— leather, coffee, spices—drifted out. Corbett entered first, Harker followed. Carter pulled the door almost shut, leaving Vance outside.

Inside, the darkness was near total. Corbett struck a match. The flame flared, revealing stacked sacks, barrels and shelves crammed with merchandise. He lit a small bullseye lantern he carried, turning the beam low. The circle of light moved over the floor, the counter and the walls.

"Check the counter," Corbett murmured. "Drawers. Ledgers."

Harker moved behind the counter and opened the drawers. Paper rustled as he examined a ledger under the lantern light. "Daily sales. Stock lists. Nothing unusual." He flipped pages. "No personal notes. No names."

Corbett swept the beam along the shelves. He looked for loose boards and false backs. He tested the weight of large sacks. He found nothing. The light caught the base of a shelf near the rear wall. Dust lay thick but disturbed in one spot. A faint drag mark led towards a stack of empty crates.

He moved the crates. Behind them, a section of the floorboard looked different, it was less worn. Corbett knelt, his fingers found a small indentation. He pried, a short section of board lifted—a cavity lay beneath.

The lantern beam pierced the darkness. Inside the hole lay a bundle wrapped in oilcloth. Corbett lifted it out, it was heavy and solid. He unwrapped the cloth.

The light gleamed on metal. A knife, its handle worn smooth—small—elegant—deadly. Etched faintly into the bone grip were the initials: *JWB*. Beside it lay a folded piece of paper, yellowed with age. Corbett unfolded it carefully. It was a playbill—*Ford's Theatre. April 14, 1865. Our American Cousin.* Beneath it, almost hidden, was a smaller slip—a torn theatre program fragment for another play—*Ford's Theatre. March 18, 1865. The Apostate*—bearing the unmistakable name: *John Wilkes Booth*. It was Booth's last performance on the stage.

Harker breathed out slowly. "Proof."

Corbett stared at the playbill—the date—the name. He saw the barn again—the smoke—the confusion. He rewrapped the bundle and placed it back in the hole. He replaced the board and stood.

"Leave it. For now." His voice was flat. "His room. Now."

The boarding house porch creaked under their weight. Carter worked the front door lock, another soft click and it opened. They slipped inside. The hallway smelled of dust and cooked food. Stairs rose to their left. Corbett pointed upwards. Carter led, testing each step for noise, Corbett followed. Harker stayed below, watching the hallway and the front door.

At the top was a narrow corridor with three doors. Corbett pointed to the door at the rear, Brown's room. Carter examined the lock, it was simpler than the mercantile's. He inserted his tools, seconds passed and another click. Carter eased the door open a fraction, he peered inside. He glanced back at Corbett and nodded. John Brown was asleep.

Corbett pushed the door open. He stepped inside, his lantern beam cutting through the dark. The room was small, a bed, washstand, chair and a trunk at the foot of the bed. John Brown lay on the bed, a blanket pulled to his waist. His breathing was slow—deep.

Corbett moved to the side of the bed. He raised the lantern and the light fell directly on Brown's face. Harker stood at the foot of the bed. Carter remained by the door, blocking it.

Brown stirred, his eyes fluttered open. Confusion clouded them for an instant—then awareness—shock. He jerked upright, scrambling back against the headboard. His hand shot under the pillow.

"Don't." Corbett's voice cut the silence. His own hand rested inside his coat, on the grip of the Colt. The lantern light glinted in his pale eyes.

Brown froze. His hand stayed under the pillow. His eyes darted from Corbett to Harker to Carter. Recognition flared—the man from the bench—the stranger buying tobacco. His gaze locked back on Corbett. The fear was raw now, stripped of the shopkeeper's mask. He saw something in Corbett's face. Something he knew.

"Who are you?" Brown demanded. His voice was rough, sleep-thickened, but tight with fear. "What do you want? Money? Take it. Take it and go." He gestured vaguely towards the trunk.

"We don't want your money, Mr. Brown," Corbett said. The name was deliberate.

"Then what?" Brown's eyes narrowed—calculating. "The sheriff? Is this about Davies? I told Pike everything. I don't know anything."

"Arthur Davies," Corbett stated. "Our associate. You met him. In the alley behind the store. Tuesday evening."

Brown shook his head, too fast. "No. I didn't. I told you. I didn't see him Tuesday."

"You did," Corbett said. The beam of the lantern didn't waver. "He was asking questions. Too many questions. About the war. About Washington. About Gettysburg. About a man named Booth." He paused. "About *you*."

Brown licked his lips. His hand twitched under the pillow. "Lies. He was a stranger. Troublemaker. Probably ran off."

"He didn't run," Corbett said. His voice remained low, devoid of inflection. "You took him to the creek. Oak Creek. Running high. Swollen. You pushed him in."

Brown's face tightened, a muscle jumped in his jaw. "That's...that's insane. Why would I do that? I'm a shopkeeper. I mind my own business."

"Because he found you," Corbett said. The words fell like stones. "John Wilkes Booth."

The name hung in the small room—heavy—accusatory. Brown flinched as if it struck him. His breath hitched—for a long moment, he stared at Corbett. The shopkeeper's pretense dissolved completely. What remained was something hunted—cornered and beneath that, a flicker of the old defiance.

"Booth is dead," Brown whispered. The words were hoarse. "Burned. In a barn. Years ago. Everyone knows that."

"Everyone was *told* that," Corbett countered. His pale eyes held Brown's. "The papers printed what we wanted them to print. A charred body. Convenient. Believable. For a time."

Brown shook his head again, but the motion lacked conviction. His eyes darted towards the window—towards escape. Harker shifted slightly, cutting off the angle to the door. Carter stood like a stone pillar.

"You're wrong," Brown insisted, but his voice lacked conviction. "You're mistaken. My name is John Brown. I run the store."

"We found the playbill," Corbett interrupted. "Ford's Theatre. April fourteenth along with the one from March 18. Your name on it. The Apostate, your last performance." He didn't move his hand from the Colt.

"We found the knife with JWB etched into the handle. Hidden under the floor. Where you hid your past."

Brown's face went pale in the lantern light. The denial died on his lips. He looked from Corbett to the grim faces of the other men. The net was real, it was tightening around him. He drew a shaky breath. When he spoke again, the tone changed. The shopkeeper was gone. The voice was lower—cooler—colder. John Wilkes Booth had returned.

"Davies," he said. The name was flat. "He was persistent. Like a dog on a scent. Asking. Digging. Showing my picture around. Asking about the leg." He touched his left thigh briefly. "He wouldn't stop."

"So you stopped him," Corbett stated. Not a question.

Brown met Corbett's gaze. The fear was still there, but now mixed with a chilling resignation and a spark of the old arrogance. "He was in the way. Asking too many questions. Threatening everything." He shrugged, a small, sharp movement. "He left me no choice. The creek...it solved the problem. Nature took him."

"Confirmation," Corbett said. His hand tightened on the Colt. The admission hung in the air. Booth had killed their man. The reckoning was here.

Brown leaned back slightly against the headboard. He managed a thin, humorless smile. "The papers said it. Plain as day. 'John Wilkes Booth is dead.' Buried. Forgotten. You should have left it buried."

Corbett didn't smile. His pale eyes burned with a cold, unwavering light. "The papers printed what we wanted them to print. To make the nation sleep. To make *you* sleep." He took a half-step closer. The lantern beam pinned Booth against the wall. "You woke up, Booth. Now it ends."

Corbett raised his left hand, a silent signal. Harker moved instantly, stepping towards the bed. Carter stepped further into the room, blocking the window. Booth's eyes widened. His hand jerked from under the pillow, clutching a small pocket revolver. He swung it towards Corbett. The ghost prepared for its final act.

The small revolver in Booth's hand looked puny against the Colt Corbett now drew. The lantern light flashed on both barrels. Booth's finger tightened on the trigger.

Harker lunged, not at Booth, but sideways, knocking the washstand hard. The pitcher and bowl crashed to the floor. The sudden noise, the shattering dishes, was a shock in the confined space. Booth flinched, his aim wavered for a split second.

Corbett fired. The roar was deafening. The bullet tore through Booth's right shoulder, he cried out, a sharp gasp of pain. The small revolver clattered from his grasp onto the bed. He clutched his shoulder, blood welling between his fingers.

Downstairs, the thunderous crash of dishes followed instantly by the gunshot jolted Mrs. Henderson from sleep. Her heart hammered hard against her chest. John Brown's room! Something terrible had happened. Fear, sharp and cold, cut through her drowsiness. She threw back her covers, her hands trembling as she fumbled for her shawl and the heavy fireplace poker beside her bed. Moving as quietly as she could, she eased open her bedroom door and peered into the dark hallway.

"Bind him," Corbett ordered. His voice cut through the ringing silence.

Carter was already moving. He pulled a rope from his coat pocket and grabbed Booth's uninjured arm, wrenching it behind his back. Booth struggled, kicking out weakly. Carter pinned him face down on the bed. He tied Booth's wrists together with swift, efficient knots. He pulled another length of rope and secured Booth's ankles.

"Leg," Corbett said, holstering his Colt. He gestured at Booth's left leg.

Carter pulled up Booth's trouser leg. He wrapped the rope tightly above the knee, around the old injury. Booth groaned. Carter yanked the knot tight.

Harker set up the washstand. He picked up the pieces of broken dishes and stacked them quietly on the small table.

"Get Vance," Corbett said. Harker nodded and slipped out the door.

Harker moved swiftly down the dark stairs, as he reached the bottom, a gasp and a muffled thud came from the hallway near Mrs. Henderson's door. He rounded the corner and froze. Vance stood, a solid shadow in the gloom, gripping the arm of a slight, struggling figure—Mrs. Henderson. Her shawl was askew, her eyes wide with terror. The fireplace poker lay forgotten on the floor. Vance had one hand clamped over her mouth.

"Easy now, ma'am," Vance said, low and urgent. "Easy. No harm."

Mrs. Henderson's eyes locked onto Harker, wild with confusion and accusation. *Thieves! Two of them! In her house!* She renewed her struggle against Vance's iron grip, a muffled cry escaping his fingers.

Harker stepped forward quickly. "Let her go, Vance. She's the landlady." Vance cautiously removed his hand. Mrs. Henderson stumbled back, gasping, her hand flying to her throat. She stared from Vance to Harker, her face pale.

"What…what is happening?" she demanded, her voice shaking but fierce. "Where is Mr. Brown? That shot…that crash…Who are you? What have you done to him?" She looked towards the stairs, fear for her tenant mixing with her own terror. "If you've hurt John Brown…"

Harker kept his voice calm but firm. "Ma'am, stay back. Stay in your room. This is federal business. Mr. Brown…he's involved in something serious. He's been injured, but he's alive. We're taking him in."

"Injured?" Mrs. Henderson's hand flew to her mouth. "Federal? But…he's just a shopkeeper! A quiet man! You must be mistaken!" She took a step towards the stairs. "I need to see him!"

Vance moved subtly to block her path. "Can't allow that, ma'am," he said, his tone leaving no room for argument. "Best you stay put. For your own safety."

Harker saw the stubborn set of her jaw, the maternal fury rising. He needed to move. "Vance, upstairs. Now. Corbett needs you." He gave Vance a meaningful look. Vance nodded and started up the stairs, his heavy tread echoing. Harker turned back to Mrs. Henderson. "Please, ma'am. Go back to your room. Lock your door. This will be over soon." He didn't wait for her response. He followed Vance up, leaving Mrs. Henderson standing alone in the dark hallway. She was trembling, listening to the heavy footsteps above, the muffled sounds of struggle, and the harsh, pained breathing of the man she knew as John Brown being dragged towards the back door.

Corbett looked down at Booth. Booth lay on his side, breathing hard. His face was pale and slick with sweat. Blood soaked the shoulder of his nightshirt. His eyes held pain and a desperate, trapped fury.

"Davies," Corbett stated. "He worked for us. His job was finding men. Traitors. Spies. Men who vanished after the war." He paused. "He found you."

Booth said nothing. He pressed his face into the thin mattress.

"Your limp," Corbett continued. "The description. The persistence. He was good. He tracked you here. He recognized you. He confronted you."

Booth remained silent. His body trembled.

"You killed a federal agent," Corbett said. The words were flat, final. "That demands one answer."

Footsteps sounded on the stairs. Harker returned with Vance. Vance filled the doorway, his gaze sweeping the room, landing on the bound man.

"Quiet?" Vance asked, his voice a low rumble.

"For now," Corbett said. "We move. Now. Before dawn."

Carter hauled Booth upright. Booth gasped as his wounded shoulder took weight. He swayed on his feet. His bound legs made movement awkward.

"Where?" Harker asked.

"The Harrell farm," Corbett said. "South of town. Abandoned. There's a barn."

Understanding dawned on Harker's face. Vance nodded once.

"Get him down the back stairs," Corbett instructed. "Avoid the street. The creek path. Move."

Carter and Vance each took an arm. They half-dragged, half-carried Booth towards the door. His bound feet scraped the floorboards. Harker went ahead, checking the hallway and stairs. Corbett followed last. On is way out, he blew out the lantern, plunging the room into darkness.

They navigated the narrow stairs. Booth stumbled. Vance held him up as they reached the lower hallway. Harker glanced towards the front. Mrs. Henderson's door was shut, a thin line of light beneath it. He could almost feel her listening, terrified, on the other side. Harker eased open the back door. The cool night air washed in. The sliver of moon above offered faint light.

They moved into the narrow alley behind the boarding house. Carter and Vance propelled Booth forward. His movements were jerky, hampered by the ropes and his injury. He breathed in harsh rasps. They turned south, following the alley towards the edge of town. The creek gurgled nearby, unseen in the dark.

The alley opened onto a path running alongside the creek. Trees lined the bank. The path was uneven dirt. Booth stumbled again, Vance tightened his grip.

"Faster," Corbett urged from behind.

They pushed on. The town sounds faded. Only the creek and their own harsh breathing filled the night. Booth's head drooped, he seemed dazed by pain and shock.

Ahead, the path curved. A fallen branch lay across it. Carter stepped over it and Vance followed. As Vance lifted Booth over the obstacle, Booth made his move.

He threw his weight violently sideways against Vance. Caught off balance, Vance staggered. Booth twisted, driving his bound feet into

Carter's shins. Carter grunted, stumbling back. Booth wrenched his arms free from their loosened grip. He hit the ground hard on his injured shoulder. He cried out, but rolled instantly towards the creek bank.

"Stop him!" Corbett yelled.

Booth scrambled on his knees and one hand, his bound legs were useless for running but propelling him in desperate lunges towards the black water. He reached the edge and plunged down the steep, muddy bank.

Corbett drew his Colt. Harker and Vance surged forward, drawing their own weapons. Carter scrambled after Booth.

Booth hit the creek—the cold water shocked him. He floundered, the ropes tangling him. The current tugged at him violently. He thrashed towards the far bank, slipping on rocks, plunging under and surfacing, coughing. The water reached his waist.

Corbett reached the bank. He saw Booth's dark shape struggling in the moonlit water. He raised his Colt.

"No!" Harker grabbed Corbett's arm. "The sound. Town will hear."

Corbett lowered the gun. His jaw tightened. "After him."

Harker and Vance slid down the muddy bank. Carter was already in the water, wading fast towards Booth. Booth saw him coming. He intensified his efforts, clawing at the opposite bank, hauling himself up through slick mud and roots. He made it over the top, vanishing into the trees.

Harker and Vance reached the far bank and climbed. Carter slogged out of the creek behind them. Corbett crossed the creek upstream where it was shallower, moving with cold purpose.

On the far side, the trees were thick. Undergrowth clawed at their legs. They listened. They heard crashing ahead—desperate—uncoordinated. The sound of a man dragging bound legs through brush.

"Spread out," Corbett ordered. "Flush him towards the open land. South."

They moved into the woods. Harker went left, Vance went right. Carter and Corbett took the center. They advanced slowly, methodically. Their boots crushed twigs as they pushed branches aside. They scanned the gloom but they saw nothing in the dark.

Ahead, the crashing sounds grew more frantic. Booth was moving but the ropes and his injuries slowed him terribly. His breathing was loud and ragged.

"Give it up, Booth!" Corbett called. His voice carried coldly through the trees. "There's nowhere left."

The only answer was a renewed burst of crashing, veering east towards the edge of the woods—towards open fields.

Harker fired his pistol into the air. The shot echoed, shattering the night silence. Birds erupted from the trees.

Booth flinched at the sound. He changed direction again, stumbling southward. Branches whipped his face and thorns tore his nightshirt. His shoulder burned. His left leg, the old injury screaming under the tight rope, threatened to buckle with every step. He tripped over a root and fell hard, he gasped and pushed himself up. He could hear them closing in, converging. He broke through a final line of brush.

He made it to open land. Moonlight silvered a wide field of stubble. Beyond it, maybe two hundred yards, loomed the dark shape of a large barn. The Harrell place. It's been abandoned for years—Isolated. It was his only cover.

He plunged into the field. The cut stalks snagged his bound legs. He fell again, he crawled and got back up. He ran, hobbling, dragging his legs, a grotesque, limping sprint. Every step sent agony through his leg and shoulder. He glanced back. Shapes emerged from the tree line. Four of them, fanning out, cutting off retreat—driving him forward.

He reached the barn, a large, double door stood slightly ajar. He threw his weight against it. It groaned open and he stumbled inside, into pitch blackness smelling of dust, old hay, and animal dung. He slammed the doors shut behind him. He fumbled in the dark, his bound hands finding a heavy timber bar. He heaved it up, dropping it into the brackets with a solid thud. He collapsed against the door, gasping, listening.

Outside, Corbett stopped at the edge of the field. He watched Booth's limping flight, the desperate barricading. Harker, Vance, and Carter reached him.

"He's in the barn," Vance stated.

Corbett surveyed the barn. It was big, built from sturdy old timber. The shuttered windows were high up. It had one door, barred now—escape was impossible.

"Surround it," Corbett said. "Cover the sides. The back. Any window, any crack."

The men moved out, circling the structure, taking positions where they could watch the walls.

Corbett walked forward alone, stopping fifty yards from the barred doors. The moon cast his long shadow across the stubble field. The night air was cold and still.

"Booth!" Corbett's voice rang out, clear and hard. "You hear me?"

Silence from the barn. Then, a voice, strained, defiant. "I hear you! What do you want, Corbett? More rope?"

"You killed Davies," Corbett said. "A federal agent. You know the penalty."

A harsh laugh came from inside. "Penalty? By whose law? Yours? You hunt men in the night like dogs! You are no lawman!"

"The law is clear," Corbett replied. "For killing a federal agent. Death. No trial. No arrest. Only execution."

Silence again. Longer this time. Then Booth's voice, lower now. "That's not the law Corbett and you know it. There's always a trial. That's your bloodlust. You were always going to kill me if you found me because you can't just walk in with John Wilkes Booth. He's been dead for years. He's just a ghost. So shoot. Shoot through the door. Be done with it. Show your courage."

Corbett didn't move. "You want a spectacle? You always did. Very well. You'll have one." He raised his voice. "Harker! Vance! Gather dry brush. Anything that burns. Pile it against the walls. All around."

Harker and Vance began pulling armfuls of dry weeds from the field's edge. Carter joined them, snapping brittle branches from a fallen dead tree near the woods. They worked quickly and silently, piling brush against the barn's weathered planks, especially around the base of the door.

Booth's voice came again, sharper now, fear cutting through the defiance. "Fire? You mean to burn me? Like an animal? Just like last tim."

"Like the murderer you are," Corbett stated. "You had your chance at surrender. You chose flight. You chose death. This is the consequence."

"You coward!" Booth screamed. The sound was raw, edged with panic. "Face me! Fight me!"

Corbett ignored him. "Light it," he ordered.

Harker struck a match. He touched it to a pile of dry grass near the barn door. The flame caught, small at first, then it licked hungrily at the dry brush. Vance lit another pile further down the wall. Carter lit a third. Orange flames began to crawl upwards, crackling, burning the dry wood. Smoke curled, gray in the moonlight, then thick and black.

The flames grew and merged. A ring of fire began to encircle the lower part of the barn. The crackle became a roar. Heat washed out, pushing against the cool night air. Light flickered across the field, painting the watching men in shifting orange and black.

Inside the barn, Booth pounded on the door. "No! Corbett! NO!" His voice was muffled, desperate. He coughed, smoke was seeping in, finding cracks.

The fire climbed higher. Flames reached the shuttered windows. Glass shattered somewhere high up. The smoke billowed out in thick, choking clouds. The timbers groaned as the heat took them, sparks flew upward like angry stars.

The light, the roar, the smoke—it couldn't be hidden. In Oak Creek, windows lit up and doors opened. Shapes emerged, drawn by the inferno glowing on the southern horizon. Murmurs grew into questions, then shouts. People pulled on coats and boots. They began to move towards the light, a growing stream of figures converging on the Harrell field. Men, women and children held back by parents—dozens—then scores. Among them, her shawl clutched tightly, her face pale with dread, was Mrs. Henderson. They gathered at the edge of the stubble field, a dark, murmuring crowd, held back by the intense heat radiating from the burning barn. Their faces were masks of shock, confusion and fear. They saw Corbett, standing alone, watching the blaze. They saw his men, positioned around the fire, weapons ready.

"What's happening?" someone yelled.

"Who's in there?"

"John Brown! Is he inside?"

"Brown? Why?"

Corbett didn't turn. His eyes remained fixed on the barn doors. The fire had engulfed the lower half. The upper timbers were catching now, framing the structure in flame. The heat was immense.

Inside, the roar was deafening. Booth choked on thick smoke. The air was unbreathable. Heat seared his skin, flames licked through gaps in the wall near him. The bar across the door felt hot under his bound hands. Panic, pure and absolute, seized him—burning—trapped—like before but this time, no escape. No heroic death just choking and searing agony.

No, he would not die like this—cowering—burned to nothing—unseen. He was John Wilkes Booth—he would be seen.

He gathered the last of his strength. He ignored the pain in his shoulder and his leg. He ignored the smoke scalding his lungs. He gripped the hot timber bar. He heaved upwards with all his might. It lifted, scorching his palms. He shoved it aside. It crashed to the burning floor inside.

He threw his weight against the burning doors. They burst open.

He emerged.

A gasp went through the crowd. A collective intake of breath. Mrs. Henderson cried out, "John!"

He stood framed in the fiery archway. The flames roared behind him and above him. Smoke swirled around him like a shroud. His nightshirt was torn, blackened and smoldering in places. Blood stained his shoulder, his face was streaked with soot and sweat, contorted in agony and defiance. He took one staggering step forward, out of the immediate flames, onto the scorched earth before the barn. He raised his bound hands, not in surrender, but in a final, desperate gesture of existence. He opened his mouth, perhaps to shout, to curse, to proclaim himself—the ghost of John Wilkes Booth.

Corbett's arm was already extended, his Colt was level. He had anticipated this, the moment of emergence. The dramatic exit Booth craved.

Corbett fired.

A single shot—precise—final.

The bullet struck Booth high in the chest. The impact jerked him backwards, his cry died in his throat. His raised arms fell. His eyes, wide with shock, met Corbett's for an instant. Then the light left them, he crumpled and fell forward onto the burning ground, just outside the barn doors—motionless.

The flames roared on. The crowd stood frozen in silence, except for the crackling fire. Horrified eyes stared from the crowd to the body, then to Corbett, who slowly lowered his smoking pistol.

A woman screamed. A low moan rippled through the onlookers. Shock turned to disbelief, then to dawning horror and grief. People recognized the shopkeeper now, despite the soot and blood. It was their neighbor, John Brown. Mrs. Henderson swayed, a hand pressed to her mouth, tears streaking her cheeks.

Sheriff Pike pushed his way to the front of the crowd. His face was pale, etched with confusion and anger. "Corbett! What in God's name have you done? That's John Brown!"

Corbett turned to face the crowd. His face was impassive in the flickering light. He holstered his Colt. "His name wasn't Brown," Corbett stated, his voice carrying clearly over the fire's roar. "He was a murderer. He killed Arthur Davies. He pushed him into Oak Creek."

Pike stared. "Davies? The stranger asking questions? Brown...he said he didn't know him!"

"He lied," Corbett said flatly. He pointed at the body. "He admitted it. To me. Before he ran. He killed Davies because Davies found out who he really was." Corbett looked at the horrified faces. "He killed a federal agent. That demands one answer. Death. I gave it to him."

The crowd murmured with grief and confusion. Their friend—a murderer? The firelight flickered on their uncertain faces. Mrs. Henderson whispered, "No...it can't be..."

"Proof?" Pike demanded, his voice thick. "You shot him down! Where's your proof?"

Corbett nodded to Harker. Harker stepped forward and held up an oilcloth bundle. He unwrapped it. The light gleamed on polished bone, a knife, its handle worn smooth. Etched faintly into the grip were the initials: JWB. He unfolded a yellowed playbill. *Ford's Theatre. April 14, 1865. Our American Cousin.* Beneath it, he held up a smaller, torn fragment of a different playbill. The name *John Wilkes Booth* stood out in bold type.

"This," Corbett said, indicating the knife and the torn playbill fragment. "Hidden under his floor. Proof of his past. And this." He pointed to the rope still binding Booth's wrists and ankles, clearly visible. "The rope Davies carried. Special issue. For prisoners. He took it from Davies. He used it to bind him before he pushed him into the creek. We found it hidden in Brown's room tonight." Corbett gestured towards the body. "It's still on him. Proof he killed Davies. Proof he was the man Davies hunted."

Pike stepped closer to the body. He knelt and examined the ropes binding the wrists. It was thick, coarse, unusual hemp. He looked up at Harker, who held up another length of identical rope taken from his pocket. Pike looked back at the knife, the playbill fragments, then at the dead man's face. Doubt clouded his eyes, then grim acceptance. He stood up slowly.

"John Brown," he said, his voice heavy. "Or whoever he was. Killed Davies." He looked at the crowd. "He confessed it to these men. The proof is here." He gestured at the rope, the knife, the playbill fragments. "He ran. He barricaded himself. He forced this end."

The crowd absorbed this. The shock remained, mixed now with a terrible sadness. The friendly shopkeeper was gone, replaced by a stranger capable of murder. The fire, the shooting, the evidence—it was too much to deny. Heads bowed, women wept quietly and men shuffled their feet, looking at the ground. Mrs. Henderson turned away, burying her face in her shawl.

The barn groaned, a section of the roof collapsed inward in a shower of sparks. The fire burned itself towards the center. The heat lessened slightly.

Pike sighed. "We need to...deal with the body. Before the fire takes it."

Corbett nodded. "Bury him here. Under the name he used. John Brown. Let Oak Creek remember the man they knew. Let the rest lie."

Pike looked at the knife and the playbill fragments in Harker's hand. "Those initials...that name...Booth. It means trouble. Even now. Even dead."

"It means nothing," Corbett said. "A ghost story. A man named Brown killed a federal agent. He was executed. That is the truth. The only truth Oak Creek needs." He looked at the items. "Burn them."

Harker hesitated for only a second. He tossed the yellowed playbill *and* the torn fragment bearing Booth's name into the roaring mouth of the barn. They flared bright for an instant, curled black, then vanished into ash. He rewrapped the knife in the oilcloth and tucked it away.

Pike called for men with shovels. Some from the crowd went back towards town—others stayed, watching the fire consume the barn. It was casting long, dancing shadows over the field and the still form lying before it.

Corbett watched as the men returned with tools. They began digging a grave a respectful distance from the smoldering barn ruins. The crowd watched silently as the hole deepened in the hard earth. Harker, Vance, and Carter stood near Corbett, watching the town bury their friend.

When the grave was ready, four men lifted Booth's body. They carried him carefully, almost tenderly, despite the ropes. They lowered him into the ground. The ropes remained—the evidence—the proof of his final crime. The proof that silenced questions about his distant past. Sheriff Pike said a few brief words. Words about John Brown—shopkeeper—neighbor. A man who did a terrible thing. The crowd murmured their agreement. Heads bowed again. Peterson spoke a few words, followed by Mrs. Henderson—then a few others spoke. They shared memories of their friend and neighbor—none of them knew the murderer. None of them knew John Wilkes Booth—the actor—the assassin.

Dirt thudded onto the body as they filled the grave with dirt. The mound rose, dark against the stubble field. Dawn was lightening the eastern sky, a pale gray washing over the scene. The barn was a heap of glowing embers and blackened timbers. Smoke still rose, thin and gray now.

The crowd began to disperse—slowly—quietly. They were heading back to Oak Creek, carrying the weight of the night. They were carrying the image of fire and death—carrying the name John Brown. Mrs. Henderson walked slowly, supported by a neighbor, her face still streaked with tears, looking back once at the fresh mound of earth.

Corbett watched the last shovel of dirt settle. He looked at the grave, then at the smoking ruin. He then looked at his men—he nodded once—a silent command—it was finished.

He turned and walked away from the grave, away from the ruin. He walked towards the woods, back towards the creek path. Harker, Vance, and Carter fell in step behind him. They didn't look back. The rising sun caught their backs as they vanished into the trees, leaving the grave and the ashes and the secret beneath the piled earth. The name John Wilkes Booth vanished with them, swallowed by the quiet morning. Only John Brown remained—buried—finished. The ghost of John Wilkes Booth will haunt Oak Creek forever.

BENEATH A DYING SUN
WESTERN SHORT STORIES
RED HOLLOW
DEADMAN'S RIDGE
LAUGHTON J. COLLINS, JR.

BENEATH A DYING SUN

WESTERN SHORT STORIES

LAUGHTON J. COLLINS, JR.

BENEATH A DYING SUN

WESTERN SHORT STORIES

LAUGHTON J. COLLINS, JR.

My Website

Social Media

Link Tree

dot.profile

Facebook

Goodreads

Authors Den

Amazon Author Page

ghost riders in the sky and other lines sample

Poem Hunter

Bluesky

Bookwire

Bookshop

Books2Read

Substack

Shadows & Light on Amazon

ghost riders in the sky and other lines on Amazon

Requiem Press

E-Mail